The Dolphin Summer

Previously published by
Carola Salisbury in Pan Books

Mallion's Pride
Dark Inheritance

Carola Salisbury
The Dolphin Summer

Pan Books in association with
Collins

First published 1977 by William Collins Sons & Co Ltd
This edition published 1978 by Pan Books Ltd,
Cavaye Place, London SW10 9PG
in association with William Collins Sons & Co Ltd
© Doubleday & Co Inc 1976
ISBN 0 330 25326 3
Printed and bound in Great Britain by
Richard Clay (The Chaucer Press) Ltd, Bungay, Suffolk

for Heather

chapter one

My name is Annabel Trewella, and I came to Falmouth, to join the steam yacht *Dolphin*, in October of 1897, which was the year of the old Queen's Diamond Jubilee.

Even in the remote village of St Finn, on the edge of Bodmin Moor, we had celebrated the Queen's sixtieth year of reign; for there was not a hovel so mean that it did not have some token of that tremendous little person in widow's weeds who ruled half the world for us; and what did it matter if the floor of a labourer's cottage was of earth, so long as it was well swept, and there was a coloured oleograph of Her Majesty over the fireplace?

St Finn's church bell rang out a peal from dawn till dusk on 20 June, and the children of the board school, where I was assistant teacher, were each given a pair of stout shoes, a handkerchief bearing an impression of the Queen, a map of the world with the Empire coloured in red, and a Jubilee mug.

For our tiny village of only seventy-two souls, cut off from the world by distance, poverty and unceasing toil, it was indeed a time to remember: as if the corner of a heavy curtain had been lifted, to reveal a wider and richer world beyond the overhung lanes and the mountains of china clay that dominated our lives. To present the gifts to the children came a party of fine ladies and gentlemen from far-off Truro: members of the School Board and their wives; all in broad-cloth and tall hats, great leg-o'-mutton sleeves, French millinery and high button-boots. They looked upon us. They gave of their bounty. The most senior dignitary among them – he was a stout, bearded man who looked not unlike the pictures of the Prince of Wales – spoke warmly of our need to trust in Almighty God and the Empire, and of our obligation to strive for the further spreading of the gospel of love and the heritage of our island race among the less favoured dark-skinned peoples of this world. Then they looked at their watches and got into their carriages – to bear witness and more gifts to the next village. The celebrations over, Jubilee mugs were stood on mantelpieces, and handkerchiefs folded away in lavender-scented drawers. The shoes were put aside carefully – to be sold at the next market day in Bodmin.

The poverty and wretchedness in mid-Cornwall was almost total. The china clay works provided a miserably paid living for the folks of St Finn and all the villages surrounding it. There was little farming in the district, for lands were held by the big families – the Trevallions, Dewaines, Lornes, Penallens and the rest – who found no profit in pouring their wealth into animal husbandry and agriculture, but preferred to let their wide acres run wild, for purposes of shooting and hunting. A few of the villagers had smallholdings, from which they wrested a few rows of potatoes and beans. They kept a few chickens in their back yards. That was all. The people did not even look like country folk, being stunted and underweight from bad diet and overcrowding, and their pale faces limned with the eternal china clay. The hopeful provisions of the Act of 1880, when Mr Gladstone had aimed for universal compulsory education, buttered no parsnips in mid-Cornwall; Mr Penbury, the school headmaster, and I, his assistant, were long accustomed to turning a blind eye to such cases as a seven-year-old who played truant to act as beater on a pheasant shoot for a ha'penny a day, or the under-age girl – already toilworn beyond her years from helping to raise a large family of siblings – who took work as a day skivvy at a distant manor house, walking seven miles there and back for a shilling a week.

Small wonder that Mr Penbury and his wife had no great difficulty in persuading me to accept the offer that came out of the blue.

It took the form of a letter, written upon embossed paper, in a prim and clerkish hand:

> St Errol House,
> St Errol,
> Cornwall
> 20 September 1897

Dear Miss Trewella,
I have been instructed by Commander Saltram to offer you the post of companion to his ward, Miss Melloney Lumley. The Commander is particularly desirous that you will find your way to accepting the position, since, as you will recall, your late half-sister Miss Harriet Cadge was governess to Miss Melloney.

Whether you decide to accept or not, I would deem it a favour if you would kindly indicate your decision at an early date. It will be necessary rapidly to fill the post, because the Commander and Miss Melloney are leaving on an extended cruise in the Mediterranean in October, and Miss Melloney's lady companion will accompany her.

Emoluments will amount to one hundred pounds per annum plus the usual perquisites. If you indicate your acceptance, I will instantly dispatch to you a railway ticket to Falmouth, so that you are able to repair aboard the steam yacht *Dolphin* some time during the second week in October.

Believe me, Miss Trewella,

Yours very sincerely, Augustus Robbins
Secretary to Commander Saltram

'But I can't possibly accept,' I told Mr Penbury, at the breakfast table. 'How will you get a replacement teacher at such short notice? Besides, I've no qualifications to be a companion to a grand young lady like Miss Lumley.'

It was Mrs Penbury who answered. She looked at me dryly over her large brown teapot.

'That can hardly be so, Annabel,' she said, 'when your sister was perfectly able to act as governess to the selfsame young lady – and must certainly have given good satisfaction, or this position would not have been offered to you. You have no reason to be modest about your attainments, my dear. I have instructed you in social behaviour ever since you came to us as a pupil-teacher at thirteen. You could mingle with any society. Besides,' she added, 'times are changing. Commander Saltram inherited the Lumley fortune, and we all know that the Lumley fortune came from trade. They are not so grand as all that.'

I smiled to myself, into my breakfast cup. Though the wife of an impoverished board school headmaster, who was glad to lodge the assistant lady teacher, Mrs Penbury took great pride in having sprung from 'gentry': the youngest daughter of a country parson, and socially far superior to her adoring and hardworking spouse.

The latter took up his wife's argument: 'You can't afford

to let such an opportunity pass, Annabel. What is there for you here in St Finn – what chance of bettering your position?'

'And what prospects of matrimony?' interjected Mrs Penbury. 'Answer me that. Or will you wish to be courted by some strutting clayman in his reach-me-down Sunday suit, and go to live in a clayman's hovel?'

'My dear,' said Mr Penbury mildly, 'I'm sure that Annabel would make a better match than that – even in St Finn.'

Mrs Penbury took the lid from her great teapot and made a great fuss and noise of stirring the contents with a large tablespoon.

'How much better?' she demanded of her spouse. 'Will she aspire to some leering smallholder who takes a fancy to her in Bodmin on a market day, and charms her heart away with his few mortgaged acres and a broken-down cow? Or, perhaps, a travelling small-goods vendor? A curate of one of the local parishes, maybe – not a gentleman, but one of the new sort? These must be the sort of matches you have in mind, Ernest – for I have espied no other quality in this corner of Cornwall. I tell you that Annabel must aspire to mixing with gentry. Or what also passes for gentry nowadays. I refer to the higher reaches of trade. My goodness, Annabel, why do you laugh?'

'I'm very sorry, Mrs Penbury,' I said, hiding my confusion by dabbing my nose with a handkerchief. 'But I have no plans for matrimony at the moment, and it amuses me that you think I should.'

'My dear, you are gone twenty-two and a fine-looking girl,' she said, 'and it's high time you did give some thought to the matter. Or is it your wish to stay in St Finn an old maid, and be still an old maid when Mr Penbury retires from the school and leaves you in charge?'

I had to agree that this prospect did not greatly attract me, and confessed as much.

'I think you should accept the offer,' said Mr Penbury. 'I really do. After a year or two in Commander Saltram's service, you would gain enough experience of the world to be able to aspire to something better than a country board school teacher.'

'I only regret that such an opportunity never came my way,' cried Mrs Penbury fervently. 'St Finn would never have seen me for dust!'

Her husband bowed his head and addressed himself to his boiled egg.

Three weeks later, on Monday, 11 October, with my carpet-bag in one hand and the cage containing my pet canary Jackie in the other, my wooden chest having been sent on ahead, I left St Finn for ever, in a dog-cart to the distant railway station.

My arrival in Falmouth was memorable for a sudden downpour of heavy rain that half-soaked my tweed dress and cape and made a poor, draggle-tailed thing of the feather in my straw boater. I managed to secure a porter, to carry my traps to a nearby waiting-room, where I sat out the rain and took stock of my position.

The instructions from Mr Robbins, the Commander's secretary, had been for me to make straight for the Town Quay in the inner harbour, and there to hire the services of a boatman who would take me out to the *Dolphin* at her anchorage. This communication – accompanied by a single ticket, second class, to Falmouth – was all I had in reply to my acceptance of the position. Nothing from Commander Saltram; but I had hoped to receive a few friendly lines from Miss Melloney, whose companion I was to become.

While the rain sluiced down upon the tar-paper roof of the waiting-room, and the pot-bellied stove in the corner hissed and sizzled, and while the grey blanket of wetness shrouded the forest of ships' masts and rigging that appeared above the station wall, I fell to thinking of the company – 'the higher reaches of trade that pass for gentry', as Mrs Penbury called them – with whom I would soon be mixing.

The key name was: Lumley. It was a household name in the West Country, even in remote St Finn; a name that was emblazoned over a chain of general stores from Taunton to Exeter and from Redruth to Penzance – or so I had been told, for I had never been as far afield as any of those places. The Lumley emporium in Truro I knew well enough from my twice- or thrice-yearly visits to the cathedral city which lay at the outer limit of my travelling experience, twenty-five miles by dog-cart.

Lumley's in Truro – for one born and bred in an area where the arrival of a travelling small-goods vendor with his donkey cart was an event to draw the whole village and most of the outlying smallholdings – seemed an Aladdin's cavern of delights. It was in the windows of Lumley's that I first saw the modes of present-day fashion displayed on life-sized wax figures; it was in Lumley's basement that I was greatly tempted to mortgage a considerable part of my financial future by purchasing, for the forbidding sum of £5 5s 6d, one of the new-style velocipedes for females, with pneumatic tyres and a hand-brake. I forget how I persuaded myself out of it.

As I understood it, an Alfred Lumley founded the family fortune with a small grocery stall in Taunton market in the thirties; but it was his son David Lumley, afterwards Sir David, who, with energy and farsightedness, seized upon the idea of providing a complete range of household goods, all under one roof, in the cities and market towns of Devon, Cornwall and Somerset. Sir David Lumley lived to hear his name on every lip and to receive the accolade of knighthood, for his charitable and philanthropic works, from the hand of Her Majesty. This much I knew because I had taken the trouble to inquire at an early age, and this only for the reason that my half-sister Harriet had worked for Sir David, as governess to his adopted daughter.

Sir David was now dead – as Harriet was now no more – and he having no issue, the estate had passed to a retired naval officer named Commander Saltram, in whose employment I now was. I knew exactly what to expect of my new master, for the Rector of St Finn had living with him an older brother who was an ex-naval officer; and there was a gentleman of similar age and background, with a wooden leg, who stomped the streets of Bodmin, and was known to all for his loud and fruity voice, his terrible temper, and for his disarming gentleness with animals and some children. I was quite prepared to like old Commander Saltram.

I had reached this point in my reflections when the tail

end of a gusty squall peeled away the sky's overcast and showed me the dramatic, greeny-grey expanse of the harbour and the craft lying there. At the same time, the rain ceased, and a thin patch of sunlight crept over the station yard. Time to find my way to the Town Quay – wherever that was.

The same helpful porter who had brought me to the waiting-room obligingly carried my traps outside to the station yard, where, he said, I should presently come upon a hansom cab plying for hire that would take me where I wished to go. I gave the man a penny for his pains and began my wait. Plenty of private carriages of all kinds clattered into the yard: broughams, victorias, dog-carts and even sleek phaetons – all seemingly to greet the arrival of the next train. But no cab for hire. And it was threatening rain again.

The first flurry of a new downpour started at the same time that an enormous gushing of steam and a squeal of iron wheels heralded the arrival of a train. Almost immediately, I saw a hansom come clip-clopping round the corner of the station yard. I waved to the driver, and he acknowledged my summons with a flourish of his whip. He was directing his cab towards where I was standing as I stooped to pick up my carpet-bag and birdcage.

'Ho there, cabbie!' a voice called over my head. Straightening up, I saw to my dismay that a man was hailing the hansom – *my* hansom.

'Excuse me, but I have already called . . .' I began.

'Give me your hand,' he said, ignoring me. 'It's muddy underfoot.' And he held out a hand to a young woman who swept past me with a frou-frou of stiffened silks and a waft of expensive scent. I had a vision of flame-coloured hair piled up under an enormous hat trimmed with bird of paradise feathers and osprey plumes; of a profile as cold and pure as marble, rising from a white throat encircled with a high collar of brilliants.

'That – that's my cab!' I faltered.

The man appeared to notice me for the first time. He was tall, thirtyish, lean-faced as an Arab and nearly as dark, with deep brown eyes that gazed down at me with disconcerting coldness.

'I think, madam, that you are mistaken,' he murmured distantly, removing his billycock hat with a gesture of frigid politeness that was really a civil way of expressing disapproval. 'I distinctly received an answering wave from the cabbie.'

'What is the matter?' demanded his lady companion. 'What *is* that creature about? Is she begging for money?'

I felt my cheeks flush hotly, and I took a firmer grip on my carpet-bag and birdcage.

'No, madam, I am not begging for money!' I cried. 'Only my right, as first comer, to this hansom.' And I reached to put the carpet-bag by the seat of the cab, the driver having opened the flaps to allow me to board – or so I thought.

'Take your turn, miss – the lady and gentleman was here first!' the driver called out to me from his high perch, and suited the action to the words, by laying the end of his long whip along the side of the cab, barring me from entering it.

'I was first!' I cried. 'I waved to you when you came into the yard – before these people had arrived – and you waved back to me.'

The driver shook his head. 'Never saw you!' he declared. 'Stand aside, and let the lady and gennleman past. Where to, sir?' he asked, in honeyed tones, of the man in the billycock.

'To the Pendennis Castle Hotel,' replied the other. And he took his companion's hand, to help her into the cab.

But I was having none of it!

'No, you shall not!' I cried.

They stared at me, all three of them: the man, the woman and the fawning creature perched up there on his box. I knew how they saw me – the man and the woman, at least; a dowdy nobody in shabby tweeds, and a wilting boater with a bedraggled feather perched on her untidy hair; I was painfully aware, furthermore, that my nose was red and that tears of anger and mortification were overspilling on my cheeks, also that my lower lip was trembling uncontrollably.

'Madam, will you permit us to pass?' he said calmly.

'What upstart impudence!' cried his companion.

'Mind your place, and stand aside!' shouted the servile

monster from on high. 'Don't you know how to behave to your betters?'

Behave to my betters! A lifetime of stern independence had set me far above that sort of attitude, and I rejoiced in my strength. If only the man had reviled me, or attempted to thrust me aside, it would have made it easier. Instead, he continued to regard me with mingled coolness and disbelief. And my legs had begun to tremble in time with my nether lip. I felt my stern independence wither.

'Are you going to allow us to board, madam?' he murmured.

'No, sir, I am not,' I breathed.

The cab driver uttered an oath and began to climb down from his box, with the obvious intention of doing what the dark man in the billycock could not bring himself to do: move me by force. I cannot imagine what the outcome would have been. In the event, I was saved by the arrival of a figure in blue.

'Well then, what's all this? Why aren't you on your way, cabbie?' The policeman had a good, open Cornish face and flaxen whiskers. I warmed to him at once.

'Officer, this is my hansom,' I cried.

'Indeed it is, miss,' he affirmed. 'I saw you hail the driver and he waved back to you. Then what's the delay, cabbie? You're holding up the circulation of the traffic.'

The contemptible jackal looked sullenly to his 'betters' for guidance.

Stiff-faced and unperturbed, the man in the billycock said: 'Madam, it appears that I have been in error, and for this I apologize.' And, taking off his hat, he backed away a pace and motioned me to enter the cab.

'Thank you, sir,' I murmured.

I caught a glimpse of his companion's face: it showed total affront, as if she had just received a calculated insult. Nor, for all his studied civility, did he look any too pleased; he struck me as the kind of man who did not much care to be put in the wrong.

A fig for them both – what were the likes of them to me?

I had put the whole incident out of my mind by the time we reached the quay. The only reminder was the sullen way in which the cabbie took his fare and a ha'penny tip without so much as a nod and a 'thank you'.

There were plenty of boatmen plying for hire on the Town Quay, and I was approached by an old fellow in high boots and oilskins, who touched a forelock and asked me where I would be taken. When I told him the *Dolphin*, he became very fussy, and called to another seaman for assistance, taking up my traps and carrying them towards his waiting craft.

'The lady's for the *Dolphin*!' he announced with pride to all and sundry. And there was a perceptible stirring of interest among the men who lolled about the ropework and boat gear. A dozen pairs of honest eyes peered out from weather-beaten faces, looking me up and down, and doubtless making inexpert reckonings of the price of my clothes, and deciding if I was an heiress or a duchess.

I was handed into the rear part of the boat, and an oilskin cape was laid about my shoulders, and another across my knees. The old boatman called for his assistant to cast off, and he bent his back to his oars, sending us out from the quay. It had begun to rain again, quite hard. The oily water near the shore was soon covered by myriads of droplets. Further out, the view was obscured by a dank mist that had descended over all, hiding the shapes of the anchored craft and all that lay beyond. The quay faded in the murk behind – and then we were all alone in an island of water and still-ness, with no sound but the splash of the oars and the call of seagulls as they circled, unseen in the mist, above us.

I marvelled that my boatman seemed to know his way with no mark to guide him; he never faltered, but rowed with steady, easy strokes, glancing from time to time over his shoulder the way we were going. Only once did we meet another moving craft: a small sailing boat that slid out of the mist and returned to it again; and a man on the deck waved us greeting.

'There she be!' cried the old boatman presently. 'There be the *Dolphin*, ma'am!'

I strained my eyes ahead. For all his age, his sight must have been keener than mine; it was some time before I made out a low-lying shape: a ghostly, insubstantial patch of whiteness forming out of the rain-mist. It rapidly took the form of a long and rakish-looking vessel with two high masts and a tall brass funnel; the hull painted all white, save for deep blue at the waterline; and a flag hanging motionless in the still air. To my eyes, the white ship was enormous, and of a mysterious and incredible beauty.

'*Dolphin* ahoy!' called my guide.

'What boat?' came a reply across the rain-flecked waters between.

'Trot-boat! Bringing a passenger aboard!'

'Come alongside the accommodation ladder!'

'Aye, aye!'

We slid under the long, overhanging prow of the yacht, past a gilded dolphin figurehead, and went the whole length of her, down a long line of gleaming brass portholes; round the curved and gilded stern where the flag hung lazily; back up the other side, to a flight of steps suspended over the water. A tall figure in brass-buttoned blue stood at the top of the steps.

So I set foot on the decks of the *Dolphin*. And the man in blue handed me up. His fingers were hard and strong on mine.

'You must be the little lady who's going to be companion to Miss Melloney. Very nice.'

He could only have been a year or two older than me, in his mid-twenties. Deep blue eyes that crinkled at the corners. Manfully bronzed and weatherbeaten. Mouth a trifle soft and womanish, and an expression – how to put it? – of a man who, by consequence of his handsome appearance, had always been used to getting his own way in all things, and especially with women. I mistrusted him on sight.

'I'm Annabel Trewella,' I replied coolly. 'Are you, sir, the captain of the *Dolphin*?' And, indeed, he looked the part, with his brass buttons and rakish cap emblazoned with an anchor set in a wreath of gold lace.

'No, I'm not,' he replied. And did I detect a hint of pique flitting across that assured countenance? 'I'm Third Officer Maugham.' The assurance came back, like the sun slipping out from behind a small and irritating cloud, and he was himself again. 'I am known to my friends as Jack,' he added with a smile that carried a wealth of meaning.

'A person can't have too many friends,' I replied flatly. 'And now, Mr Maugham, would you be so kind as to inform Commander Saltram and Miss Lumley that I have arrived?'

'The Commander's not aboard,' he replied sulkily. 'He's expected tomorrow. But Miss Lumley's been living aboard for the last week with her nurse. I'll take you to her. You there...!' he broke into a harsh shout, and a sailor in a wide-brimmed straw hat dropped a mop with which he had been attacking the already gleaming white deck and came running. 'Take the lady's gear down to number seven cabin on B deck! And look sharp about it!'

The man padded off, bearing my carpet-bag and birdcage. I looked at Third Officer Maugham: he was watching me slyly. It struck me that he was searching for signs of my admiration at the overbearing way he had addressed the poor sailor.

'And now, sir,' I told him, 'if you will kindly escort me to Miss Lumley, I shall be glad to get in out of the rain.' One had to be firm, I felt, with the bumptious Mr Maugham.

He led the way through the door and down a wide, panelled staircase that immediately banished any sensation of being in a seagoing vessel. The steps were covered with plum-coloured carpeting that was thickly-piled and yielding. The handrails were of gleaming brass and finely wrought. At the bottom of the staircase was a marble statuette of a lightly-draped pagan girl seated upon a dolphin, from whose open mouth gushed a jet of pure water that rose on high, and returned in diamond droplets to an awaiting bowl of marble. The lighting was by electric lamps, discreetly shaded. In a lifetime of mid-Cornwall, I had only known such signs of luxury from the pages of the more fanciful novels.

My guide paused by the fountain, indicating it and our surroundings.

'Splendid, isn't it?' he declared. 'What a blessing it is to have plenty of tin, eh? They say old man Lumley spent a cool quarter of a million on the *Dolphin*, and heaven knows what on fitting her out. I say, I hope that we shall soon become very good friends. You know, there's nothing like a long sea voyage for cementing firm friendships.'

The handsome and conceited Mr Maugham gazed at me intently. He had removed his cap, revealing a smooth head of chestnut hair slicked down with macassar oil.

'May we continue on our way, Mr Maugham?' I asked him coldly.

He scowled.

'You may be glad of a friend before the voyage is over,' he said sulkily.

'Indeed?' I murmured.

'They're a strange lot,' he said. 'You'll find that out soon enough, Miss Trewella. I don't know them well – haven't been in the *Dolphin* long – but you won't have to be cooped up aboard this yacht with them for very long before you'll understand what I'm trying to tell you.'

He gave me a very intense look that was quite different from his usual expressions of conceit or petulance; and all at once I had forgotten the luxury about me – and was only aware of the cold, grey sea that lay only just beyond the thin steel skin of the vessel. The recollection made me shudder.

'What,' I asked him falteringly, '*are* you trying to tell me, Mr Maugham?'

But he would venture no more confidences, and I was left with the disconcerting feeling of having been the unwitting eavesdropper to a fragment of conversation that it would have been better for me not to have heard.

We went through a double doorway, my guide standing aside to let me pass first.

'Here we have the saloon,' he said.

I stared in unashamed awe. The great saloon of the *Dolphin* – it stretched the width of the vessel and was three times as long as the width – added to the sensation, begun by the sumptuous stairway, of one's being in a situation of the most extreme luxury on dry land. A single carpet of oriental appearance covered the entire floor, and hanging drapes in matching colours shielded the portholes, which were swagged with lace curtainings. All round the polished mahogany panelling of the walls were hung gilt-framed paintings of classical and marine subjects. There were oval tables adorned with exquisite vases bearing most elaborate floral arrangements, china, and glassware, fanciful clocks of marble and gilt, waxen fruits, silver cigar boxes and dishes containing sugared almonds and bon-bons. And everywhere potted palms and aspidistras cascaded in rich abundance.

'How ... wonderful!' I cried aloud.

'So refreshing to hear someone expressing sincere delight,' came a voice from behind a bank of aspidistras to my right: a low and musical voice that carried a hint of merriment. 'Step forward and let me see you.'

I obeyed. Melloney Lumley was sitting on a pink sofa with her tiny, slippered feet stretched out on the cushions. I had an immediate impression of smallness, neatness; of life and vitality; an irrepressible gaiety. Dazzling eyes of an unbelievable largeness and blueness looked out at me from a delicately-complexioned face. Her mouth was small, and seemed on the point of breaking from a smile into laughter. Her hair was the colour of spun flax, highlighted with gold; she wore it in an unfashionable Greek chignon – for, as I was to learn, Melloney Lumley was no slave to fashion or custom. She was clad in an oyster-coloured silk gown unembellished by jewellery or decoration of any kind.

She reached out a slim arm and patted a cushion by her feet. 'Sit down beside me, Miss Trewella,' she smiled. 'Do you know, you're not one bit like poor dear Harriet to look at, but then, you were only half-sisters.'

'Harriet resembled her father and I mine,' I told her. At closer quarters, I could see the true quality of Melloney Lumley's complexion – which seemed quite flawless, like that of a young child, though she must have been at least four years older than I; something like twenty-six or seven. She looked not a day over seventeen.

'Poor Harriet,' she said. A shadow fell across the brightness of her smile, and I saw the beginnings of a tear forming in the corner of her eye. 'I still miss her greatly. She was so strong, you know. So reliable, with the sort of shoulder that was made to cry on. I called her ... "my Guardian Angel".' She looked away, touching away the tears with her fingertips. When her face turned back to me, the smile had returned, and the eyes were dancing again. It was as if Melloney Lumley had the secret of being able to lift the curtain of even the deepest gloom and reveal the sunlight that lay behind. I have seen her do it a thousand times : this, the first time, was a memorable and heart-warming experience. 'But – now I have you, Annabel Trewella,' she said simply.

I could have hugged her then. Instead, I contented myself by taking her slim, cool hand in mine.

'Thank you for saying that, Miss Lumley,' I whispered.

'You will call me Melloney,' she said with a mock frown. 'I'll have no standing on ceremony in this ship. What do you say, Mr Maugham?'

Third Officer Maugham, who had been standing to attention with his cap under his arm, gave a start and looked confused.

'Er ... quite so, ma'am,' he replied. It came to me that the handsome Mr Maugham was clay in the hands of Melloney.

'My dear Annabel,' she cried, 'you must forgive me for not offering you refreshment after your journey. Will you have some tea? No, what am I thinking – it's much too early for tea. Besides, the occasion calls for a celebration. Mr Maugham, be so good, please, as to ring the bell and summon the steward.'

This was done, and a white-jacketed waiter appeared.

'Champagne!' cried Melloney. 'And three glasses!'

A large bottle was brought, and three glasses filled till the foaming wine overflowed on to their silver tray.

Melloney raised her glass, looked towards the officer and me.

'My friends,' she cried gaily, 'I give you the toast – "to the *Dolphin* summer!"'

'The *Dolphin* summer!' answered Mr Maugham, and I also repeated the toast – but with total puzzlement.

To say that I had never before taken champagne in a mid-afternoon of an October Monday would be to understate my case; I had, in fact, never before even seen a glass of champagne, let alone raised one to my lips.

'The *Dolphin* summer,' said Melloney, 'refers to the coming voyage to the North African coast. The whole thing is an idea of my darling guardian. He has the notion that I am too delicate for these cold and uncharitable climes. So there is to be no winter. Winter is banished. Instead, we are having an extra summer in the sun of the Mediterranean. A *Dolphin* summer, do you see?'

'And we'll not be back till spring,' declared Mr Maugham, draining his glass. 'But now, ladies, I must ask you to pardon me. It's past six bells in the afternoon watch, and the hands must be kept at work.'

Melloney gave him a brilliant smile and said: 'Mr Maugham is such a comfort, Annabel. This you will discover. With Captain Pelly and the other officers ashore, as they are now, Mr Maugham is the senior officer aboard. And he manages the yacht so capably. I never feel a moment's qualm with him in charge.'

The subject of her compliments puffed out his chest and flushed with embarrassed delight under his weatherbeaten bronze.

'One does one's best to do one's duty, ma'am,' he declared. 'But there's really nothing to supervising the running of a vessel at moorings' – he coughed delicately – 'not to a fellow who was cadet of his year and one of the youngest officers to hold a Master's ticket in the Mercantile Marine.'

'I think you're a credit to the Marine,' said Melloney. She flashed me a gay, mischievous glance.

'I must return to the upper deck,' said Mr Maugham. 'Your servant, ladies.' He bowed and departed.

Melloney smiled at me, and when his footfalls had faded away, she said: 'Jack Maugham is not a wicked man. On the other hand, he is not one of the virtuous men who figure as heroes in the more uplifting modern novels. Did he flirt with you?'

'From the very first,' I told her. 'As soon as my feet touched the deck.'

We both laughed.

'Really,' she said, 'one shouldn't encourage him.'

'Or tease him,' I said.

The blue eyes flared suddenly. My lightly-hinted reproof had touched its mark; but her amusement quickly returned.

'Yes, I do tease him,' she admitted. 'But, do you know, the conceited fellow is never aware of it? I promise you, Annabel, that if one were to tell him that he's the greatest sailor since Lord Nelson and the handsomest gallant since Lord Byron, he would swallow it like a kitten taking cream, and ask for more. How nice it must be to have such a simple and uncomplicated nature as dear Jack Maugham! A bit of flattery here and a mite of encouragement there, and his afternoon is made. Why, he'll be quite civil to those poor sailors for the rest of the day. What a pleasure it is, to be able to spread so much happiness so easily!' She flung back her lovely head and laughed so infectiously that I joined in.

Afterwards I said: 'I understand that the Commander isn't coming aboard till tomorrow. I hope he'll approve of me when we meet.'

'For sure he will,' she declared. 'And you'll like him too. Most people find him rather an old bear, but he hides a kind heart under that quarterdeck gruffness.'

'A gruff old gentleman with a heart of gold! Do you know, that's just how I imagined him to be?' And I went on to tell her about the Rector's older brother and the peg-legged gentleman in Bodmin.

She nodded. 'You have painted a perfect word-picture of him,' she said. Her eyes danced with amusement. 'He doesn't snore in church like your rector's brother, nor does he smite lamp-posts in passing with his walking stick like the other old salt, but he has his peculiarities. For instance, he...'

I never did hear Melloney's list of Commander Saltram's peculiarities, for at that instant a voice called from the door and someone swept in.

'Melloney, my darling girl – who are you talking to? Why aren't you resting?'

The newcomer was a tall, somewhat stout lady in black bombasine. Her greying hair was drawn back under a widow's cap of the kind favoured by the Queen. Her expression was a mixture of benign worry and amiable despair. Her voice echoed her manner: it died at the end of every phrase. She did not look to be a very happy sort of woman; but one, nevertheless, who tried to rise above her melancholy.

'Nanny dear,' said Melloney affectionately, 'come over here and meet Annabel Trewella, who is poor Harriet's half-sister. Annabel, this is dear Nurse Amy Bagley, who has been my nanny for all my life that I can remember.'

'From the first day you came into St Errol House,' said Nurse Bagley, taking her by the hands and gazing at her fondly. 'When you were but a poor little month-old mite with barely the strength to suck.' Her eyes, which were dark and searching, flickered over the glasses on the silver tray by the couch. 'Oh, my dear heart, don't tell me that you've been drinking that champagne again? Not champagne, Melloney' – her voice fell away to a dying whisper – 'not after what Doctor Weems told us! Not after the Commander's strict instructions!' She stood back from Melloney and regarded her in mingled horror and dismay.

'Only a sip, Nanny,' breathed Melloney, eyes wide and pleading. 'Just a few drops at the bottom of a glass, to welcome the arrival of Annabel Trewella.' Her hands, released from the nurse's, lay upon her lap. I noticed – and I hoped that Nurse Bagley did not also notice – that she crossed her fingers when she told the fib, in a very child-like manner that was quite unselfconscious.

Nurse Bagley sniffed, and deigned to notice me for the first time.

'How do you do, miss,' she said, amiably enough. 'Very glad to see you. It will do Melloney good to have a companion of around her own age. She's lived too long in the pocket of her old nanny, and there's precious little company in this vessel that I find suitable for my darling girl.' She concluded this remark by cocking her eye towards the deck above – and I imagined that she was probably referring to Third Officer Maugham.

'I was remarking,' said Melloney, obviously glad to get off the subject of the forbidden champagne, 'how little Annabel resembles her half-sister. Do you see any resemblance, Nanny?'

Nurse Bagley's brooding eyes swam over me. 'There's something of Harriet Cadge in her,' she pronounced. 'And that was intended as a compliment, miss. A finer young woman than your half-sister never drew breath upon this wicked earth.'

'Thank you, Nurse Bagley,' I murmured.

'Call me Nanny,' she said. 'They all do, even the sailors. And now, my lovely' – turning to Melloney and holding out her hands – 'I'm going to ring for Flack.'

'Oh no, Nanny!' cried Melloney. 'I don't want to go to bed.'

Nurse Bagley reached to pull a bell-cord. 'Time for your nap,' she said firmly. 'And early to bed with you after a light supper. The Commander and the guests will be aboard tomorrow, and you want to be strong and well enough to welcome the company and join them for luncheon.' The soft-footed steward coming in answer to her summons, she said to him: 'Fetch Able Seaman Flack.'

Able Seaman Flack proved to be a massive young fellow with a ginger beard, low forehead, and hands and arms like hams that were all covered in a fuzz of red hairs. He was neatly dressed in seaman's slops, and his huge bare feet were clean and white.

Melloney sighed. 'Goodbye, Annabel,' she said. 'I don't suppose I shall be seeing you till tomorrow. So tiresome. Still, tomorrow will soon come.' And her face lit up like sunshine coming through cloud.

'Rest now and play tomorrow,' pronounced Nurse Bagley. 'Take Miss Melloney up, Flack,' she directed.

With a gentleness that belied his fearsome appearance, the big seaman stooped, and, taking Melloney in his arms, lifted her from the sofa.

'See you tomorrow, dear Annabel,' said my new companion and friend. 'And I'm so glad you came.'

Too taken aback to speak, I could only assemble a feeble smile in reply; and I watched Able Seaman Flack carry her carefully out of the saloon, with the nurse following.

This was something I had not known, never guessed: that Melloney Lumley was unable to walk.

My cabin was on the same deck as that of the great saloon, nearer the front end of the yacht, and reached by a staircase leading down from the boat deck, where four long lifeboats were kept. It lay at the end of a corridor that contained three other cabins each side. No sound came from them and I saw no one, so I presumed that I had no near neighbours. On questioning the sailor who escorted me, I confirmed that there was aboard only what he referred to as a 'skeleton crew', and that the Captain and the rest of the officers and sailors would be back on duty in the early morning, to take the yacht alongside the quay to await the arrival of the owner and his guests. He showed me how to put the electric lamps on and off, and – an even more dreamlike novelty – how to work the telephone, which, he said, connected with the Chief Steward's pantry and would summon refreshments, valeting service and so forth, at any hour of day or night. I shook my head in wonderment.

My cabin was decorated in blue: blue oriental carpet, blue velvet curtains, and a deliciously soft blue quilt on the bunk. Nor was that all: I had a bathroom of my own, leading off from the main cabin, with an eau-de-nil bath and a silvery mask of a dolphin whose open mouth gushed hot or cold water, or a combination of both at the turn of the taps. I had decided to take a bath there and then, when a ring of a bell made me all but jump out of my skin. It was the telephone. I approached it with great trepidation, it being a machine that I had never handled before in my life, lifted the handpiece as I had been instructed, and put it to my ear.

'Chief Steward speaking, ma'am. Will ma'am be requiring tea?'

'Why yes,' I faltered. 'That – that will be very nice, thank you. Where do I go for ... ?'

'The tray will be brought to your cabin, ma'am. Will ma'am be aboard for dinner, or is ma'am dining ashore?' —

'I – I'm not going ashore,' I told him.

'The steward will bring a dinner menu with the tea-tray, ma'am. Might I suggest that ma'am peruses it at her leisure and telephones her requirements later?'

'Yes – yes, I'll do that,' I said.

'The menu, I hasten to add, is merely an indication. A few

suggestions to assist ma'am.' The voice added with a very considerable touch of pride: 'Any dish that ma'am requires – *any dish at all* – is available aboard the *Dolphin*.'

It sounded like a challenge, and not one – considering my slight acquaintance with gastronomic elegancies – that I would be likely to be taking up on that particular occasion.

I replaced the telephone handpiece. 'We really are living in style, Jackie!' I cried. The canary whistled back at me.

So I postponed the heady delights of my dolphin bath till I had taken tea (served on a huge silver tray, with a three-piece tea-set of hallmarked silver, and covered porcelain dishes containing hot buttered toast and muffins ditto; porcelain plates of cucumber sandwiches, Dundee cake, seed cake), and after I had bathed, I changed into my only other outdoor costume, of grey velvet, and went out on deck to see Falmouth harbour.

Night was falling. The rain had stopped and the mist had lifted with it. Lights were going on all over the town, along the quays, and among the tall ships at the dockside. As I gazed about me, pinpoints of light were revealing the whereabouts of lonely hamlets and farms on distant hillsides. The world was winding down; and I was coming to the end of one of the most momentous days of my life – a day of great change.

But not quite the end ...

At eight o'clock I was discreetly summoned, by telephone, to dinner in the saloon. And there I sat, all alone, at the end of a long table that had been set there for one. The Chief Steward, one Dacres – a man of enormous size, with a lot of gold lace and whiskers – presided over the service which I received from three underling stewards. From a huge menu of great complexity which had been delivered with my tea-tray, I had made the choice of one single dish: a dish of which I had not only never heard, but – being somewhat deficient in the French language – had not the slightest idea of its composition.

It was called: *Pintadeau rôti et flambé à la riche*. I enjoyed it very much. I have tasted many exotic dishes since then, both aboard the *Dolphin* and elsewhere, but they have never dimmed the memory of the time I sat in solitary state and dined off guinea fowl.

It must have been the slight motion of the yacht in the tideway that woke me up; an almost imperceptible dipping and rolling from the wake of a passing fishing boat, returning late to harbour from the catch, perhaps. I stirred and turned over, after re-establishing my whereabouts in an unaccustomed bed, as one will.

It was while composing myself for slumber again that I heard – *it* . . .

The sound of weeping; of some fellow human being in a paroxysm of heart-rending grief or misery. And near at hand!

I sat up, cocked my head, till I was able to establish the direction from which the sounds were coming – and they seemed to be coming from beyond the wall behind my bunk, the opposite direction from the door and the corridor that led to the upper deck.

The weeping was broken, from time to time, by outbursts of incomprehensible muttering, as if the sufferer – and it was a man – was trying to come to terms with his misery by telling it to himself over and over again.

By the moonlight that filtered in through the porthole, I slipped out of my bunk and crossed to that wall through which the sounds seemed to be coming. As I did so, the suffering man gave a deep and expiring groan that faded away into silence. It was repeated. Again – silence.

No sound, then, but the gentle slapping of water along the ship's side below my porthole.

I crept back into my bunk; and some prompting of childhood's terror caused me to pull the sheets over my head, to shut out the sounds of night's uneasy phantoms.

chapter two

I was awakened again, in the dawn light, by the rattling of
heavy chains on an iron deck, the hoarse cries of men and a
clanging of bells. Then the whole vessel gave a shudder, and
I heard the pounding beat of a powerful engine. There was a
sensation of motion. The *Dolphin* was moving.

Mist still lay over all, shutting out the hills whose shapes
the lights of last night had described; but from my porthole,
through which I looked, crouched on my bunk with my
dressing-gown wrapped about me, I was able to see the grey
water sliding past, and the boats in the anchorage.

Presently, we began to turn. Presently, all Falmouth passed
in front of me: the empty streets, towers and steeples, rooks
in high trees, the docks. There was a slight bump – and the
yacht came to rest beside a pier. Bells tinkled again. I distinctly heard a cry: 'Finished with engine!' A patter of bare
feet on the deck above my head, and a gangplank was pushed
in place, spanning ship and shore. Right outside my cabin
porthole. I should have a grandstand view of the owner and
passengers coming aboard.

I identified the owner quite soon...

He came after I had had breakfast (boiled eggs and coffee,
all served in silver, on silver, in my cabin): a tall, thick-set
man of around sixty, with fierce blue eyes, brick-red cheeks,
and whiskers of a glaring whiteness. He stomped up the
gangplank, staring about him with a proprietorial air, yachting cap set jauntily aslant. So this was Commander Saltram.
He looked terrifying – but likeable. Just as Melloney had
described him.

I stayed in my cabin through the middle of the morning,
and every time there came the sound of footsteps on the gangplank I rushed to see who had arrived next.

Mostly it was provisions: sacks, boxes and casks borne on
the backs of seamen and porters. There was luggage:
splendid-looking trunks and military chests; ladies' hat-boxes
and portmanteaux of calf and crocodile. I wondered how
many passengers would be coming on the voyage, and

whether any of them would be notable or famous; or the aristocracy, or even royalty. The splendours of the *Dolphin* were quite equal to coping with the needs of such elevated personages, surely.

It would have been at about ten o'clock that footsteps brought me again to the porthole, and I saw ... *them*. The couple with whom I had had the embarrassing wrangle in the station yard the previous afternoon!

He preceded her up the gangplank, assisting her with a hand on her elbow. He was dressed as before, in broadcloth and a billycock; she was wearing another enormous creation of millinery surmounted by a dove-coloured bird with extended wings, and an extremely smart suit of grey and white stripes that admirably set off her excellent figure. The same flame-coloured hair; the same cold arrogance. How I envied her.

It was no use ...

I said as much to myself in the mirror. I should have to go to Commander Saltram and confess that I had had a public quarrel with two of his guests; furthermore, that I had bested them in what for them must have been particularly humiliating circumstances. And I must confess before I was brought face to face with that couple, to the hideous embarrassment of all concerned. I must tell the commander – and immediately resign.

There came a discreet tap on my door. I opened it, to one of the stewards.

'Commander Saltram sends his compliments, ma'am, and would Miss Trewella be so good as to come and see him now.'

I tarried only to pick up a clean handkerchief and tuck it in the sleeve of my blouse. A last glance at myself in the mirror: I was pale and tragic-looking, and my blue serge skirt was shiny at the hips. No matter – it was good enough to wear back at St Finn board school.

The steward led the way: up the stairs and along the boat deck; past the tall brass funnel and in through an entrance beneath the bridge. It was like a march to the scaffold. I closed my eyes and wished myself far away when he paused and tapped on a door. There was a muffled response. The door opened.

'Miss Trewella, sir,' said the steward.

He looked up from his desk at the far end of the cabin, his lean, dark face betraying nothing of shock or surprise – nothing to match my own expression. The deep brown eyes took me in, from head to foot, without so much as a flicker.

The billycock hat was perched at a corner of the desk. Sending for me must have been almost the first thing he thought of after coming aboard.

Commander Jason Saltram then got to his feet and treated me to a brief nod that carried with it neither distaste nor recognition – only bland blankness.

'Good morning, Miss Trewella,' he said. 'Please be seated. I regret that, since summoning you, a small administrative crisis has arisen. But, if you will bear with me in patience for a few minutes, I will quickly deal with it.'

The crisis concerned one of his guests who had missed the train from London. He had taken up the telephone that stood on his desk and was speaking into the mouthpiece; speaking – by some modern miracle of communication between ship and shore – to the Station Master of Falmouth railway station.

With his profile turned to me, I had the opportunity of studying him: he was like a compressed spring: all pent-up energy. The very hand that held the earpiece of the instrument was as taut and sinewy as the claw of a hawk.

No elderly retired sea-officer he. I had deceived myself in my predictions about my new employer. And it came to me, then, how I had been ably assisted in the self-deception by the impressions which Melloney Lumley had given me. No wonder her lovely blue eyes had danced with merriment when she had spoken to me of her guardian; of his age and infirmities – age and infirmities, indeed!

The man at the other end of the telephone wire had just delivered a lengthy explanation, to which Commander Saltram had listened with a deadly kind of patience. Then he replied.

'Let me make this clear,' he said. 'I am not remotely concerned that Lady Topsham and her maid were late for the train at Paddington Station; nor for the reasons why your people at Paddington were unable – or unwilling – to hold back the train till their arrival. I am only concerned that Lady Topsham is brought here immediately. Here is what you will do: you will telegraph your people at Paddington and instruct them to put on a special train – at my expense – for Lady Topsham and her maid to be conveyed to Falmouth at express speed. When that is done, you will immediately telephone me and inform me of the train's estimated time of arrival. Do you have any questions? No. Good.'

He put the earpiece back on its hook. His brief address had been delivered – for all its forcefulness – in a bland and imperturbable manner; as if it was the most natural thing in the world to order special express trains, as if they were as readily available as three-farthing loaves. Calm and imperturbable still, he turned back to me.

'You are younger than I imagined,' he said. 'But then, your half-sister was considerably older. It must be – let me see – nine years since she passed away. And she would have been your present age then. You do not greatly resemble her, Miss Trewella, do you know that?'

'So I am told, sir,' I answered nervously. 'I don't remember her very well. She was away in service most of my childhood, and I only saw her occasionally.'

'As at the time when your mother died,' he said. 'I recall that she asked for leave to attend the funeral and settle you in a foster home. My uncle – the late Sir David Lumley – was very happy to grant her request. Harriet Cadge was much liked by the family. By Melloney, by all of us. I, personally, admired her greatly. She had – how shall I put it? – an inner fortitude in adversity which any man would have been proud to own.'

It seemed odd to be sitting there, listening to that strange and rather alarming man, talking about the half-sister whom I had scarcely known. To tell the truth, I had not greatly liked Harriet, nor had I thought that she was particularly fond of me. It was the old story of the widow who remarried to provide a new father for her child. My own father – Harriet's stepfather – had died soon after my birth, leaving our mother worse off than before, with two mouths to feed instead of one. Harriet had had to go out in service at an early age. Her natural qualities had lifted her up; she had educated herself and had become a governess, a person of refinement. I tried to recall her face the last time I saw her – when she came to kiss me good night after settling me in at a foster home, before returning to the Lumleys, to illness and to death – but nothing came.

I remembered one thing...

'Harriet wrote me a long letter,' I told Commander Saltram, 'while she was dying. She was very brave. Hardly mentioned herself; she seemed only concerned with me and my future life. She begged me to work hard at my books and to become a teacher.'

'And this you did,' he said. 'I am right in saying, if I have been correctly informed, that you have been a credit to her and have taken advantage of all your opportunities.'

I dropped my eyes before his searching gaze and said: 'When she died, Harriet left me her life savings, which were enough to pay my foster parents till I was of an age to leave and take the post of pupil-teacher at St Finn. Thanks to Harriet, I've always enjoyed a measure of independence. Without that, I would have been nowhere. I owe her everything.'

He nodded. 'I am satisfied, Miss Trewella, that I made a good choice in offering the post to the half-sister of Harriet Cadge. You do not look alike, but you have shown yourself to be similarly worthy and industrious.' The dark eyes flared briefly, and my heart missed a beat. 'I also know, from personal experience, that you are not without something of her inner fortitude. You are willing to fight for your rights.'

It was the first allusion he had made to our previous meeting.

'I – I'm sorry for what happened at the station, Commander Saltram,' I whispered.

'Why so?' he demanded. 'Why should you be sorry? You were entirely within your rights.' He added with a wry smile: 'I rather fancy, however, that my dear friend Miss

Topsham does not take such a liberal view of the occurrence. She was – quite annoyed. But she will get over it.'

'I – I hope so,' I said fervently.

'Miss Trewella,' he said, 'I should like you please to turn round and look at the portrait hanging on the bulkhead behind you.'

I obeyed him.

'I believe you have already met my ward?'

'Why, yes. Yes!' I cried. 'And that's her. That's Melloney.'

It was a gilt-framed painting of a young girl on a grey horse: she was a flaxen-haired, merry-eyed slip of a thing dressed in formal black riding-habit that seemed entirely unsuitable for one of her looks; she should have been wearing Greek draperies, with flowers twined in her hair; young Diana the Huntress. It was indeed Melloney – the young Melloney scarcely out of childhood – in all her thrilling liveliness and gaiety.

'That is my ward at the age of fifteen,' he said soberly. 'As she was when your sister first knew her. Before she had ... the accident.'

'Accident?' I glanced towards him; he was looking down at his hands. 'I didn't know ...'

'She was thrown from a horse – the selfsame grey in the painting,' he said. 'It was not thought at first that she had suffered serious injury. But her condition rapidly deteriorated. Now she has to be wheeled, or carried, everywhere.'

'How awful!' I cried. 'That one so lively and beautiful should ...'

'Life is frequently cruel, Miss Trewella,' he broke in harshly. 'And it is not given to all of us to know the full extent of the cruelties that lie in store for us – for which we should give profound thanks.' So saying, he reached into a drawer of his desk and took out a calf-bound volume and laid it before him. 'I am going to ask you a special favour, which you may well see fit to refuse, Miss Trewella.'

'What would that be, sir?' I asked him in trepidation.

'I am going to ask you solemnly to swear upon this Bible that you will keep a confidence which I propose to share with you. That you will never repeat it to a living soul, till the time comes – as come it will – when the secret is a secret no longer. Are you willing to do this?'

'Gladly, sir!' I cried. 'But I would keep any secret that you reposed in me, Bible or no Bible.'

'I would prefer a formal oath,' he replied. 'Not because I have any doubt that you will break your word, but because, as you will soon appreciate, the gravity of the matter demands it.'

With that, I laid my hand upon the Bible and gave the promise he required. And when I had done this, it seemed to me that an expression of relief flitted across his uncompromising countenance; the look of someone who is about to shed – or share – an intolerable burden.

'What do you wish to tell me, Commander Saltram?' I asked gently.

He crossed over to the far side of the cabin, by the porthole, where he paused and looked out broodingly.

'I have brought you here to be companion to my ward, because I hope – and indeed I believe – that you will be the faithful companion and friend that your sister was also,' he said.

'I will do everything in my power,' I told him.

He nodded gravely, and turned to face me.

'There never was woman who stood so in need of a friend,' he said. 'As you will realize when I tell you that Melloney, who has known almost constant pain for the last ten years, has scarcely begun her martyrdom. Her torments will increase, Miss Trewella. In twelve months, or less, they will become intolerable. Shortly after, that lovely girl will die in agony!'

'No!' I cried in horror. 'No – it can't be so!'

He turned his back on me again, directed his gaze broodingly at the figure in the portrait.

'She doesn't know,' he said. 'She must never know. Death, when it comes, must take her unawares.'

'But – can't something be done?' I asked him. 'Physicians have made such strides in the last few years. Surely ...'

'Her case is hopeless!'

'Surely, somewhere ... abroad ...'

'She has been to the leading specialists of Europe and

America! My God, Miss Trewella, with the fortune at my disposal, do you think that I would have stinted in obtaining the finest opinions available in the world? Our family doctor has taken her to see the top physicians and surgeons dealing with such cases. Only last month she came back from Geneva. This very week she has been in London, undergoing the most rigorous examinations. The verdict has been the same everywhere: *Hopeless!*'

'And she has no suspicions about ... about ...' I could not bring myself to finish.

'That she is doomed to die? – none at all! She has been told that the pain must increase before it gets better, nothing else. Her courage and cheerfulness – as you have seen – are boundless, an inspiration to all who come into contact with her. And so it must remain. She cannot be allowed to suffer the ultimate agony of hopeless despair.'

My eyes were brimming with tears of pity. I gazed upon the laughing face in the painting; imagined the boundless energy and love of life that had so inspired the artist; shrank away from the thought of all that beauty and vitality being condemned to a cruel death and an untimely grave.

'No, Commander Saltram!' I cried. 'Melloney must never know! The time left to her must be filled with every kind thought and action that love and friendship can bestow. And I promise that I will do my own best to help make it so.'

He took my hand, which felt small and helpless inside the hard grasp of his. The very dark and brooding eyes gazed down at me intently.

'So be it, Miss Trewella,' he declared. 'It will be a pact between us; the two of us, sharers of the terrible secret (for apart from Dr Weems, the family physician and Nurse Bagley, no one else knows the full truth): that we will devote ourselves to making Melloney's last months as free of hurt as is possible. At least she will never know what it is to be lacking in affection; never experience the loneliness of despair. It is for this reason, you see, that I have arranged this present cruise. As soon as Dr Weems received confirmation from the Geneva specialists that the case was hopeless, I conceived the idea of giving Melloney what might well be the last summer vacation of her life: a winter cruise in North African waters. A false summer... a *Dolphin* summer.'

'I'll do everything in my power to make the *Dolphin* summer perfect for her,' I said.

He nodded. 'I know I can rely on you,' he said. 'I have carefully chosen a small party to accompany us, including Miss Topsham, a lady of Melloney's age. Your own duties will be light, for Melloney tires very easily and will need to rest for a great deal of the voyage. Later, when we reach the warmth of North Africa, you will be able to accompany her ashore on various sightseeing excursions. I trust you won't find it too dull, Miss Trewella,' he added anxiously.

I assured him, with perfect truth, that I would not.

Commander Saltram courteously dismissed me with the instruction to join him and the others for luncheon at one o'clock in the saloon, for, as he said, I should be having my meals with Melloney and their guests. Even as I was taking my leave of him, a message came over the telephone from the railway station to say that the special train bearing Lady Topsham and her maid was due to leave Paddington immediately and was to be expected in Falmouth at a quarter to five in the afternoon.

I wondered what relation this Lady Topsham was to the insufferable flame-headed beauty referred to by Commander Saltram as 'my dear friend Miss Topsham' – she who was not taking his liberal view of the incident in the station yard. Were they mother and daughter, perhaps? In any event, her ladyship would not be in Falmouth in time for luncheon – that hurdle which I so soon had to surmount. I also fell to wondering, while getting myself ready for the ordeal, what the beautiful Miss Topsham was to the Commander and what he was to her. Was it likely that they were affianced? Strangely, I found the idea disquieting – though why this should have been so was quite beyond me.

At a quarter to one, changed into the modern brown dress that had been my Sunday best in St Finn, I made my way to the saloon: down the sumptuous stairway and past the spouting dolphin and its attendant nymph, the shaded lights, the air of careless luxury. And my heart pounded with sheer nervousness.

I saw her – Miss Topsham – almost immediately. And the more easily because she was still wearing the extravagance of dove-coloured millinery on her head. Our eyes met across the long apartment. She paused in the act of speaking to her companion. Her flawless face hardened.

'My dear Oriana' – it was the Commander who stood by her, together with another man – 'may I present Miss Annabel Trewella, who has come to be Melloney's companion? Miss Trewella, meet Miss Oriana Topsham.'

The mask of beauty betrayed nothing of her feelings save a total contempt. Greeny-grey eyes swam up and down my attire, taking in the plain silver ring that had belonged to my mother and the jade brooch that had been left to me by Harriet – the only items of jewellery that I possessed in the world. What she saw seemed to confirm her in her opinion.

'How do you do?' she said, and looked away. Clearly, it was beneath her contempt even to allude to our previous encounter – for which, let it be said, I was profoundly grateful.

Commander Saltram indicated his other companion.

'And this is Mr John Bennett, of Boston, Massachusetts,' he said.

'Delighted, ma'am.' The American's voice was warm and deeply-inflected, reminding me of the soft burr of the mid-Cornish voice.

'How do you do, sir,' I said, giving him my hand. He was tall – tall as the Commander – and wore a tweed Norfolk jacket and knickerbockers with the easy grace of a frontiersman. I was particularly taken by his eyes, which were grey, flecked with hazel, and brimming with good humour.

'And this is Dr Weems,' said the Commander. 'Our family physician, and surgeon-extraordinary for the duration of this coming voyage.'

'Your servant, Miss Trewella.' The doctor had a pleasant, lazy-sounding voice; with a pleasant, sleepy-eyed countenance to go with it. Sandy-haired, bespectacled, gentle.

'My ward you have already met,' concluded the Commander.

Melloney was reclined, as before, on the pink sofa. She was wearing a simple gown of a dull golden colour that enhanced her peach-bloom fairness. She held out her hands to me, smiling with a sudden, heart-warming joy.

'Dear Annabel,' she said. 'Come and sit beside me and meet Sir Gregory Topsham, who is not only a Knight of the Bath, but also an Admiral – and, to paraphrase Mr Gilbert, a right good admiral too!'

'Your servant, ma'am,' cried the Admiral, implanting a kiss upon my hand in the most gallant manner imaginable. He was the fierce, naval-looking gentleman in his sixties whom I had seen coming up the gangplank that morning: the one I had assumed to be the elderly, retired Commander Saltram. I cocked an eye towards Melloney, who was obviously trying hard not to dissolve into laughter.

'Do you not have a strange feeling, dear Annabel,' she said teasingly, 'that you have met Sir Gregory before?'

'Indeed, ma'am?' boomed the Admiral, fixing me with a quizzical glance. 'And where was that, pray? Were you at Cowes Regatta this year? Were you among the guests aboard my flagship HMS *Neanderthal*? Was it then that we met, eh?'

'I'm sorry, Sir Gregory,' I told him, 'but we really haven't met before. 'It's just that' – I shot Melloney a sharp, reproving glance, and it was to her credit that she had the grace to colour up and lower her eyes – 'you remind me of at least two other naval gentlemen – though neither so distinguished as yourself.'

The Admiral showed a very fine set of teeth in a broad grin. 'You turn an excellent compliment, ma'am,' he cried. 'I am happy to make your acquaintance. And I may tell you that you will certainly be receiving an invitation to join my party at Cowes *next* year.'

It was then that the tuneful throbbing of a gong announced that luncheon was ready, and the guests began to move towards the long table that stewards had set down the centre of the saloon. Miraculously, the giant Able Seaman Flack appeared as if from nowhere and took up Melloney. She smiled mischievously at me over his massive shoulder and nodded towards the Admiral.

'You have made a conquest, Annabel dear,' she said.

Commander Saltram took his seat at one end of the table, and Melloney was set at the other. Chief Steward Dacres indicated where the rest of us were placed. I was on Melloney's left, and Sir Gregory was opposite me, on her right. My other neighbour was the American, Mr Bennett.

There was a late-comer: the captain of the *Dolphin* – a stout, red-faced man with four rings of gold lace on his cuffs. He bowed to the company when our host introduced him as Captain Pelly, and took his place on the Commander's left, opposite Oriana Topsham and next to Dr Weems. We were eight.

Captain Pelly muttered his way through a brief Grace before Meat; instantly a small army of stewards swept in from the kitchens, bearing covered dishes which they laid on an enormous sideboard. Menu cards were then presented to every guest.

My heart sank – as I gazed in dismay at the length and breadth of the bill of fare. And – of course – it was all written in French. A swift glance round the table showed me that the others were contemplating their choices with the air of people to whom such things as French menus the size of novelettes are part of the warp and weft of daily life; and I was determined not to make a fool of myself. I would choose something, willy-nilly, and eat it with every appearance of enjoyment.

My eye ran down the huge card. It seemed to me that *Caprice Saint-Sylvestre* had a nice round and satisfying look about it – on the printed page, at least. That would do for me.

'So confusing, Miss Trewella,' murmured Mr Bennett on my left. 'I scarcely know where to begin. As a guide, might I ask what you have chosen, if anything?'

'I'm having – that,' I told him, pointing to the item of my choice.

The American nodded sagely. 'And how right you are, Miss Trewella,' he pronounced. 'One of the great classic desserts of France. Perhaps the finest cake recipe ever devised to delight the discriminating palate.'

'Don't tell me it's ... cake?' I whispered.

He nodded gravely. 'I'm afraid it is,' he whispered in return.

'Thank heaven you told me. I would have looked a fine goose, sitting here and eating cake with the rest of you on your meat course. I – I'm afraid, Mr Bennett, that my French isn't of the best.'

He gave a conspiratorial glance to his left, where Oriana Topsham was deep in conversation with the Commander. 'Nor, to tell the truth, is mine,' he confessed. 'But I can just about find my way through a menu. Tell you what, Miss Trewella: what say if I choose for the both of us? – after due consultation between us, of course.'

'Nothing would make me happier, Mr Bennett,' I told him with heartfelt relief.

'Fine,' he said. 'So how about we both begin with this item – which, unless my uncertain French is leading me right up the garden path, I take to be our old friend the humble pickled herring?'

'Pickled herring – lovely!' I whispered.

His hazel-flecked eyes twinkled. 'I could be so wrong, Miss Trewella,' he warned. 'What do we both do if it turns out to be frogs' legs after all?'

'We will accept defeat,' I replied, matching his mood. 'And we will eat them up, every scrap.'

'Bravo!' cried my new friend.

Conversation was general during the first course. It was while this was being cleared that Sir Gregory – who had been immersed in Melloney's charms – looked round and addressed his host at the far end of the table.

'Well now, my dear Saltram,' he boomed. 'This cruise upon which we are embarking – do you have an itinerary, or are you simply pointing the ship's bows towards the sun, to sail on till we touch the Happy Isles and see the great Achilles? – as Lord Tennyson put it.'

'Our itinerary is a little more precise than that, Sir Gregory,' the Commander replied dryly. 'And Captain Pelly, who has prepared the charts, is better qualified than I to furnish the company with the details. If you would be so kind, Captain.'

'Hem!' Captain Pelly regarded us all from under bushy

eyebrows. 'We sail on tomorrow's tide,' he said. 'It is my hope to raise Gibraltar by the seventeenth, unless the autumn gales in the Bay of Biscay make it advisable to put into La Rochelle, or even into Lisbon. After a stay in Gibraltar for refuelling and sightseeing, we shall proceed eastwards into the Mediterranean, hugging the African coast...'

I had an urge to pinch myself, to prove that I was really present, then and there: I, Annabel Trewella, orphaned board school teacher of mid-Cornwall, who had never in her life set foot further than Truro before this outlandish episode: this strange chain of circumstance that had brought me to a luncheon table in a millionaire's yacht, about to eat – at the recommendation of Mr John Bennett of Boston, Massachusetts – a dish of exotic meats that would have taken a month's pay of a china-clayman; and listening to the names of far-off and dreamlike places that I was soon to see with my living eyes...

'We will put in at Oran, in Algeria,' the Captain was saying.

'Oran I know well,' declared Sir Gregory. 'And you too, I fancy, Saltram, when you were with the Mediterranean Fleet.'

The Commander nodded. 'That was in ninety-four and ninety-five,' he said. 'When I was first lieutenant of *Royal Conqueror*. I made a great friend there of Commandant de Belleisle of the Foreign Legion.'

'Ah, the Legion!' cried Oriana Topsham, clasping her hands and allowing an expression of rapture briefly to occupy the porcelain perfection of her countenance. '*Les beaux sabreurs!* I do hope we have the opportunity of meeting your friend, Jason.'

Commander Saltram did not seem to catch her remark; he was looking into the middle distance with an intense expression in his unbelievably dark eyes.

'I remember one magical night,' he said, 'when Armand de Belleisle brought horses for us, and we rode across the desert to Sidi-bel-Abbès. All through the night. Under the stars of heaven. With half a hundred Spahis riding escort. It was dreamlike. Fantastic.'

I felt my pulse quicken at the image his words conjured up in my mind: I seemed to see them – shadowy figures thundering across the silent desert, their long cloaks streaming in the moonlight. I stared at the speaker, entranced.

All at once, our eyes met. My heart skipped in mid-beat, and I looked away in confusion.

'What topping fun!' trilled Oriana Topsham.

A slight confusion on my right made me look towards Melloney, who seemed to be choking on a mouthful of food; but I guessed – when she winked at me over her handkerchief – that she was only suppressing a giggle.

'Don't you think it sounds topping fun, Annabel?' she whispered to me when she was able.

I nodded – and the strange instant had passed by.

Sir Gregory took a deep draught of his wine, dabbed his lips, and said: 'I recall how highly you were regarded in the Mediterranean Fleet, Saltram. It's a great pity you're not still on full pay. The Navy needs you, my dear fellow. There'll be war before the century's out, never fear.'

Mr Bennett said: 'You are referring to the situation in South Africa, Sir Gregory – you think the aftermath of the Jameson Raid will eventually bring you to war with the Boers?'

The Admiral eyed the speaker coldly. 'No, sir, I am *not* referring to South Africa,' he growled. 'And any disturbance in that area would scarcely deserve the distinction of being called a "war". If the Boers continue to make trouble, they will speedily be crushed with a brigade of cavalry. That, sir, will be the end of it. And the Royal Navy, sir, will not be concerned in the matter.'

'Then who is to be your enemy in this war that will herald in the twentieth century?' persisted my neighbour.

'*Germany.*'

It was Commander Saltram who answered the American. All eyes turned towards him.

'Saltram's right,' said the Admiral. 'For all that he's Her Majesty's grandson, the German Emperor did not appear at the Diamond Jubilee celebrations, and this for the same reason that his yacht *Hohenzollern* has not been seen at Cowes since ninety-five – because he wasn't invited. I tell you there's a widening gulf between our two countries that will not be bridged in the lifetime of anyone present.'

'You may be right, gentlemen,' commented Mr Bennett. 'But all the signs convince me that you will soon have a war on your hands in South Africa – and that it will not be a simple matter of bringing a few Boer farmers to heel with a sabre charge and a whiff of grapeshot.'

Sir Gregory stared at my neighbour, affronted, his brick-red cheeks taking on a purplish tinge, and one glittering blue eye narrowed to a pinpoint.

'Sir!' he growled at length, 'I am aware that you are of the Transatlantic persuasion, and I think you should realize that the system here has greatly improved since we lost the American colonies. In short, sir, we are vastly better at the business of putting upstart colonials in their place!'

Mr Bennett smiled. 'I'm sure you are, sir,' he said. 'And you have certainly been given plenty of opportunity for practice.' He ticked off his fingers one by one. 'There was the Indian Mutiny in fifty-seven; the Maori Wars of sixty and sixty-three; the small problem you had in Abyssinia between sixty-seven and -eight, with another Maori War in the latter year. As for successive troubles in the Sudan ... and I have named only a few ...' he spread his hands and beamed amiably at the furious Admiral.

'One might be excused for thinking that you consider the British to be incapable of keeping their many houses in order, my dear Bennett,' said Commander Saltram wryly.

'I'm sorry, Saltram. I speak only as I have been informed.'

'You are remarkably well informed, sir,' said the Admiral with more than a ghost of a sneer. 'You are, no doubt, a diplomat or a politician of some sort. One of the smarter fellows who move in and put matters to rights after the fighting men have done all the work.'

'No, sir, I am not one of that sort,' replied the American blandly. 'I am a draper.'

'A – *draper*?' exclaimed the Admiral. 'Did I hear you aright, sir – did you say ... a *draper*?'

'A draper!' cried Melloney, clapping her hands with glee.

'How divine! You didn't tell me you were a draper, Mr Bennett; you led me to understand that you were an ordinary old multi-millionaire.'

'I'm sorry to have misled you, ma'am,' said Mr Bennett with a broad grin. 'But it was quite unintentional. To get the record straight, my father is an ordinary old multi-millionaire and my uncle likewise. I am merely one of their employees. And we are all drapers.'

'Mr Bennett is too modest about his family's achievements,' said Commander Saltram. 'And I would further put the record straight by reminding the company that the firm of Charles Bennett and Sons is, of course, the largest and most celebrated chain of drapers and mercers in North America.'

I was amused to note that my neighbour's announcement, enlarged upon by the Commander, had a curious effect upon the guests round the table. Captain Pelly and Dr Weems gazed upon the American with a new respect, while Oriana Topsham was quite unnecessarily patting her flawless side-curls, puffing out her leg-o'-mutton sleeves and arranging her lace cuffs – with an eye on Mr Bennett. Melloney was all excitement. Only Sir Gregory appeared unmoved by what he had heard about the American's connections, and continued to glare at him with distaste.

'Are you over here on holiday, Mr Bennett, or are you here on business?' asked Captain Pelly.

'I seem to be combining a little of both,' smiled my neighbour. 'At least, that's how it has turned out.' He glanced towards the Commander, as if for guidance.

'No point in making a secret of the matter, Bennett,' said the other. 'I should tell you all that our Transatlantic friend has come over, on behalf of his family firm, to make an offer for the purchase of Lumley's.'

'Buy Lumley's!' It was Melloney who made the exclamation. 'Jason! You're not going to sell Lumley's!' Her smooth cheeks had turned quite pale, and her eyes were already brimming with tears.

All eyes turned to the Commander, who bowed his head and began to butter a piece of bread roll.

It was Mr Bennett who answered for him. 'Commander

Saltram has so far refused to discuss the matter with me,' he said. 'Instead we have become great friends, and he has invited me on this trip. I've accepted the invitation. Firstly, because I like Jason Saltram as a friend. Secondly, because – and I might as well out with it – I still have hopes of making a deal for the purchase of his firm.'

'Jason darling, you must sell!' cried Oriana Topsham. 'It's the chance of a lifetime. You'll still be incredibly rich, and free to go back into the Navy, where tremendous opportunities await you. Father's quite sure you could have a ship of your own in no time!'

'Jason already has a ship of his own!' cried Melloney in a strained, tearful voice that nevertheless carried a note of proud defiance. 'He has the *Dolphin*!'

It was a meal that ended with awkward silences strung together with half-hearted attempts on the part of those I would call 'the lesser players' to introduce some commonplace subjects for conversation – but all to no avail. Everyone was too conscious of Melloney's anguished face at the end of the table, and of the way her eyes remained averted. It was obvious that she was praying for the end of the luncheon, and my heart went out to her. I was among those who declined dessert; and the gathering broke up soon afterwards, Commander Saltram taking leave of all of us, with a stiff bow for the company and an anxious glance at his ward.

'I think I should like some fresh air,' announced Melloney.

Able Seaman Flack bore her out on to the poop deck, at the rear end of the yacht; Nanny Bagley arrived with a full-length sable coat into which she fussily wrapped the invalid, insisting that she wear the Russian-style hood attached to the garment.

I went to my cabin for my warm coat and shawl. When I arrived back on the poop deck, Flack was setting up a reclining chair for me beside Melloney, who was having her pulse taken by Dr Weems.

'How is she, Doctor?' asked the nurse in her mournful voice. 'The poor darling should never have been subjected to the ordeal of a formal luncheon party. She should have had a quiet snack in her cabin with Nanny.'

'You fuss too much, Nanny,' said Melloney. 'Everyone fusses too much.'

The doctor relinquished his patient's wrist and gave a lazy smile. 'A short rest in the fresh air will work wonders,' he pronounced. 'We will all leave you in peace with Miss Trewella.'

And this they did.

Though mostly open to the elements, the poop deck was screened on each side by wide glass panels and the deck above – which was the boat deck – extended over the part where we were sitting. The afternoon sun had conquered the morning mist, setting the wrinkled wavelets a-sparkle and picking out the colour of every autumn leaf of the wooded slopes at the far side of the harbour. A seagull glided gracefully towards us, settled upon the top of the flagstaff – and immediately became a lumbering, inelegant bird with over-large feet. Melloney and I laughed to see him.

I turned to regard her: her face had resumed its peach-bloom pink-and-whiteness, framed in the rich black fur of the hood.

'Are you feeling happier now?' I asked.

She nodded bravely. 'In my heart of hearts, I don't really believe that Jason would ever sell Papa David's business,' she said.

'You would hate it – if he did?' I asked.

'I don't think I would ever get over it,' she replied. 'To understand that, you would have to have known Papa David.'

'Tell me about him,' I asked her.

The seagull gave a hoarse cry and rose from the flagstaff with a frantic beating of wings: almost immediately he was a thing of grace once more.

Melloney said: 'Papa David was the kindest man who ever lived. My earliest memories are of him: of the time I lay in a scarlet fever, with his gentle face never far from me; how he would put anything aside – any business, however pressing and important – to listen to my childish prattlings. When one's very young, these things don't mean much; it's only in later years, in moments of reflection, that one appreciates the inner worth of an enormously rich and busy man who would stop everything to mend a little girl's doll. In big things, as in small, he was all heart. Lumley's was more than a business to him: it was a sacred trust, handed down to him by his father, to keep whole and prosperous – for the sake of the hundreds of small, ordinary people for whom it provides a livelihood. Papa David would never have sold Lumley's. He would rather . . . he would rather have cut off his right arm. The idea of selling his work-people into the hands of strangers . . . foreigners . . .'

'I'm sure that, as you said, Commander Saltram feels the same as you about his uncle,' I told her.

'Jason's different,' she said. And a shadow passed across her lovely features. 'He only succeeded to the estate by default, because Papa David had no direct heirs. He resented having to come out of the Navy; he never speaks of it, but I know it's so. And he can't wait to go back . . .'

Her voice trailed away. We sat in silence. A large bank of cloud was drifting slowly towards the sun: I told myself that we would go below when that happened. Meanwhile, it was strangely pleasant to sit and do nothing.

Footfalls on the deck above our heads . . .

A woman's light tread, and the heavier step of a man.

Voices . . .

'What time is Mama's train due in?' The affected drawl of Oriana Topsham.

'Shortly before five, Saltram tells me. I must say it's a very civilized mode of travel – by private train. A style of living to which one could easily become addicted. What do you say, my dear?' This was the Admiral.

I exchanged glances with Melloney, who flashed a mischievous smile and put a finger to her lips for silence. We were to be eavesdroppers then, and with some reluctance on my part: I have always felt that eavesdroppers are at a grave disadvantage, inasmuch as they are condemned to hear, without the opportunity of protest, everything that is delivered to them, whether good or bad. In view of what followed, I blame myself for not putting this point of view to my companion.

Oriana Topsham made no direct reply to her father's comment, instead she said: 'I simply cannot get over that absurd outburst from that hysterical creature at luncheon.'

'Melloney, you mean? Can't say that I would call it an outburst. She got a trifle het up, that's all, poor little gel.'

'Little girl? She's no girl, Father. She's older than I am, for all her simpering ways and her simple flowing frocks.'

'Oh come, my dear. That's a harsh judgement on a cripple who's simply making the best of herself. Personally, I find her entirely charming and attractive to gaze upon. Full of spirit, too. Brave little filly.'

While Sir Gregory was speaking, Melloney put on an expression of syrupy charm, fluttering her eyelashes and pouting her lips. She then quickly changed her mime to a grimace that would have done justice to a prizefighter, and was obviously meant to represent spirited bravery. I pressed a handkerchief to my mouth to prevent myself from laughing out loud.

'In my opinion, Father,' said Oriana Topsham, 'your "brave little filly" is a calculating baggage who squeezes every last ounce of advantage from her condition. She cultivates poor health with the care and devotion you lavish upon the carnations you grow on the stern-gallery of your flagship. I tell you, the woman's no more than a professional invalid. And she's ruining Jason's life and career.'

I looked away from Melloney, fearful of what I should see there. I was prompted to call out: to warn that loose-tongued wicked creature to be silent. Coward that I was, I hesitated to do so.

And then it was too late: from the uncharitable, Oriana Topsham moved to the unspeakable.

'Oh come, my dear,' protested the Admiral. 'Saltram is only carrying out his obligations to the gel...'

'She's destroying him!' snapped Oriana Topsham. 'If it hadn't been for her, Jason would never have left the Navy, but would have sold Lumley's as soon as it came into his hands. For all that he's related to the Lumleys, Jason's a gentleman.'

'I don't like to see a gentleman mixed up in trade,' growled the Admiral. 'Makes one wonder what the country's coming to.'

'He left the Navy to continue to provide a home background for that woman – that scheming cripple! And you do realize, don't you, Father, that she's not related to him? She doesn't even own the name she uses. She's nothing but a ... a *foundling*!'

Melloney's hand came out and took hold of mine. It was trembling, and I gave it a comforting squeeze. Her face was averted from me, pressed to the sable fur of her hood. I saw only the angle of her cheek, now pale, down which coursed a single tear. At that moment, I could cheerfully have choked the life from out of Oriana Topsham.

That was the close of the hideous episode. Their footsteps passed along the deck and their voices faded to silence.

'We shouldn't have heard that,' whispered my companion. 'One just shouldn't hear things like ...'

'Oh Melloney!' I cried.

Her head was against my shoulder, and my arms about her.

'But it's true,' she sobbed. 'Every word. I *am* ruining Jason's life and career. If it hadn't been for me, I think he would have sold Lumley's already, and given up St Errol House, the *Dolphin* and everything. He doesn't need these things; he only keeps them going for my sake. And, as that awful woman said, I'm nothing to him. Just a ... just a ...'

I laid my hand across her lips, to silence her.

'No, Melloney,' I cried. 'Don't say those things.'

'I wish I were dead,' she whispered brokenly against my hand. And she repeated it again: 'I wish I were dead.'

I thought of the secret I held in my heart: the secret given me by Jason Saltram, and sworn to concealment upon the Holy Book. And, knowing that her awful heart-cry was doomed to be fulfilled, I wept with her.

It was some time before Melloney had composed herself sufficiently to allow me to summon Able Seaman Flack, who came and bore her to her cabin. Nanny Bagley was there to receive her, and the faithful nurse's sharp eyes soon discerned that her beloved charge had been crying. By the sharp glance I suffered from those berry-black, sombre eyes, I gathered that I had been judged and found guilty of causing the upset. Neither Melloney nor I, of course, alluded to the real reason.

'No sitting up to dinner for you this night, my darling girl!' cried Nanny Bagley, taking off Melloney's pink kid button-boots and chafing her feet. 'And it's straight to bed as soon as you've had a cup of tea and a biscuit.'

'I'll see you in the morning, Annabel,' said Melloney, squeezing my hand. And her eyes lit up. 'Don't forget we sail with the morning's tide. We're leaving, Annabel! Out into the wide sea, and away to the wonderful *Dolphin* summer!'

I felt elated when I left her: she had that power, the ability to shut out darkness and admit light. By the time I reached my cabin, I had forgotten the agonizing episode on the poop deck. As soon as I opened the door, I sensed that something was amiss. My elation was swept away like snow before the sun of springtime.

The birdcage was uncovered. The piece of American cloth lay on the carpet beneath it, as if it had fallen off. Or had been taken off and thrown down.

'*Jackie!*'

His perch was empty: no sign of the little bird. I swiftly crossed the cabin and reached up to the cage.

It was not empty; the small bundle of yellow plumage lay at the bottom, below the perch and swing, tiny claws relaxed in death, bright eyes shut for ever.

I opened the cage door and took him out. He was quite warm still. The little head lolled brokenly.

How could it have happened? That someone could have come into the cabin while I was absent, removed the American cloth, opened the cage door, and deliberately and maliciously ...

I put the idea out of my mind; it was totally unacceptable to me. I had no enemies aboard the *Dolphin*. No one who could possibly have such an insane hatred towards me as to destroy that little scrap of life. Some sudden malady must have struck at Jackie and taken him.

So I wept a few tears and put him in an old cigar box in

which I had brought my sewing materials. And I weighted the box with a pretty, blue-flecked stone that I had picked up, one summer's day, on a Cornish beach; then tied the lid with a blue hair-ribbon.

The autumn evening was already closing down upon Falmouth, and the lights were making long reflections in the oily water, as I went out to the poop deck. No one was there to see me drop the box into the harbour, where it sank immediately.

I did not stray from my quarters again that night. The Chief Steward telephoned to ask if I should be attending dinner in the saloon at eight, or if I required it in my cabin. I declined both suggestions and asked only for a cup of tea, which was brought to me on the inevitable silver tray.

I sat down by lamplight and wrote goodbye letters to everyone I knew : to the Penburys, to the old couple who had been my foster-parents before I went to St Finn, to a former fellow pupil-teacher who had married and gone to live in Truro. I told them all about the *Dolphin* summer, and guessed how they would envy me my coming experiences. Finally, having written myself into a state of sleepiness, I took a hot bath and went to bed.

But sleep was long in coming, despite all; for my waking thoughts remained strong, and were forever returning to the lovely, tragic woman whose companion I now was. Her face loomed large in my mind's eye; and beyond it I saw the darkly sardonic countenance of Jason Saltram.

I heard the throb of a fishing boat's engine as it put out to sea; the slight disturbance of its passing caused the *Dolphin* to roll gently at her ropes. The rocking motion must have carried me away, for I knew no more till morning light flooded in through the porthole.

No uneasy phantom had disturbed my rest. If the unknown man had wept again in the dark hours, his agony had passed unheard by me.

chapter three

The morning of Wednesday 13 October brought a light rain and mist that miraculously lifted by ten o'clock and revealed the West Country's most beautiful harbour in all its glory of wooded hills and shaded inlets. At midday exactly, the *Dolphin* cast off her ropes and slid out on the ebb tide, watched from the quays by a sizeable crowd of well-wishers.

A telephone call from the Chief Steward courteously advised me that Miss Melloney was awaiting the pleasure of my company on the poop deck, where a buffet luncheon was to be served in order to allow the guests to enjoy the prospects of leaving harbour and setting off across the English Channel.

I clad myself warmly and repaired to the poop deck where I found Melloney in a sheltered spot, wrapped in her sables and hood, and reclining on a wicker settle amid a cascade of silk cushions. She greeted me with her habitual dancing-eyed delight and a hand-squeeze. With her were Dr Weems, Sir Gregory and Mr Bennett. The menfolk bowed to me, and the American handed me his binoculars and directed me to feast my eyes on the beauties of St Mawes harbour and village opposite, which, he said, would presently be opened to our view as we came out of the inner harbour of Falmouth and into the main stream. I was focusing the glasses in this direction (and acutely conscious of Mr Bennett's closeness and the tangy scent of the distinctive cologne he was wearing), when a sudden flurry of greetings heralded the arrival of Commander Saltram, Oriana Topsham, and a marvellously turned-out lady of middle years whom I correctly assumed to be her mother.

'Lady Topsham,' said the Commander, 'I think you know everyone except Miss Trewella, who was not at dinner last evening.'

Her ladyship graciously gave me her gloved hand and contrived to look agreeable while staring straight through me. I had no doubts that her equally haughty daughter had apprised her of my position among the guests aboard the *Dolphin*, and she accorded me just that amount of attention – and no more – of which she considered me to be worthy. Then, dismissing me from her mind, she turned a more interested glance to Melloney, through a lorgnette.

'And how are you, my dear?' she asked. 'I missed you when I came aboard, and again at dinner. It was with some difficulty that I was dissuaded from coming round to see you in your cabin, to feed you a little soup and perhaps chat to you for a while.'

Melloney was quite straight-faced, but I saw an imp of secret mischief sparkle in her dazzling blue eyes as she meekly replied. 'What a beautiful thought, Lady T. I had no idea you'd taken up doing good works. Do you dispense a lot of soup and chit-chat?'

Her ladyship looked a little uneasy, as if she was not quite sure if she was being teased or not. 'I deem it my duty,' she said, 'to perform the obligation of sick-visiting, particularly to members of Sir Gregory's fleet and their families. I am always well received, I must say.'

'Perhaps,' commented Melloney, straight-faced still, 'perhaps the poor sailors and their families believe that anyone so grand as an admiral's wife has the healing touch – you know, the way kings and queens were once supposed to be able to cure scrofula by the laying on of hands. Have you ever tried it, Lady T? I don't suppose you'd have much of an effect upon scrofula – but you might make some small inroads on, say, toothache. Or a runny nose.'

'Well, really, I . . .' Her ladyship looked about her, as if for guidance. Commander Saltram provided a timely diversion by calling to the attendant stewards to provide champagne for his guests. This he followed with a reproving glance in Melloney's direction.

'I adore champagne!' she cried, quite uncontrite.

The Commander himself poured a quarter of a glassful and handed it to her. I was close enough to hear him say: 'And that is all you are having today, my dear Melloney. More than this and you will not only be disobeying doctor's orders, but also teasing my guests even further. I am not very pleased with you.'

Despite the mildness of his rebuke, he really looked quite angry. Melloney only pouted and did not look one bit put out; but it seemed to me that his manner was overly harsh to a poor stricken girl such as she.

As for Lady Topsham, she darted an indignant glance in Melloney's direction and turned to address her daughter; but we had not heard the last from the admiral's wife on that memorable occasion.

Mr Bennett touched my shoulder. 'There you see St Mawes Castle coming up on your left, Miss Trewella,' he said. 'And its sister stronghold of Pendennis Castle guards the other point on the right. Between them lies Black Rock, which we shall leave on our right, or starboard, hand.'

By then, the *Dolphin* was turning into mid-channel and pointing towards the glittering strip of open sea that lay between the wooded headlands. As we gathered speed, white water surged away behind us, and I felt an almost imperceptible rocking motion.

'Do you suffer from sea-sickness, Miss Trewella?' asked Dr Weems, who had joined us, champagne glass in hand. 'Am I to put you on my list of potential patients? I have a most effective preventative draught that never fails.'

'I really don't know, Doctor,' I confessed. 'This will be the first time I have ever been to sea.'

'I am convinced that sea-sickness is hysterical in origin,' said the doctor with his slow, lazy smile. 'And you seem very much the phlegmatic type to me.'

'You're very wrong,' I assured him. 'I'm really a bundle of nerves, and can imagine myself into almost any state.' Then, all unbidden, I had an impulse to confide in the *Dolphin*'s surgeon. 'Do you know, the first night I spent aboard here, I imagined that I heard a man sobbing his heart out in a nearby cabin. And I'm not so sure it was imagination.'

No one else had heard my remark; Mr Bennett had moved just out of earshot. Dr Weems' gentle eyes clouded with mild puzzlement behind his thick-lensed spectacles.

'Did you now?' he said slowly. 'A sobbing man, eh? Now, that was a very odd thing to hear, Miss Trewella.'

'There goes Black Rock!' came an interruption from Commander Saltram, as a rocky fang of an islet slid past down the right side of the yacht some five hundred yards distant. 'Ladies and gentlemen, regard it well: it's the nearest you'll come to England for another six months.'

Glasses were raised to Black Rock, and Mr Bennett threw the dregs of his champagne over the side in what he described as 'a libation to Britannia, Mistress of the Seas' – a gesture that won him a much overdue glance of approval from Sir Gregory.

'I'm hungry,' announced Melloney.

The stewards brought forward a buffet table laden with cold meats and concoctions of every conceivable variety. And more champagne, together with other wines both red and white. Looking to Mr Bennett for guidance, as before, I accepted his suggestion of a cold lobster with salad. Folding chairs and tables had been set up, and Mr Bennett and I made a trio with Dr Weems; the Topshams and the Commander shared the other table, and Melloney remained reclining in her wicker settle.

All Cornwall was on our right: hills and headlands bathed in the October sunlight, and so clearly that it seemed as if I could reach out and touch each leaf and pebble. The *Dolphin* had increased speed: we were fairly flying past a four-masted sailing ship labouring on under full press of canvas. The scene was set for Lady Topsham to dominate the conversation, which she did at once.

'Commander,' she began in a loud voice, 'I must repeat my thanks for your prompt attendance upon my needs. The private train from Paddington saved me over an hour's wait and the tedium of an absurd thing that was due to stop at every station along the line. I should never have arrived in time for dinner.'

'A great pleasure to have been of service, my lady,' murmured the Commander.

Her ladyship gave an arch smile, looking about her so that we should have its benefit. 'Speaking of service rendered,' she said, 'the reason I missed my express in the first place was because I had to carry out a small commission for our host. Isn't that so, Commander?'

Jason Saltram had not the sort of face that could accommodate an expression of embarrassment, but it came close to it; his expression darkened, and he looked down at his plate. 'That is so, my lady,' he growled.

'A small errand,' cried Lady Topsham, 'of a most exciting nature. Isn't that the truth, Commander?'

The reply came in a deep murmur. 'Some might think so, ma'am.'

Her ladyship continued: still smiling, still apparently unaware of the resentment she was clearly causing to the object of her comments. 'I must tell you all that I received a telegraph message from the Commander yesterday morning, asking me to call at Cartier's the jewellers and collect a certain item, to bring down with me. True, Commander?'

'Yes,' he confirmed curtly.

'Mama,' interposed Oriana Topsham. 'Perhaps Jason doesn't wish it to be known that...'

'Quite so, my dear,' boomed the Admiral. 'Clara, I think you should not...'

But Lady Topsham was not to be denied the pleasure of telling her story. She swam sedately through all opposition, like a swam through a flock of milling farmyard ducks, driving all before her.

'A most splendid item of jewellery,' she told us. 'I doubt if even Her Majesty, nor yet the Tsarina, has a piece to match it. I wonder if I dare ask the Commander to show it to you all?'

There was a denial on Jason Saltram's lips. 'Your ladyship, regrettably, I...'

But she would have nothing of it. 'I know he is carrying it with him,' she said with a syrupy coyness, 'for I saw him take the box from his pocket when he came on deck, and reassure himself that its precious contents were still intact.'

'Oh, come on, Jason!' cried Melloney. 'Be a sport and put us all out of our misery. Our appetites have been so whetted by Lady T's story that I declare, if you don't satisfy our curiosity, I shall call upon the other menfolk to bind you to the mainmast and commit an act of piracy upon your pocket!'

Not even this lighthearted approach softened the grim-faced manner with which Jason Saltram dipped into the pocket of his yachting jacket and brought forth a small leather jewel box which he laid on the table before him. I followed the movements of his lithe, brown fingers as they nimbly tripped the catch. The lid of the box flipped open.

'Oh! How gorgeous!' cried Oriana Topsham with un-ashamed delight.

'It's – very pretty,' said Melloney in a tight little voice.

It was a ring: a diamond ring, with a large central stone surrounded by a collar of smaller diamonds. It was inexpress-ibly beautiful and expensive-looking, a ring fit for an em-press. It was – very obviously – an engagement ring.

'And now do you see why I was delighted to carry out the Commander's commission and collect it from Cartier's?' asked Lady Topsham of us all. 'Can you not imagine what dis-appointment it could have caused if I had refused?'

All eyes were upon Oriana Topsham, whose marble cheeks had taken on two spots of bright colour. She was watching the ring, and the tip of her small tongue came out and moistened her nether lip.

'It would have been – a great shame – to have left it be-hind,' she murmured.

No one gave a thought for Melloney – no one, that is, but me. I glanced at her covertly, to see what effect, after her first reaction, the incident of the ring was having upon her. She was watching the Commander – and her blue eyes told me nothing.

Jason Saltram broke the spell by snapping shut the small box and replacing it in his pocket.

'If you will excuse me, ladies and gentlemen,' he said, rising, 'I must go up and join Captain Pelly on the bridge, to approve the course we must set for Cape Finisterre, which – as you may know – is the north-westernmost point of the Iberian peninsula. For your information, we estimate to pass close by it at noon the day after tomorrow.'

He bowed, and left us. Oriana Topsham, who had watched the return of the ring to his pocket with disappointment, turned and flashed an angry glance at her mother. Lady Topsham's mask-like face was washed of all expression; she gazed after the Commander's retreating figure with the wistful air of a puppet-master whose favourite doll has refused to dance on strings and has gone off on its own.

'Will someone please summon Able Seaman Flack?' murmured Melloney. 'Excess of fresh air has made me feel rather faint. I should like to go to my cabin.'

Flack arrived, and took her up. Doctor Weems made to follow after them – and so did I.

'Don't come with me, Annabel,' whispered Melloney, squeezing my hand. 'When the doctor's done with me, I should really much prefer to be alone for a while.' Her eyes were sad and my heart went out to her as I watched Flack carry her towards the gangway of the boat deck.

The *Dolphin* had changed course, and was now heading straight out to sea, so that Cornwall was all behind us and receding fast. The party on the poop deck had broken up. The Topshams had gone below – to discuss the incident of the ring, I didn't doubt. Only Mr Bennett remained: he stood, leaning on the stern rail, by the fluttering British ensign, looking back along the white-flecked wake, where the seagulls swooped and screeched.

'Well, Miss Trewella,' he said. 'Looks as if this trip's going to end with wedding bells. Can't say I'm surprised. What do you say?'

'I'm afraid I don't have any views on the subject,' I said rather frostily.

'It's a very suitable match,' he said. 'I gather that Jason Saltram owes his rapid advancement in the Navy so far to Sir Gregory's patronage. How much more will the Admiral not do for his son-in-law? Do you find me cynical, Miss Trewella?'

'The thought had crossed my mind, Mr Bennett,' I replied.

He grinned disarmingly. 'You're darned right I'm cynical, ma'am. And I can't afford not to be; with a multi-million deal to put through, I'm clutching at every last bit of cynicism I can make stick. Yes, ma'am! When my friend Jason marries Miss Topsham, I'm banking on the fact that she's going to get him out of Lumley's and back into the Navy so fast that he won't feel it happen.'

'Really?' I replied.

'Cynicism and self-interest aside,' said Mr Bennett, 'I still think it will be a good match. She's a nice girl: beautiful, elegant, make him a good wife... I sure wouldn't fancy that Lady Topsham for a mother-in-law! No, ma'am!'

Despite myself, I had to smile. 'She might improve on acquaintance,' I ventured.

He shook his head firmly. 'If you really believe that, Miss Trewella,' he said, 'it only goes to show you've got a beautiful disposition, to match your beautiful face. That woman's a dragon – that's what she is, a regular dragon. And this is what makes me uneasy: my old man always says to me, "Son, always look at the mother before you propose to the daughter." And that's the only doubt I have about the wisdom of my friend Jason Saltram marrying Miss Topsham.'

'That isn't what worries me,' I murmured, half to myself.

He shot me a keen look. 'You mean how's Melloney going to take it?' he said. 'You're right – she isn't going to like losing her guardian one bit.'

He stared back towards the wake, and I studied the profile of the gentleman from Boston, Massachusetts. Mr Bennett was shrewder than I had thought. Really quite shrewd.

By mid-afternoon we had seen the last of England and were ploughing southwards through a smooth sea that did no more than lightly rock the *Dolphin* in her passage. I looked forward to a good night's sleep, lulled by the gentle motion; and only hoped that poor Melloney would be similarly blessed.

At about five o'clock I went down to my cabin. It was just getting towards dusk, and the corridor lights had been put on. My bunk had been made and the coverlet turned back; the cabin was dusted, tidied and polished like a new pin.

I opened the top drawer of the chest of drawers to take out a clean handkerchief – and immediately saw that someone else had been there!

Now, I am not an excessively tidy person, but my tidiness follows a certain pattern which I can immediately recognize. Because I am very sensitive to colour, it matters more to me that a drawer full of assorted small linens are grouped according to their colours than that they are piled particularly neatly.

That drawer held three piles of handkerchiefs, all standing as neatly as platefuls of cut sandwiches; but all higgledy-piggledy as to colour, with blue-edged ones in the same pile as reds, whites mixed with coloureds, and so forth. Someone had taken them all out – and put them back again.

It was the same in my trinket drawer. The bits and pieces: cotton bobbins, scraps of material for patching, darning wools – they had all been taken out and put back again with what was to me a false neatness.

Further examination made it quite clear that everything I owned had been carefully turned over and examined – and then put back again.

Why? – I asked myself. Why?

I sat down to think it out. The chair faced the porthole and the lace curtains were drawn aside, to show a view of the grey sea sliding past under the darkening sky. It also showed something else. My skin prickled. The hairs at the back of my neck stood up, one by one; I distinctly felt them.

I went over to examine the glass of the porthole. Its centre was faintly misted, as when a person breathes upon the chill surface. And written upon the mist as if with a fingertip, were two stark words:

HELP ME!

Even as I stared, bemused and frightened, the misting was fading from the glass, and the message dying before my very eyes.

A message from – whom?

It sounded like the despairing cry of a soul in torment; and this brought me to think of the man who sobbed in the night. And the phrase: HELP ME! – that suggested the heartcry of a prisoner, a captive. But who was he, or she, this prisoner? And whose captive?

A little later, the cabin steward brought a message from Nurse Bagley, who had sent him to tell me that Melloney had a slight fever and would not be dining with the company. I took this as a hint from Melloney that I was under no obligation to attend either – and asked the steward to bring me a light supper in my cabin. I also asked him – as a sudden afterthought just as he was leaving – if he had a passkey to the cabin door, or would it inconvenience him if I locked up and took my key when leaving the cabin? The young fellow – he was no more than a lad – said he indeed possessed a master-key, and raised his eyebrows in surprise at the idea of a passenger aboard the *Dolphin* locking against intruders. Eyebrow-raising butters no parsnips with me, and never has. Let him think what he liked. After what had happened to poor Jackie, followed by the prying into my belongings and the message on the porthole glass, I was for keeping out intruders.

So I spent my first night at sea alone in my cabin, where I did a bit of needlework: refurbishing an old petticoat with some oddments of lace I had bought in Bodmin market. You may be sure my mind had plenty with which to occupy itself during the purely mechanical task. One decision I arrived at during the evening was that I should say nothing to anyone about the strange message, or anything that might be connected with it. I decided that this was best for everyone's sake, particularly for Melloney's.

I retired early to my bunk, and the gentle motion soon turned me to sleep. The sea grew rougher, rough enough to waken me about midnight. As I lay there, listening to the creak of the cabin panelling and the hissing of the waves sliding past outside, I distinctly heard it: the anguished sobbing of the unquiet prisoner. It lasted for only a short time, then faded away: just as the cry for help had faded with the insubstantial mist upon which it had been written.

In the days and nights that followed, I slid easily into the routine of shipboard; so easily, indeed, that one might have thought I had seafaring blood in my veins; though, to my knowledge, my family had never strayed from mid-Cornwall.

Still, I suppose that all West Country folk – indeed, all the inhabitants of our islands – are never so far from the sea as not to have had a sailor somewhere in their distant ancestry.

One thing of which I was quickly grateful: I found myself immune to sea-sickness, and had no need of Dr Weems's draughts. Not so Oriana Topsham: I was uncharitable enough to notice, with some wry amusement, that whenever the motion of the yacht caused the stewards to attach little wooden railings – they are called 'fiddles' – to the sides of the saloon table at mealtimes, to prevent the plates and dishes from slipping into one's lap, the admiral's daughter remained in her cabin. On the other hand, I was sorry to learn that poor Melloney suffered occasionally from the same complaint, especially in the evenings, and never appeared at dinner throughout the passage to Gibraltar. In consequence, neither did I, but took a light supper in my cabin, which suited me better.

Routine of shipboard – as far as the passengers were concerned – began at eight o'clock in the morning, or 'Eight Bells' as I quickly learned to call it, since it was heralded by four strident double-strokes of the ornamental brass bell that hung under the awning of the poop deck. Eight bells brought me delicious-smelling coffee, Melba toast, marmalade, Cornish farm butter and clotted cream – delivered on a huge silver tray by the cabin steward, together with a daily report from the Captain, copied out, as I knew, by the Commander's secretary, Mr Robbins, in the Ship's Office every morning. I have one with me still, dated Friday, 15 October, 1897. The stiff card is creased and crinkled, and the ink smeared from immersion in salt sea-water, but it can still be read. Mostly composed, it is to be imagined, with an eye to the interests of the nautically-inclined gentlemen among the saloon passengers, it tells how we were steering a course of south, south-west at a speed of ten knots – inclement conditions having made it necessary, for the sake of the passengers' comfort, to reduce speed slightly; in consequence of which, we should not be passing Cape Finisterre till two in the afternoon, and our estimated arrival at Gibraltar would now be 11 a.m. on Monday the eighteenth. The report also carries a postscript to the effect that Mr John Bennett shared with Miss Annabel Trewella the £5 sweepstake prize for the nearest guess to the yacht's twenty-four-hour run from midday to midday. In view of the fact that Mr Bennett both gave me the figure and financed my entry into the sweepstake, that £2 10s was surely the most easily-earned money I had ever received in my life.

Breakfast over, I bathed, dressed and – after locking my cabin door – went for a stroll on the upper deck. As the first saloon passenger about, this always won me interested glances from the sailors at work, cleaning, polishing or plaiting ropes and wires – things which, to my observation, sailors seem to be doing all the time; and, on one occasion, a message from Captain Pelly, presenting his compliments to Miss Trewella and would she honour him by her presence on the navigation bridge?

The Captain handed me up the ladder to his holy of holies, which was a mass of brightly-polished instruments set among a baffling array of brass and copper pipes. There was an able seaman at the great steering wheel, and Third Officer Maugham stood at his elbow looking very self-important. He had the gall to wink at me.

Captain Pelly was a kind gentleman with an old-world gallantry that I found extremely flattering. It needed only for me to show the slightest interest and he rattled off the astonishing facts and figures involved in keeping a sixteen-hundred-ton steam yacht at sea in the Year of Grace eighteen hundred and ninety-seven. In addition to himself and four watchkeeping officers, he told me, the *Dolphin* required no less than nineteen seamen of all grades, from boatswain and carpenter to ship's boy, to handle her. And the great coal-burning boiler and the steam engine that drove her slender prow so sleekly through the waters of Biscay – they were ministered to by a chief engineer and two assistant engineer officers, plus firemen and greasers to the number of twelve. Warming to his theme, Captain Pelly asked me if I realized that the Chief Steward required six assistant stewards and cooks to attend to and feed the passengers? – nor did he consider himself any too well staffed. To round off the crew were a steward and cook to look after the yacht's officers, and two cooks for the sailors. In all, eight officers and forty-one men.

For me, who had had some acquaintance with modest housekeeping in the school house at St Finn, and had seen Mrs Penbury trying to square her yearnings for the genteel existence with a housekeeping allowance of eight shillings a week, the scale of living aboard the *Dolphin* was like that of another world. Eight officers and forty-one men – to look after and transport around the seas a mere handful of pampered people and their servants (and I considered myself one of the latter), and at a cost of – Captain Pelly himself whispered the figure into my ear, after making sure that neither his third officer nor the sailor at the wheel could overhear – £714 a month, for wages, stores, and coal. And this figure took no account of the sumptuous food and wines consumed in the saloon.

I have said that I regarded myself as a servant aboard the *Dolphin*. Indeed, this was my position: that of a higher servant, comparable with, say, that of child's governess. My half-sister Harriet must have enjoyed a similar status at the Lumley mansion at St Errol: the privilege of eating at table with her charge, of being allowed to address Melloney by her first name, of being treated with some deference by Nanny Bagley and the other paid staff.

During the five days' passage to Gibraltar, I did not see all that much of Melloney – and this to my regret, for I had quickly grown fond of her; and how could it have been otherwise? – she with her breathtaking gaiety, her dancing wit, the entrancing shifts of mood from shadow to sunlight – always towards the sunlight. She would come on deck shortly before luncheon. If Nanny, Dr Weems, or her guardian were not about, she would call for champagne for the both of us, and would sip hers with the guilty haste of a little girl stealing jam from her mother's pantry. On fine days, we all sat down to lunch in the saloon, with Lady Topsham occupying Commander Saltram's right and Oriana on his left.

Every day after our departure from Falmouth, as soon as she appeared for the first time, I found my gaze being dragged inexorably towards the third finger of Oriana Topsham's left hand; and I am quite sure that everyone else did the same, particularly Melloney. But Thursday followed Wednesday, and waxed into Friday; Saturday came, too – but still that glorious ring of diamonds did not appear on her finger. It occurred to me that Jason Saltram was perhaps waiting for our arrival at Gibraltar before making his gesture of betrothal. John Bennett, during an after-luncheon chat and a stroll we enjoyed together on the boat deck on – I think – the Saturday afternoon, put forward the cynical view that Lady Topsham's overbearing and indiscreet behaviour when we were leaving Falmouth had had the reverse effect from that which her ladyship had intended: instead of encouraging the would-be swain into making an early declaration, Jason Saltram had taken fright; had seen the image of his would-be mother-in-law behind the face of his beloved – and that the diamond engagement ring would presently find its way back to Cartier's whence it came.

Mainly because Melloney was obliged to take a rest after luncheon and seldom appeared for tea, I found myself thrown more and more into the company of the gentleman from Boston, Massachusetts. John – I drifted into calling him that at his own request, but only when we were alone – walked with me, taught me to play several two-handed card games at the saloon table, and genuinely put himself out to be a pleasant and amusing companion. With John, I felt none of the strain that I experienced in my relationship with the other-passengers – excepting Melloney. Thanks to Mrs Penbury's firm tuition, I am possessed of all the superficial trappings of gentility: I know how to murmur 'how do you do' when introduced; I can handle my knife and fork; and I would never dream of interrupting a gentleman when he was addressing the company. At this level, living in close quarters with people so grand as the Topshams and Commander Saltram presented no great embarrassments. But, though I never drank from my finger bowl, nor ate peas off my knife, I was hideously aware of the unbridgeable gulf that yawned between us: a gulf hollowed out by money and position, and the things that money and position bring in their train – like the lordly assurance that the world is ordered for one's benefit; that the 'lower orders' are happy – indeed, grateful – to pander to one's every whim; and the belief that the lavish display of one's possessions, one's jewels, horses, houses, yachts, give rise not to un-Christian envy on the part of the deprived, but to pleasure and admiration.

John Bennett was quite different from the others. Though, from casual things he let drop, it was clear that he had been born with a whole canteen of silver spoons in his mouth, into a family who could probably have bought and sold the Topshams and the Lumleys together, he seemed quite unspoilt and unaffected. There was none of the Topshams' snobbishness; none of Commander Saltram's calm arrogance. I grew to like him very much.

My only other occasional companion during the first days out from Falmouth was Third Officer Maugham, who would sometimes meet me on deck and stroll with me. He improved on acquaintance, as most people will. Beneath the brashness and conceit was a man who – rather surprisingly – was somewhat shy and uncertain of himself. I gathered that he was an only son, sent by his widowed mother at considerable sacrifice to nautical college, in order to follow the footsteps of his father who had been the commander of a crack Atlantic liner. Despite being, as he said, very well-qualified in his profession, I got the impression that Jack Maugham felt insignificant in the giant shadow of his distinguished sire, and that, deep down, he would have been happier in some other occupation.

This was only an impression that I had from three or four brief meetings – no more. Maugham took his meals with the other officers, whose saloon was also used by Nurse Bagley, the Commander's secretary and Lady Topsham's lady's maid. I had little opportunity to get to know him better.

Little opportunity, and – as an evil fate willed it – even less time.

I retired early, as usual, on the night of Sunday, 17 October. From the Captain's daily report, we had learned that the *Dolphin* was due to sail close by Cape Trafalgar in the early hours of Monday morning, and there had been some talk – mostly between John Bennett and the Commander – of going out on deck when the yacht actually passed through the historic area where Lord Nelson gained his famous victory. With much eyelash-fluttering, Oriana Topsham had implied that she, also, would like to be called on deck at eight bells of the middle watch, 'to honour the Immortal Memory', as she put it; a suggestion that Melloney had squashed with the wry comment – accompanied by a mischievous twinkle in my direction – that bad weather was expected during the middle watch and that 'darling Oriana' would do better to stay in her bunk with a couple of opium pills to keep her company.

In fact, the *Dolphin* was rolling quite heavily while I was preparing for bed, as the movement of the water in my hand-basin amply demonstrated, and the creak of the panelling was so loud that I remember thinking, with some relief, that it would shut out the sounds of the sobbing man, if he were to begin.

It was then – and I had just kicked off my bedroom slippers – that the telephone bell rang out with a sudden insistence that made me start with alarm.

I crossed to the instrument; took it down from its hook.

'Miss Trewella, this is Jack Maugham. I must see you. Urgently. Privately.' The Third Officer's voice was strained and urgent. It was also hushed – as if he was in fear of being overheard. I recalled that he would be speaking from the Chief Steward's pantry, which should have been closed at that hour.

I thought of the hour. 'Can't it wait till morning?' I asked him. 'Surely there's nothing that . . .'

'I've got to see you!' he whispered hoarsely. 'Listen . . . I come off watch at midnight. Meet me on the poop deck just after twelve. Be there – please. It's terribly important. There's something you must know. Something terribly' – he seemed to be searching for the word – 'terribly *puzzling!*'

The instrument gave a click in my ear and went dead. I replaced it on the hook, and met my own reflection in the mirror opposite. I looked pale and drawn – but in a rather romantic and interesting manner. All unbidden, I seemed to hear again a remark that John Bennett had made – surely in jest – to the effect that I must have a beautiful disposition to match my beautiful face.

Enough of that, I told myself...

What was amiss with Jack Maugham? Why had he found it necessary to communicate with me at such a late hour? And to make a midnight assignation with me? I had last seen him – I thought back – at about four o'clock that same afternoon, when we had passed with the exchange of a nod and a smile on the boat deck. No sign, then, of anything troubling him to such an extent.

'Something terribly important...something I must know ...something terribly *puzzling*!'

One thing I knew, and I knew it with great clarity: notwithstanding the lateness and inconvenience of the hour, despite the discomfort of turning out of a warm cabin at the witching hour to go out into the blustery night, and even bearing in mind the sheer impropriety of meeting a young gentleman alone at such an hour – taking one thing with another, nothing on earth would prevent me from keeping the assignation. My female curiosity was aroused to such an extent that the prospect of waiting – I cast a swift glance to the clock – a whole two hours and forty minutes to hear what it was that Third Officer Maugham could not wait till daylight to divulge was going to be the worst possible form of torture.

I resolved to make the best shift I could with curbing my impatience. Hopeless to attempt to lie down and rest till midnight; I should either lie in an eternity of boredom, or else fall asleep till the morning sun awakened me. So I took out my needlework again, and applied myself to what I had overheard the *Dolphin*'s sailors describe as 'me bit of make-and-mend': patching up my old petticoats and refurbishing a torn shift. And my mind worried busily all the while at the question before me: what would I learn from Third Officer Maugham at midnight?

It came to me quite quickly, of course: the probability that what was troubling Jack Maugham was likely to be of a piece with the things that had been troubling me.

In particular: the strange message on my porthole, coupled with the searching of my belongings; the inexplicable fate of my poor little canary; the mystery of the man who sobbed in the night.

Yes, I told myself, that was it: Jack Maugham had just recently stumbled on the reason behind all these strange doings. And he was puzzled.

Perhaps he hoped that I should be able to provide him with the additional piece of evidence that would solve that puzzle. It was a theme for speculation as I plied my busy needle for two hours and forty minutes.

For the passengers' comfort, the ship's bell was not rung to mark out the passing half-hours of the watches between dawn and dusk. It was in silence that I left my cabin at twelve o'clock, locking it behind me as usual, and making my way down the corridor to the boat deck and beyond. The rolling had abated, and with it the sounds of motion: nothing but the gentle, faraway throb of the great steam engine and the rush of waters slipping past us in the darkness.

I was agreeably surprised to find that the night was warm, even balmy; and I supposed it to be because we were rapidly passing into sub-tropical climes. The sky above the decks – freshly-scrubbed and gleaming white in the moonlight – was spangled with diamond constellations of many stars, and the air smelled like champagne.

There was no sign of anyone on the boat deck; only the wink-ing lights at the mastheads and another cluster of brightness at the navigation bridge. I paused at the rail, by one of the long lifeboats, and looked out across the ever-moving waters, with their hidden depths of shadow and secret caverns of bright luminosity.

I was standing there, drinking in the beauty of the night, when I quite distinctly heard a loud cry: a man's cry, sharp and instantly quenched. Coming from the direction of the stern, from the poop deck. Or perhaps I had been mistaken; had it not sounded more like the call of a seagull? We were close to land. Yes, it must certainly have been a seagull.

One reached the poop deck by means of a covered companionway that led down from the rear end of the boat deck. I passed out of the moonlight and into shadow as I descended. At the foot of the companionway was a short corridor – also unlit at that hour – which led out on to the open poop.

It was while negotiating this corridor, with one hand against the wall to guide me and my eyes fixed firmly on the rectangle of moonlit sky ahead of me, that I had ... *the sensation of someone passing me in the opposite direction.*

'Is that you, Mr Maugham?' I asked.

There was no reply; but the impression of being close to another living and breathing person was very strong. I paused; reached out a hand, in order to touch ... whoever was there. My fingertips met only the empty air. Almost immediately after that, it seemed as if the apparition had taken flight, and I was alone.

I went out on to the moonlit poop deck. There was no one there. No Third Officer Jack Maugham. Only an empty flag-post traced against the night sky, and the luminous white wake stretching behind us into the secret darkness.

I waited about half an hour for Mr Maugham, and then it grew chill on the open deck. With a shiver, as if someone had just walked over my grave, I turned and found my way back to my cabin.

The steward woke me early, with the apology that, though it was only seven bells, we were approaching the Strait of Gibraltar. A very fine sight to behold, he informed me. And the gentlemen were already on deck with their spy-glasses.

The view from my bathroom porthole, which looked out from the left-hand side of the yacht, presented me with a stretch of coastline that could not have been more than four miles distant, with a small white town and a lighthouse on a promontory; and beyond that, a range of mountains set against a startling azure sky. This was southern Spain.

I skimped my breakfast, and my toilette also, cramming my unruly hair under a straw hat and tying a scarf over all, wrapping a shawl about my shoulders, and rushing out on to the boat deck.

'Miss Trewella, ma'am!' It was Captain Pelly waving to

me from the navigation bridge. 'May we have the pleasure of your company, dear lady?'

Commander Saltram was on the bridge, tall and lean in navy blue; he nodded gravely to me and returned to examining the Strait ahead through his telescope. John Bennett was present also. He took my arm and led me to one side of the bridge.

'Look down there at our escorts, Annabel,' he said, pointing.

'Dolphins!' I cried.

Two graceful, black-backed shapes were cavorting along beside the yacht, close by our bows; plunging in and out of the foaming wake, for all the world like boys at play. Every so often, one of them would take a deep dive clean under the vessel, and its companion would follow; then both would reappear, leaping high out of the water, as if to let us all know that they had returned.

'They'll follow us right through the Strait,' John informed me, 'till we reach Gibraltar breakwater, then they'll break off and escort another vessel back out into the Atlantic. I guess some international commission should be set up, to reward them for their services.'

'They're lovely!' I cried. 'What do they eat?'

'Fish,' said John. 'Being mammals, that doesn't make them cannibals. Why, here comes Melloney. Hi there, Melloney! Good morning!'

She was all in buttercup yellow and pretty as a picture, and Able Seaman Flack carried her along the boat deck, setting her down upon a reclining chair by the rails just below us. I waved down to her and she blew me a gay kiss in reply. Nurse Bagley was with her: she treated us to a grave nod.

'Isn't it lovely?' cried Melloney.

'Have you seen the dolphins?' I called back.

'No! Where? Oh, Annabel, aren't they beautiful?'

From the poop deck came the strident clang-clang of the ship's bell: four double strokes.

'Eight bells,' said the officer who was standing by the helmsman. 'Quartermaster, go and present my compliments to Mr

Maugham. Remind him that he is due to take over from me for the morning watch, and that I should like to be relieved on time for a change, if this does not impose too great a strain upon his resources.'

'Aye, aye, sir.' The man departed, grinning.

'If you look almost directly ahead, Miss Trewella,' said Commander Saltram, 'you will presently see the Rock of Gibraltar coming into view round the far headland. Take my telescope. That's the ticket. Lay the end of it on my shoulder, close your left eye and squint through with your right.'

He had turned his back to me, and the end of the long telescope was resting on one of his broad shoulders. He was so close to me that I could see the weave of his yachting jacket, the texture of his dark skin, the gleaming short hairs that rose above the white shirt collar.

'Do you see the Rock?' he asked.

I closed my left eye, as I had been told. To my surprise, my hands were trembling. Looking through the telescope was rather like peering closely into a goldfish bowl; but suddenly my eyes adjusted to the vision, and I saw the distant, rocky point on our left as hard and clear as if I were standing there. Something loomed beyond: a grey, domed shape rising out of the blueness.

'I see it!' I cried excitedly. 'The Rock!'

A puzzled voice said loudly: 'Can't understand it, sir. Mr Maugham ain't in his cabin and nowhere to be found. Don't look as if his bunk's been slept in, either.'

Quite distinctly I felt a chill feeling creep over my skin, and my scalp seemed to crawl. I lowered the telescope, and met the surprised gaze of Jason Saltram's dark eyes.

'Is there something the matter, Miss Trewella?' he asked.

'Third Officer Maugham,' I faltered. 'He's missing.'

'So I hear,' he replied. Then, turning to the sailor, he demanded: 'Pipe round the yacht for him. He may have gone to the officers' saloon for a cup of coffee before coming on watch.'

'I've piped from fore to aft, sir,' replied the sailor, wide-eyed. 'And Mr Maugham ain't nowhere to be seen.'

There was a moment of tension so keen that you could have reached out and touched it. Captain Pelly and the Commander exchanged glances, and the latter nodded.

'Stop engine!' barked the Captain.

'Stop engine!' was repeated down a voice-pipe.

There was an immediately noticeable change of sound to the ship's engine, and the hissing of water lessened. We came slowly to a halt.

'When was he last seen?' demanded Captain Pelly, turning to the other officer. 'Who had the middle watch?'

'Davies had the middle, sir. He relieved Maugham five minutes before midnight, you may be sure. He's very punctual – not like Maugham.'

'That's right, sir. Maugham stood watch with me and we were both relieved before midnight,' said another. The rest of the yacht's officers, attracted by the hue and cry, were coming up on to the bridge, and sailors were crowding on to the boat deck, looking up at us and muttering together.

'Has anyone seen him since midnight?' demanded Captain Pelly.

There was no reply. The Captain looked to his employer, and Jason Saltram nodded again.

'Make steam for full speed!' cried the Captain. 'Starboard your helm – and back the way we came!'

Some time later, racing back along the track we had taken, I collected my thoughts and laid them out. When I had examined them, I decided what best to do – which was to tell John Bennett everything I knew and suspected.

chapter four

There was hardly a breath of air in the high-ceilinged room in the police station off Gibraltar's main street, though the windows were open and shielded from the sun's glare by striped awnings on the outside. A fly was buzzing somewhere above my head. A carriage clattered over the cobblestones that lay beyond the narrow garden with its enclosing railings and palm trees.

The police inspector remained with his head bowed over some papers on his desk. He had not spoken to me since waving me to the chair before him and courteously begging my indulgence while he made a note of something.

Presently, he looked up with a smile: a big man in his middle forties with a heavy moustache in the military style, eyebrows to match, and a slight paunch that overtopped the cummerbund he wore under a short uniform coatee.

'This is a bad business, Miss Trewella,' he said slowly. 'A bad business indeed. Unless the poor fellow has been picked up by a passing fishing boat – and, in view of the weather, I do not rate the chances very highly – I feel that he must have perished. From his fellow-officers of the *Dolphin* I learn that, though a man of quite powerful physique, he was not a very adept swimmer. It is an oddity I have many times observed among those who follow the seafaring profession.'

I said: 'I – I can't believe it's happened.'

The long search to seaward that the *Dolphin* had continued at full speed for several hours had yielded the sight of nothing but a few scraps of driftwood, floating bottles, and some coconut shells. No Jack Maugham – dead or alive. At noon we had run into the beginnings of a gale that rendered any further search both impossible and useless; so Captain Pelly turned his vessel and ran before the gale to Gibraltar – where he immediately informed the authorities that a member of his crew had been lost overboard.

And now, the following day, I had been summoned to explain my own part in the tragic business. John Bennett was waiting for me outside in the hallway of the police station.

'You have stated to my subordinate, aboard the *Dolphin* last evening,' said the inspector, referring to his notes, 'that you were only slightly acquainted with this young officer?'

'That is so, Inspector.' I could see what was coming and dreaded it.

'You were not, by any stretch of the imagination what one might call' – one blue eye probed me from under a raised, bushy eyebrow – 'close friends?'

'No,' I said. 'Mr Maugham was the first to greet me when I first came aboard the *Dolphin*. We met on deck several times during the passage from Falmouth, when we strolled and chatted.'

'And that was the sum of your acquaintance with this unfortunate young man?'

I nodded. 'Yes, Inspector.'

He glanced down at his notes again. 'Now, I am informed that Maugham was on duty on the bridge from eight p.m. till midnight – which is referred to in nautical circles as the first watch. In consequence of being the junior officer and the one with the least experience, he always kept night watches with the First Officer. And did so on this occasion. Hem.' He riffled through his papers and found another sheet. 'According to the statement given by First Officer Crane, it was at about nine p.m. that Maugham left the navigation bridge to make a tour of inspection of the vessel – a routine procedure carried out at least once during each watch, either by the junior officer or the duty quartermaster. He would ensure himself, during the course of this inspection, that the navigation lights were burning correctly, that the fire-fighting appliances were in place, that the crew were all turned-in in their hammocks, and such routine matters concerning safety and discipline. Miss Trewella, I think you are able to enlighten us about another action that Third Officer Maugham performed on that occasion.'

I gave a start at the suddenness of his last remark, and was uncomfortably aware of the probing blue eye.

'Yes,' I said. 'Mr Maugham telephoned me in my cabin.'

'That would have been at – let me see – nine-fifteen, you

said. And he would have made the call from the telephone connection in the Chief Steward's pantry – which compartment he would have visited as part of his tour of inspection. And he made an assignation with you, Miss Trewella.'

'Yes,' I murmured in a tiny voice that did not sound like mine.

'To meet on the poop deck, at midnight, after he came off watch. And you kept your part of the assignation.' The eye probed me from head to foot, and noted how my hands were clenched tightly together on my lap, so that the knuckles showed whitely. 'Now, why did you do that, Miss Trewella?'

'I was ... curious,' I whispered.

'*Curious!*' He looked down at his notes. 'This officer, this young man with whom you only had a slight acquaintance, telephones to make a midnight rendezvous, giving as a reason the fact that there is something you must know ... something terribly important ... terribly puzzling. Now, I have to tell you, Miss Trewella, that I find it very strange that a young lady in your situation did not tell the young gentleman – and in no mean terms – that this terribly puzzling information could very well wait till morning.'

'I – I suppose so,' I admitted lamely. 'But he made it sound so important that I ...'

'Unless' – he interrupted me – 'unless Third Officer Maugham's message had a special import for you ... *taken in conjunction with other matters that were, perhaps, troubling your mind?*'

'No!' I replied so sharply that my voice, ringing loudly in the high-ceilinged room, shocked even myself. His eyes widened with surprise. 'I – I mean it wasn't like that,' I added lamely.

'You have no idea of the subject about which Maugham wanted to speak with you?' he asked.

'No,' I replied truthfully – though, if his eyes had not been upon me, I might have crossed my fingers, as I had seen Melloney do.

'So there was nothing else – no other matters puzzling or troubling you; matters that you confided to Third Officer

Maugham – which would have caused him to make the assignation and you to keep it because you were – as you put it – curious?'

'No, Inspector,' I replied with less than the complete truth.

He looked disappointed in me, sighed, and rose to his feet as an indication that the interview – interrogation – was over.

'There will shortly be an inquest, Miss Trewella,' he said. 'And you will be called upon to attend and give evidence to the coroner. I understand that the *Dolphin* is to remain in Gibraltar for some few days, so there should be no question of having to delay its departure on your account.'

I nodded meekly. 'Yes, Inspector.' Let him only permit me to go, I told myself, and I would agree to anything.

He accompanied me to the door, holding it open for me. His bulk towered above me as I slipped past him.

'One thing more, Miss Trewella,' he said. 'If, by chance, anything else occurs to you – as, for instance, if you were to recall a conversation or incident that might have accounted for Maugham's telephone call . . .'

'I will let you know, Inspector,' I said.

He bowed. 'I am at your service any time, Miss Trewella,' he said.

I seemed to feel his eyes boring into my back, and the sensation lent an unsteadiness to my tread, as I walked down the hall to where John Bennett was waiting for me, a straw boater under his arm and carrying a walking cane.

'How did you get on?' John asked me in a low voice.

I turned, to see the door of the inspector's office quietly close behind him. He had, indeed, watched me progressing the whole length of the hall.

'He – the inspector – knows that I'm holding something back,' I whispered. 'He leapt on to it at once! John, I'm not so sure I was right in taking your advice. I feel like going straight back in there, to tell him everything.'

The hazel-flecked eyes remained bland. He took me by the arm. 'Not now, Annabel,' he said. 'Later, if you like. But first let me buy you some tea. And while we're having tea, we'll talk the whole thing right through again, and see what it all adds up to – this significant evidence that you're keeping from the police.'

The teashop was in Main Street, a narrow, crooked and twisty thoroughfare that runs through the centre of Gibraltar town, which itself skirts the foothills of the high-shouldered peak that seems to rise straight out of the plain and the almost encircling sea. Main Street I found to be noisy, jostling, exciting: full of proud-stepping Spaniards, sly-looking Levantines, white-clad and whiskered Jack Tars; and children – barefoot, wide-eyed and laughing – children everywhere.

The teashop was set back a little, in a small square fringed with shady lime trees; and we sat at a wrought-iron table in the open shade and watched the crowds go past, while a smiling old *señora* plied us with tea and toasted crumpets, cucumber sandwiches and seed cake.

'It's like we never left England,' grinned my companion. 'You folks never cease to amaze me. You spread yourselves all over the globe, but you don't consciously change a thing; the subject peoples keep their ancient customs – with your customs grafted on top. Cricket matches and curry. Seed cake and a distant view of the Sierra Nevada. Crazy – but it seems to work, though I wonder for how much longer.'

'We were going to talk,' I reminded him, 'about those things I should have told to the inspector.'

'My pardon, Annabel,' he said. 'Let's start with Maugham's warning when you first met: when he muttered darkly that you'd be glad of a friend aboard the *Dolphin* before the voyage was through' – he beamed and laid a hand on mine – 'and, incidentally, Annabel, he was sure right in that assertion, was he not? And you have got yourself a friend in me, have you not?'

'Yes, John,' I said, gently disengaging my hand. 'You are my very good friend. Now can we please continue the discussion? You were saying?'

'Third Officer Maugham,' he continued, 'had already been twice threatened with dismissal for inefficiency before the *Dolphin* summer was even dreamed of. I had this from Captain Pelly. It seems Maugham had all the right qualifications, the book knowledge of seamanship and all that, but his heart wasn't really in it. What you'd call a round peg in a square hole.'

'But he wanted very badly to succeed,' I said, remembering.

'Then don't you see, Annabel? – this puts his remark in a very different light. This was the remark of an aggrieved employee. A guy with a chip on his shoulder about the boss-man.'

A very small girl came up to our table, dragging a basket nearly as tall as herself, full of white jasmine flowers. She prattled a few words of Spanish, and John took a bunch of jasmine and pressed a shilling into her small brown palm. I was amused to see her test the coin with a bite of her teeth as she struggled away. John handed me the flowers.

I thanked him and said: 'Very well, John. I accept your explanation for Maugham's warning. But what about the search among my belongings – who went through all my things with a fine tooth comb?'

He looked embarrassed – as indeed he had looked embarrassed when I had first mentioned it to him the day before.

'The cabin steward did it,' he said. 'Who else?'

'The steward?' I echoed, astonished.

He gave a small cough and said: 'Annabel, I guess you unpacked your own baggage, put it away in drawers, hung up the dresses and the like in the wardrobe. Am I right?'

I stared at him uncomprehendingly. 'Of course I did. Why would I do other...?' then I saw my mistake. Back came a half-forgotten pronouncement I had once heard from the lips of my social mentor, Mrs Penbury, and I repeated it: 'The gentry don't unpack their own things. If they don't travel with a personal valet or lady's maid, it becomes the task of the host's servants.' And I bowed my head, feeling a complete fool.

He said: 'Right. Finding you'd unpacked, the cabin steward would feel that you'd done his job for him, but he'd still check through to see if there was anything that needed to be laundered or pressed.' He grinned, and in such a candid and self-mocking manner as to remove any overtones of snobbishness from his remark: 'That's the way well-heeled folk are indulged throughout Europe, Annabel. And likewise in Boston, Massachusetts, I would add.'

'All right,' I said. 'The steward went through my things. But who wrote the message on the porthole glass?'

He shook his head. 'I can't explain that, Annabel,' he said seriously.

'And my pet canary?' I persisted.

He passed his hand across his brow. 'Annabel, Annabel,' he murmured, 'you realize what you're trying to say?'

'Jackie was alive and well when I left the cabin at a quarter to one to go down to luncheon,' I said evenly, being determined not to sound as emotional as I felt. 'When I came back, his cage had been uncovered and he was freshly dead. I thought at the time – but I forced it straight out of my mind – that it seemed as if his little neck had been wrung.'

'But you didn't keep his body?'

'No.'

He spread his hands. 'So what can I say? We'll never know now. We'll never have any better evidence than this impression you had in a moment of shock and grief at the loss of your little bird. Is that enough evidence to present to the police? That – and a message that faded in mist?'

'The sobbing man!' I cried desperately. 'What about the man who sobs in the night?'

He sighed. 'Annabel, I have to tell you that I've checked around. There's a framed plan of the *Dolphin* in the officers' saloon. From it, I discovered that there are two cabins immediately behind the forward bulkhead of your cabin – in the direction from which you say you hear the sounds. On enquiry, I was told these two cabins are both unoccupied this voyage. However, it's possible that the sounds could have travelled through the air-ventilating system which stretches the length of the yacht and could act as a sound tube or voice-pipe. In which case your sobbing man could be almost anywhere.'

I looked straight into those flecked grey eyes. 'John, you think I'm just being a silly, hysterical woman, don't you?'

He shook his head. 'There isn't a scrap of silliness in your pretty head, my dear,' he said. 'I think you've taken the disconnected items of evidence – the things you've told me about – and composed in your mind a lurid, but perfectly logical explanation. I can guess the sort of thing.'

'Tell me,' I demanded, intrigued, despite myself, to find out how much he had guessed about the working of my mind. 'Tell me about my lurid, but perfectly logical explanation.'

'A prisoner!' he said. 'Your whole approach to this thing suggests that you believe there's a prisoner somewhere aboard the *Dolphin*. Someone shut away, either for his own safety or for everyone else's.'

'John! You've looked right into my mind!' I exclaimed in wonder.

'A prisoner who gets out from time to time,' he continued. 'A captive who sobs himself to sleep in the dark hours. Isn't that the picture you've conjured up behind that fine, handsome brow? And when you take it out and look at it, doesn't the whole thing sound unlikely?'

'Yes,' I admitted. Could a secret horror of the night stand up to such calm examination in the sunshine of the Mediterranean afternoon?

'And there's a better explanation,' he said. 'Do you know that, among the seamen, engine-room staff and stewards of the *Dolphin* there are no less than ten lads under eighteen, and three of those are under fifteen and making their first voyage? What more likely than that your "weeping captive" is simply a homesick boy who cries himself to sleep nights?'

'That never occurred to me . . .' I said, suddenly feeling very foolish.

'Now you see why I advised you to say nothing of it to the police,' he went on. 'Tell the inspector, and he'd be obliged to act. Armed with your allegations, he'd have to question the passengers and crew as to whether they harmed your canary or went through your belongings. Do you want that? Do you seriously want him to ask Jason Saltram if he sobs himself to sleep nights?'

'No!' I cried out in horror, and two English ladies at the next table turned to regard me, one of them through a monocle.

'Or Admiral Sir Gregory Topsham, maybe?'

We both laughed together at the absurdity of the thought, which won us both another glance of disapproval from the English ladies.

'And now,' said John Bennett, 'we will share the last piece of this fine seed cake and then I'll call a carriage to take us back to the *Dolphin*.'

The carriage was similar to the one that had brought us to the police station, and of a pattern which seemed to serve as a public vehicle in Gibraltar: a four-wheeled chaise not unlike a victoria, but with a flat-topped sun-roof, and drawn by a single horse. Our driver was an intensely Latin-looking individual, who, sizing up John and placing him as an obviously rich American, declared that his name was Arthur Mendoza, a Gibraltarian and a British subject, and that he would be proud to take the lady and gentleman for a grand tour round the first outpost of Her Majesty's Empire, at a special price of two shillings and sixpence.

'Some other time,' responded John, handing me into the carriage. 'For the present, will you please convey us to the *Dolphin* yacht alongside the South Mole?'

'Yes, sir!' cried Arthur Mendoza, urging his horse forward. 'We going along Main Street and I tell you all the things of interest. No extra charge.'

John looked at me and squeezed my hand. 'Feeling better now?' he asked.

I nodded. 'You're right. You were right from the first, and I'm glad – for everyone's sake – that I kept my silly fears to myself. Thank you for coming with me today, and being at hand to steady me when my courage failed.'

'That,' said the gentleman from Boston, Massachusetts, 'is what friends are for.' He relinquished my hand, and I liked him for that.

'We are coming to the cathedral,' intoned our driver and guide, from the side of his mouth, over his shoulder. 'Cathedral of St Mary the Crowned, called the Spanish Church. Used to be Moorish mosque till Spaniards capture Gibraltar, knock down mosque and build cathedral. When British capture Gibraltar, Spaniards bombard Rock and knock down cathedral. British build it up again. I – Arthur Mendoza – was baptized there. God save the Queen!'

The narrowness of the street and the height of the surrounding buildings, with their shuttered silence, meant that we were mostly passing through shadow; but every so often – as when we reached an open square a little later – the low afternoon sun shone upon us like a blessing.

'Convent Place and residence of His Excellency the Governor,' Arthur Mendoza informed us. 'The building was once a house of the Franciscans. All things pass. Nothing remain the same.'

John and I exchanged a smile about our philosophical driver.

'All things pass,' said John. 'The shadow of our small horrors will go away. Life goes on. We shall put the tragedy of poor Maugham behind us. I spoke with Jason this morning. He particularly doesn't want Melloney to be worried about it, and the *Dolphin* summer will continue as scheduled.'

I nodded vigorously. 'Yes, yes! Nothing must stand in the way of Melloney and her *Dolphin* summer. Nothing!'

I thought back to the occasion of my first meeting with Jason Saltram and how our hands had joined in a solemn compact to make Melloney's last months full of affection and free of all hurt.

The recollection of that moment sent a curious sensation through my body, a sort of shudder, as when someone walks over one's grave. I loked down at my right hand, and touched its palm with the fingers of my other hand. Almost immediately, I had another remembrance, another impression: I was standing on the bridge of the *Dolphin*, with the telescope in my hand, Gibraltar Rock a smudge rising out of the horizon, and Jason Saltram's broad shoulder turned towards me . . .

'I guess this would be the barracks, Mendoza?' John's voice shattered my strange reverie. A large Union Jack stirred limply above a high gate, and two kilted and pith-helmeted Highlanders stamped up and down, bayonet-tips agleam in the fitful sunlight and shadow of the plane trees.

'That is so, sir,' confirmed our guide. 'St Jago's Barrack, sir, and Southport Gate and Trafalgar Cemetery.' We rattled under an ancient archway that marked the end of the street, and were out in the blinding sun of the Mediterranean afternoon. To the left of the archway in a place of shadows, were a jumble of humped graves and old headstones. 'There lie Nelson's sailors who died of wounds in the great battle,' said Arthur Mendoza, pointing with his whip, 'and there is Alameda Gardens, where everyone take *paseo*, which is Spanish custom of walking up and down in evenings ...'

As we were borne through the sunbaked dockyard, past the grey shapes of warships, and repair basins resounding to the strident clang of hammer on steel, I allowed my mind to wander along new and forbidden paths, in which the tall and forbidding figure of Jason Saltram figured very largely.

What did I know of him?

That he was undeniably attractive, in a cold and domineering way; and a more impressive man than any I had ever met before. Not that that was any criterion – I who had never set foot outside the villages and dusty lanes of mid-Cornwall, save for occasional forays to Bodmin and Truro – I had responded, from the very first, to the masterful energy that lay within him. The impression he gave me was of a wild beast tamed by the force of his own mind and will.

And he was to marry Oriana Topsham. The announcement could not much longer be delayed. For all his professed concern for Melloney, this action was going to ruin the short time left to her. Could he not see that? Was he truly so blind?

John Bennett was addressing me: I brought my thoughts back to the there and then.

'I'm sorry, John,' I apologized.

'You were miles away. I was saying that the *Dolphin* will be taking fresh coal aboard some time during our stay in Gib. It usually takes a whole day. It's a filthy job and there's a lot of cleaning up to be done afterwards. Jason was hinting to me that he was taking us all on some sort of outing – a day's picnic – while the coaling takes place. And here we are, back at the *Dolphin* already. And isn't that Melloney I espy on the poop deck?'

The sleek white yacht lay like some lovely great seabird at

rest by the jetty, with coloured flags fluttering bravely all over her from figurehead to gilded stern and across all the tall masts. Melloney was a splash of pink tulle in the shade of a white canvas awning that now stretched over both ends of the vessel. She was reclining in a deck-chair, asleep. Seated by her was Nanny Bagley in her black bombasine and widow's cap; she paused in her devoted task of lightly fanning her sleeping charge, and gave us a doleful smile as we alighted from our carriage at the bottom of the gangway. John paid off our loquacious driver. The Second Officer came down the gangway and saluted me.

'Commander Saltram presents his compliments, ma'am, and would Miss Trewella be so kind as to attend him in his cabin?'

My heart seemed to give a treacherous lurch, and my breathing quickened. 'Yes, of course.'

I could have wished to have had time to go to my cabin and change out of the grey tweed jacket and skirt – my best, and the only really smart day-costume I possessed, but, as I had found, much too heavy for a sub-tropical Gibraltar afternoon – and into something cooler, or even to have dabbed some eau de Cologne on my forehead and wrists; but I did not dare to keep Jason Saltram waiting, as I guessed those all-seeing, dark eyes must have sighted us coming the whole length of the South Mole. Calming myself as best I was able, by taking several long, deep breaths, I went up to the boat deck. His cabin door was open, with a white muslin curtain across the opening. I tapped on the side of the door.

'Come in, Miss Trewella.'

He rose to his feet from behind the desk and greeted me with a grave nod. There was a tea-tray laid for two before him.

'Did Bennett take you to tea in the town, or would you care to join me?' he asked, placing a chair for me by the desk.

'I – I'd love another cup. So – refreshing,' I replied breathlessly, feeling like some great raw-handed country girl in the presence of this fastidious man in his trim cabin, with its spare elegance of decoration, its pieces of rich silverware, paintings and nautical instruments.

'Indian or China? Milk? So you have returned from seeing

the police. I trust that all went well and that they will not be troubling you again.'

He handed me the delicate cup and saucer. I took them carefully and said: 'I don't think the inspector will want to see me again. But I shall have to give evidence at the inquest.'

'The inquest – yes.' His brow darkened and he scowled into his cup. 'Concerning the communication – the telephone call – that you received from Maugham?'

'That's right.'

'Tell me, Miss Trewella. I have to confess myself somewhat puzzled. Was Maugham in the habit of telephoning you in your cabin?'

All unbidden, my hands began to tremble. 'No, he never did it before,' I murmured.

'There was no – *liaison* – between you?' He rapped out the word, accompanying it with a penetrating glare of his shadowed eyes.

'Oh!' I cried.

The cup and saucer fell from my hands that had suddenly become incapable of control, and shattered in pieces on the Persian rug at my feet. I was on my knees in an instant, dabbing with my handkerchief. His gleaming boots were a bare few inches from my scrabbling fingers.

'Get up! Get up, woman!' he shouted. 'Confound it, I employ servants in this yacht!'

I obeyed him, scarcely daring to meet his gaze, for I knew that the look he threw at me was of contempt almost beyond bearing. I sank meekly into my seat again as he pulled the bell-cord that brought a steward almost immediately.

'Sir?'

'Clear up that confounded mess, and look sharp about it!' grated Commander Saltram in tones of bleak savagery, without turning from the porthole through which he was staring, his back turned towards me.

'Aye, aye, sir!' The man stooped and picked up the pieces of broken cup and saucer, and, rolling up the rug, tucked it under his arm. 'Will that be all, sir?'

'Get out!'

The steward departed hastily with the soiled rug and scraps

of priceless china : I was alone again with my tormentor.

A long silence, during which time I felt the last of my fortitude ebb away, so that all that remained was a desperate desire not to break down in tears. And then, without turning round, but still keeping his back to me, he said, in a flat and expressionless voice :

'Following on the secret that I confided in you in Falmouth, I have to tell you that I do not intend Melloney to be in any way put out by the tragedy of Maugham's end. The subject will simply not be discussed, and I shall be grateful for your co-operation in this.'

'Yes, Commander,' I replied in a very small voice.

'Tomorrow ...' he began, when there came a tap upon the door jamb. 'Yes, who is it ?'

'Weems, Commander.' The doctor put his head round the side of the curtain. The Mediterranean sun had attacked his normally ruddy complexion and his face was glowing like a beacon. 'Can I have a brief word with you ?'

'I'm busy, Weems.'

'It's rather important. It concerns Melloney – Miss Lumley.'

Jason Saltram nodded. 'Very well.' And to me : 'Will you please excuse me, Miss Trewella ?'

I rose quickly, only too glad to be gone. His parting remarks only halted me for a few moments at the door.

'Miss Trewella, you will wish to accompany the party who will be departing immediately after breakfast tomorrow, to spend the day on the upper part of the Rock. Can you ride ?'

'Yes,' I told him. 'I was brought up on a farm, and learned to ride a pony almost as soon as I could walk.'

'Good.' The ghost of a half-smile softened the corners of his firm lips. 'You will only be called upon to handle a donkey, but a certain degree of expertise is needed.' He turned to the doctor. 'And now, Weems ... ?'

Hateful! I told myself. He was hateful. How could I ever have deceived myself that he was attractive? Domineering – yes. Frightening – yes. And cuttingly, brutally rude. How dared he to suggest that Jack Maugham and I had had – what was his word? – a liaison? I blinked away the angry tears and strode purposefully along the boat deck, with the intention of going below to my cabin and soothing my overheated mind and body in a cool bath. But I was forestalled. Nanny Bagley appeared at the top of the companionway leading down to the poop deck, called and waved to me.

'Melloney wants a word with you.'

I followed her down to the shaded poop, where Melloney was stretching herself like a newly-awakened kitten in her reclining chair.

'Hello, Annabel,' she smiled. 'You look cross. Didn't you enjoy your trip ashore with John Bennett? Did he try to hold hands or kiss you, or have I been misinformed about American gentlemen? You can go now, Nanny darling, and run me a bath. I'll have Flack bring me presently.'

Alone together, I said to her: 'Mr Bennett behaved perfectly properly – which is more than can be said for the Commander.'

'Oh, has Jason been acting the old bear again? What a bore he can be. You mustn't take any notice of him in his growly mood. I don't. For instance, he's perfectly capable of growling that I can't go on the picnic tomorrow. Is Dr Weems with him now, Annabel?' She looked anxiously at me, and I had the feeling that it was to put this question that she had sent for me.

'Yes, he is. Melloney...' I laid my hand on her smooth brow. It felt hot. 'Are you feeling all right?'

'Perfectly all right.' She made a moue, wrinkling her perfect small nose. 'Dr Weems makes such a fuss all the time. If he's advising Jason that I mustn't go on the picnic tomorrow, I shall pull faces and act thoroughly cross, too.' She glanced sidelong at me, her eyes brimming with laughter. This was Melloney at her most entrancing. All my resentment faded.

'I'm sure it will be all right for you to come tomorrow,' I promised her. 'Dr Weems looked quite cheerful when he called to see the Commander.'

'I'm sure, too!' She took my hands and looked at me. 'Oh, Annabel, I'm so happy today.'

'And you make me happy too – just to be with you,' I told her truthfully.

'Fortunately,' she said, 'the Admiral and his Lady won't be

with us tomorrow. They are taking luncheon with His Excellency the Governor!' So saying, she turned up the end of her nose with the tip of her forefinger and, with marvellous economy of expression, put me instantly in mind of both Lady Topsham and her daughter, so that I laughed aloud. She continued: 'However, we shall have to put up with Oriana. But that won't be quite so hard to bear, since the poor wretch seems to have quite lost all her intolerable smugness, and her eyes are fairly dropping out for a sight of that long-awaited engagement ring her mama has promised her.'

'Melloney! You're cruel to poor Miss Topsham,' I chided her mildly, thinking how fortunate it would be for her – and how compassionate on the part of Jason Saltram – if her guardian's engagement and subsequent marriage to the insufferable Oriana Topsham were postponed till...I could not bring myself even to frame the thought without an effort of will...till she was beyond all hurt.

Melloney seemed about to reply to my remark when a shadow passed over her features. Her mouth quivered, her eyes clouded, her hand flew to her side, and she gave a sharp cry of pain.

'Annabel!' she breathed.

I put my arm about her, and in the same instant I heard footsteps on the companionway: Dr Weems was already on his way down to us; when he saw Melloney, his movements became more urgent.

'What's happened?' he asked.

'She – she seems to have had some sort of seizure,' I told him.

'Get Flack here at once!'

I went up on the boat deck and called to a passing sailor to fetch Able Seaman Flack. He rushed off, bare feet pounding. When I returned again, Melloney was lying back in her chair, eyes closed, moaning faintly. Dr Weems turned back one of her eyelids and gave a grunt.

'Is she...is she...?' was all I could say.

'A few hours' sleep in a darkened room will put her to rights,' he said quietly. 'Ah, here comes Flack. Take Miss Melloney up, there's a good fellow. No need for you to come,

Miss Trewella. You can safely leave this to Nurse Bagley and myself.'

Melloney did not appear at dinner that night, but I sought out Dr Weems, who informed me that his patient was making a brave recovery from the attack, and would be in a fit state to go on the morrow's picnic.

That night, in the dark hours just before dawn, I heard again the bitter moans of the weeping man.

The steward woke me at seven o'clock. Long before then, the sounds of padding feet on the deck above, coupled with the ringing of bells and the throb of the yacht's engine, revealed that we were on the move. But not for long; by the time I was enjoying the delicious coffee and freshly baked roll, and reading the Captain's daily report, the vessel was still again. From the report, I learned that we had just moved a short distance to the coaling wharf, where the process of 'coaling ship' would take place as soon as the saloon passengers had departed for their day's outing. To stimulate our appetites for the latter enterprise, Captain Pelly had composed a flowery itinerary, which I have kept – though it is ruined by salt water like all the rest ...

The party will ascend a road on the eastern side, which rapidly turns into a mule track as the Upper Rock is neared. From this high vantage point will be observed – should the weather be not inclement – a panoramic view of the Strait, with the northern fringe of the great African continent a bare 15 miles distant and Mount Abyla which, with Gibraltar Rock, were the Pillars of Hercules famed in the ancient myths.

Pausing to observe the antics of the famous Rock Apes (species *Macacus inuus*), the party will descend to a pleasant plateau at the southern end, named Windmill Hill Flats, where luncheon will be the better enjoyed for having abandoned the stimulating but somewhat vertiginous heights of the Upper Rock ...

The day looked hot and sunny, and the sky an unblemished blue. Mindful of the exertions ahead of me (riding a donkey, not to mention riding a donkey at 'vertiginous heights'), I put on a simple white blouse with not over-generous sleeves, and a serviceable black serge skirt. For headgear: my old straw boater with its bedraggled feather. When I took stock of myself in the mirror, I knew for certain what I had come to suspect: that John Bennett's compliments about my face only went to show what a kind person he was. Was there ever such an ill-assorted collection of features got together in one countenance? And too scrubbed and healthy-looking by far! As for the hair! – coarse and black as horsehair and forever falling down because pins would never stay in it. I thought of Oriana Topsham's Dresden shepherdess fragility, and despaired. How Mrs Penbury could have imagined that, with my attributes, I would ever improve my matrimonial prospects by mixing with the 'gentry' was beyond all belief. I sighed, took up my reticule, and went out on to the deck.

John Bennett and the Commander were standing by the gangplank, both dressed in white drill. They both saluted me.

'Good day to you, Miss Trewella,' said Jason Saltram. 'We are just awaiting the other ladies' pleasure. As soon as they present themselves we set off' – he gestured to the quay – 'and the coaling will begin.'

A mountain of coal stood some distance from the end of the gangway, where the *Dolphin*'s sailors and a party of villainous-looking Latins were grouped, watching us. In every man's hand was a small basket of plaited rush, presumably for carrying the coal. They seemed impatient to begin. 'Will the job be finished by sundown, Saltram?' asked the American.

The other nodded. 'Earlier,' he said. 'I have promised a bonus of five shillings to each member of the crew, and half-a-crown to every Spanish dockyard-matey, if the coal is all loaded and the yacht repainted from stem to stern by six. It will be done. Ah, here comes Oriana. Good morning, my dear. How charming you look.'

Oriana Topsham was dressed as for a garden party at Buckingham Palace, as I had seen the mode in the pages of illustrated magazines, in a gown of lilac silk and white lace, with a confection of French millinery on her head that must have cost the sacrifice of a whole aviary of coloured birds. Her perfect features, behind the tight veil that enclosed them, were expressionless as ever; despite which, I would have sworn that her eyes were slightly pink-rimmed, as if from weeping, and there was a slight tremor in her voice when she addressed the company.

'Good morning, Jason. Mr Bennett. Miss – er – Trewella.' She scarcely spared me a glance.

'We are just waiting for Melloney and her entourage now,' said John. 'And here she comes!'

She was travelling in a makeshift litter, composed of one of the dining chairs from the saloon, with two stout poles connected to it, with which she was borne aloft on the shoulders of Able Seaman Flack, and another sailor of like build. She was in pale lemon yellow and a saucy straw adorned with lemon bows. She looked as pretty as a china doll under the shade of her parasol. Dr Weems and Nurse Bagley came after. I noticed that he was carrying a leather shoulder-bag – a reminder that he was her personal physician, charged with the doleful task of watching over the dying girl. I remembered this – and it was as if the sun had gone behind a cloud that had appeared from nowhere to mar the perfection of the sky.

'The steeds await you, ladies,' cried Jason Saltram. 'Let's be off.'

A sailor stooped his back to give me a step-up on to my donkey, which looked a docile-enough creature. Nurse Bagley was unceremoniously lifted on to hers by two grinning big fellows. Jason himself assisted Oriana to mount up. She looked extremely out of place on a little black donkey in her garden party rig-out: when I turned my face to hide a treacherous smile, I met Melloney's glance and she gave me a broad and extremely vulgar wink. For an awful moment, I thought she would make some outrageous comment about poor Oriana – but she changed her mind.

'Full speed ahead, the picnic party!' cried Jason Saltram.

We set off: Jason and John leading, with Oriana following and me after her. Behind me came Melloney and her litter, with Nurse Bagley coming after, and Dr Weems leading her donkey. A long train brought up the rear, comprising Chief Steward Dacres and the six stewards and cooks of his department, with three additional donkeys carrying hampers and wine coolers – the rich fare upon which we should be feasting later in the day.

Cries of delight went up from the waiting seamen and Spaniards.

'Three cheers for Commander Saltram and his guests!'

Three cheers rang out. And then: 'Set to, lads! Let's have the old *Dolphin* coaled and right as a trivet afore the ladies and gentlemen return!'

Scarcely had we left the wharf and begun to mount the steep street beyond, with its high-walled houses that clung precariously to the foothills of the great rock, than sailors and Spanish workmen were racing back and forth across the *Dolphin*'s gangplank, bearing the coal baskets on their heads. Even by that time, a black cloud of dust was rising high above the pristine whiteness of the great yacht. No wonder, I thought, that the saloon passengers were all set ashore; no wonder they had to repaint the vessel afterwards.

We were above the town, and the Strait stretched in a carpet of shimmering blueness that was only marred by occasional tiny wavelets. The bulk of a flattened pyramid dominated the far, African shore.

'That's Mount Abyla,' said John Bennett, pointing, and slowing his pace till he was beside my donkey's head. 'You're looking particularly stunning this morning, Annabel. Poor Oriana! – you make her look like a well-kept grave.'

'Rubbish!' I told him. 'You're gulling me, John, and it will profit you nothing.' But such is the honeyed tongue of the male animal that I was half inclined to disbelieve the evidence that my own eyes had perceived in my mirror, and felt the better in consequence.

He slapped my donkey on the rump, grinned at me, and waited for Melloney to overtake him. Turning, I saw him address her. By the way she burst into laughter, I guessed that he had repeated to her the remark that he had made to me.

Jason Saltram remained in the lead, pacing nimbly up the steep slope, his walking stick swinging with every stride, his back as straight as a ramrod. Oriana Topsham never looked round; it seemed to me that she never took her gaze from him.

We were well on to the Upper Rock, negotiating a narrow track just wide enough to take a carriage. To our right, the ground sloped steeply away in broken earth and limestone studded with thorn scrub and olive bushes. Below all that, the illimitable sea whispered shorewards. Above, the heights grew ever nearer and more awesome. We were as remote from the teeming life in the town and dockyard below as a caravan crossing the deserts of the moon. I was filled with a sense of exhilaration, a remoteness from reality, that I had never before experienced.

'Is it much further, Jason,' wailed Oriana Topsham. 'I'm beginning to feel rather dizzy, and the sun's much too hot to be either pleasant or comfortable.'

'Not much further, Oriana,' he replied – and was I mistaken, or did I notice a slight tightening of his lips, as if in exasperation? He pointed upwards and ahead, to where the winding track gave a final flourish and disappeared beyond the summit of the crest. 'When we reach there, my dear Oriana,' he said, 'you will behold a sight that will repay all your discomfort. I would go so far as to say that you will recall it with wonder for as long as you live.'

Oriana was not convinced. 'I am not one for views,' she replied petulantly. 'Mama and Papa made a great to-do about my accompanying them to Venice the Easter before last. "Such views as you never saw," they said. For myself, I was quite unimpressed, and that is not to mention the dreadful smell of the place! No – whatever your vista, Jason, I doubt if the memory will stay with me for as long as you boast.'

'We shall see,' he replied coldly. And I was not mistaken; he was irritated with her to a degree that was almost beyond his bearing, so that he strode on ahead at a swifter pace, and furiously thwacked his stick against every large rock that he passed and sliced the heads off several inoffensive thorn shrubs.

There was a chuckle at my elbow. John Bennett had moved up beside me again. He had obviously overheard the exchange between Jason and Oriana, and was grinning to himself.

'I'll wager you five pounds to a single strand of your magnificent raven hair, Annabel,' he murmured, 'that the eagerly awaited engagement is going to go unannounced for quite a while longer, if not forever. Yes, ma'am!'

I silenced him with a fingertip to my lips and stole a hasty glance to the back of Oriana's head. She gave no sign of having overheard John's comment.

Melloney's voice rang out in the clear air: 'I'm thirsty. When we reach the top, I propose that we toast the Rock of Gibraltar with a glass of champagne. Do you agree, Jason?'

But Jason Saltram was out of earshot, striding the last few yards to the crest; and when he reached there he stood, shielding his eyes against the sun's glare and looking out towards the east. Seized with an impulse, I tapped my mount's flank and urged him forward with a cry of 'giddup'. Never allowing my gaze to waver from the tall figure in white above me, I overtook Oriana Topsham – ignoring her affronted stare – and set my donkey at a smart jog-trot up the steep, rocky slope.

Jason turned, hearing my approach. He smiled with approval to see me.

'Well now, Miss Trewella,' he declared. 'Take a look and tell me that you at least are impressed.'

I halted my mount beside him – and looked out. An exclamation died on my lips. My hair and cheeks were fanned by a new wind that swept over the crest of the great Rock: a wind that blew from out of the sun, down the whole length of the Mediterranean Sea that was spread out before me.

My eyes were assaulted by a blueness of an intensity that dazzled the vision. It was a total blueness composed of sea and sky; a united blueness, stretching from heaven's zenith to the distant horizon, and extending downwards from the horizon to the place beneath my feet. I had the impression of being suspended high in the air, or of soaring like a bird over the earth.

Then I looked down – and if Jason Saltram had not laid a restraining hand on my arm, I think I might have fallen.

The eastern face of the great Rock – unlike the western side, up which we had made a tolerably easy ascent – was an almost sheer precipice: a descending sweep of silver-grey limestone that ended in white water among the jagged fangs at its base.

'It's four hundred feet and more down there,' said Jason Saltram. 'You are standing on the very crest of one of the Pillars of Hercules!'

'It's terrifying,' I breathed, finding my voice at last. 'Terrifying and wonderful! I wouldn't have missed this moment for the world!'

He nodded. 'It is a moment to remember.'

A breathless stillness passed by. After what seemed like an eternity, there came the rattle of donkeys' hooves on stone, and the rest of the party joined us on the crest. Oriana Topsham was still in the lead. She took one look over the dizzy magnificence of the eastern side and let out a most unladylike screech.

'What a perfectly horrid place to bring us, Jason,' she said, when she had recovered from the first shock of our staggering surroundings. 'The authorities shouldn't permit people to come. It surely isn't safe.' And she edged her donkey well away from the edge. 'I simply loathe heights,' she added by way of explanation.

'I'm sorry, Oriana,' said Jason Saltram simply.

'I love heights!' declared Melloney, leaning from her chair to stare down towards the sea's edge far below. 'I have a mystical compulsion to step out into space and beat my arms like the wings of a bird. I half believe that I would be lifted up, by a sheer act of faith and will.'

'What a perfectly ghastly thought!' was Oriana's comment.

'Do you think so?' asked Melloney. Her face was grave and serious, in that child-like way she had. 'I don't find it in the least unpleasant. I think ... I really think that, if the sands of my life were fast running out, I would prefer to step out into space and beat my arms like wings. Then I would either become a bird and rise to meet the sun. Or else ... a quick end.'

I met Jason Saltram's eyes at the same instant that a shudder passed through my frame. I saw my own thought mirrored in his eyes . . .

Did Melloney know . . . had she guessed her fate?

It was John Bennett who – typically – broke the tension by tactfully changing the subject.

'Hey!' he cried. 'If I'm not mistaken, Saltram, there's a large company of ships approaching from the east!' He pointed to where a flat cloud of black smoke had begun to form above the sheer blueness of the horizon.

Jason Saltram smiled, as if relieved to put aside the dark thought that the two of us had silently shared. 'I have to tell you that this is the principal reason for my traipsing you all the way up here, my friends,' he said. 'What you have just sighted, my dear Bennett, is the approach of the Mediterranean Fleet, which is expected in port shortly after noon.'

Jason took out his watch and consulted it. 'I estimate,' he said, 'that we shall have time to continue along the path that follows the western side, taking in a look at the apes on the way, and arriving at the plateau of Windmill Hill Flats just as the Fleet rounds the southern tip of the Rock. We shall get a splendid view.' He glanced towards Oriana with an apologetic smile. 'And you will find it not half so terrifying as up here on the crest, my dear Oriana.'

Oriana responded gratefully. 'Thank you, Jason,' she murmured. And a becoming pinkness suffused her cheeks.

'I'm thirsty,' said Melloney flatly. 'And I'm not moving till someone gives me a glass of champagne.'

'Tch, tch! You are a terror, my darling girl,' said Nanny Bagley reprovingly. 'What is Dr Weems going to say?'

But no one asked Dr Weems's opinion; and when a magnum of champagne was opened by Chief Steward Dacres, the *Dolphin*'s physician took a glass with the rest; and toasts were drunk to the Rock of Gibraltar, the Mediterranean Fleet, and the passengers and crew of the *Dolphin* yacht.

I also drank a private toast, alone with myself and my astonished heart. And I threw the dregs from my glass over the dizzy edge of the great rock as a libation to the jesting gods who had looked down upon the Pillar of Hercules and cruelly decided that I, Annabel Trewella, should choose this occasion to realize that I loved, had probably loved from the first, and would certainly love for ever, the forbidding male animal known as Jason Saltram!

I have a recollection that we actually saw and commented upon the famous Gibraltar Rock apes, but it meant very little to me at the time.

I seem to remember that we came upon the apes grouped together on the western slope: about a dozen of them, and two of the females had babies at their breasts. They were shy and quite unapproachable; as soon as we drew close, the leader of the colony called shrilly to his followers and urged them to retreat up the slope; then he remained in the rear, urging them on and snarling defiantly back at us. The last we saw of the apes, their dark, shambling forms were disappearing over the crest and down to the sheer eastern precipice, where, as one of the stewards was able to tell us, they took refuge on an isolated shelf that is known to Gibraltarians as 'The Monkeys' Alameda'.

But, as I said, it meant very little to me. All my thoughts were elsewhere, and my mind was in a turmoil.

I was in love ...

That was the first certainty. The knowledge had come to me when I had stood with Jason Saltram on the crest of the great Rock and he had pronounced the words: 'It is a moment to remember'; a remark that he had made without so much as a glance in my direction, but which had cast a light on the inner recesses of my secret heart and showed me how I felt.

The second certainty was that my love was quite hopeless. A whole way of life, of class, manners, background and education lay like an unbridgeable abyss between Commander Jason Saltram and me. I might be willing to reach one trembling hand across that gulf; but he, a man with all the bigotry of his sex and class, would never consider it in his wildest dreams. To him, I was a creature of the lower orders, an employee, a piece of not very valuable and easily replaceable domestic equipment. Furthermore, he was also contemplating marriage to Oriana Topsham; despite all appearance to the contrary, might already have decided to present her with the ring that very day.

Forget it ever happened, I told my sad heart. For everyone's sake. I had come to terms with this, shortly before noon, when we descended a steep slope which brought us to a small plateau near the southern tip of the Rock. This was the place called Windmill Hill Flats and, as Jason had told us, it provided a splendid view of the approach to the harbour. The plateau ended abruptly in a sheer cliff face, below which Gibraltar Rock ended with a point and a lighthouse.

The Mediterranean Fleet was in sight, and coming up fast: two long rows of silver-grey leviathans, with smaller craft fussing in lines each side. Great columns of smoke pouring skyward. Long white furrows ploughed through the sea's smooth blueness.

John had his binoculars to his eyes. 'Do you see, Saltram?' he cried. 'They are performing a manoeuvre!'

Jason was watching also. And I was watching him, noticing the pride and delight in his face as he gazed upon his former comrades and their ships.

'They are manoeuvring into single line for entering harbour,' he said. 'See, the flagship has lowered a flaghoist giving the order, and the cruisers and battleships will form up behind her. By Jove, that was well done! They move as one!'

'I'm so proud,' gushed Oriana Topsham. 'Such beautiful ships!'

'*Dolphin* is prettier than any of them!' declared Melloney with a catch in her voice.

The cooks and stewards had spread tablecloths on the flat rocks in the centre of the plateau and unloaded the hampers of food upon them. This done, they joined the rest of us, looking out at the approaching fleet. The nearest ship was now less than half a mile distant.

'I count six battleships and three large armoured cruisers,' said John.

'The first three are of our newest Admiral class,' replied Jason. 'Fourth in the line-of-battle comes my old ship *Royal Conqueror*, God bless her! See how well she is keeping station, Bennett? Such faultless helmsmanship is only achieved by unremitting practice. Well done, *Royal Conqueror*!'

'Is that the flagship in the lead, Saltram?' asked John.

'Yes. See the flag of St George at her masthead.'

As the great flagship drew abreast of where we were standing, the sound of a strident brass band came across the sparkling blue water towards us, and the unmistakable strains of 'Hearts of Oak'.

'The Marine band is playing on the quarterdeck,' said Jason. 'Do you see them, Miss Trewella?'

'Magnificent sight!' cried John Bennett. 'What ships!'

'The sure shield of Britain and the Empire!' declared Jason. From the corner of my eye, I saw his hand go stiffly to his yachting cap in a salute. John following suit by removing his hat and laying it across his breast.

The lines of giant ships were streaming past us now, so close together that they almost seemed joined. From our high vantage point, we were looking down on to their snow-white decks, to the long grey guns, the flags snapping at every masthead, the tiny figures sprinkled about the floating cities of steel.

'God save the Queen!' I heard the cry of Chief Steward Dacres. 'And three cheers for the Fleet, lads!'

His cooks and stewards led the cheers, in which everyone joined, myself included. John Bennett met my glance and grinned: he was loyally cheering with the rest.

The last of the ships swept past, trailing her white wake in the dazzling blueness, and the shrill notes of a bugle came across the open space in a brave farewell as she rounded the point and followed the others towards the harbour.

It was all over. I felt a distinct sense of anti-climax.

'Ladies and gentlemen,' announced Chief Steward Dacres. 'Luncheon is served.'

'I'm famished,' said Melloney. 'Flack, would you be so good as to carry me over to where the food is?' She rolled her eyes in my direction and smiled mischievously. 'It may be all very fine and large for a sailor's daughter like darling Oriana, but I thought the naval review was never going to end.'

'Where is Oriana?' asked Jason.

'What?'

'I can't see her,' said John. 'Oria – na! Where are you?'

'You men!' snapped Jason to the cooks and stewards. 'Drop what you're doing and search the plateau for Miss Topsham.'

There was nowhere to search. A few flat rocks, a bit of scrub here and there, a piece of low wall running along part of the southern end. Suddenly, all unbidden, I felt a cold chill of dread start at the nape of my neck.

Nowhere to search – but still we searched.

I was to provide the answer to the question that must have been in everyone's mind. I looked over the low wall, but only in order to see if there was a ledge on the other side, behind which (and it would have been totally out of character for the stiff, unbending Oriana) she might possibly have been hiding, as if to tease us.

There was no ledge; immediately over the wall, the edge of the plateau fell away in a sheer drop for two hundred feet or so to the lower level.

I saw her. She was lying directly below me – beneath the very spot from which she must have fallen: a crumpled heap of lilac and white: flame-coloured hair lying loose; one slender arm reached out to scrabble.

I cried out in horror, and they rushed to join me from all sides: the cooks and stewards, John Bennett; I saw Jason's shocked face.

And someone was screaming. It must have been me.

chapter five

The *Dolphin*'s ensign, which had been lowered to half-mast for Third Officer Maugham, was made to serve the same sombre duty for Oriana Topsham. The afternoon of her funeral, which was on the following day, the menfolk departed from the quayside in a black landau hung with mourning plumes. I watched them go: Jason and the Admiral, John Bennett and Dr Weems; and a party of sailors who were to act as pall-bearers followed after it in a brake.

Lady Topsham had collapsed on being told of the tragic end of her only child, and had been moved to the Governor's residence at the invitation of His Excellency. She and her husband were to stay there till their return to England by the next available steamer. They were to accompany us no further on the cruise; for them, as for Oriana, the *Dolphin* summer was spent.

The distant bell of the Anglican cathedral tolled out the sum of Oriana's years in the hot afternoon. I heard it with Melloney, in the shade of the poop deck. She had scarcely spoken since the tragedy. Despite the mutual dislike and resentment that had existed between them, and although what Melloney had overheard Oriana say about her must have wounded her deeply, my companion was driven into a most profound depression by the other woman's death. She lay in her deck-chair, eyes fixed on the grey slope of the great rock that soared above us, oblivious of all but her secret thoughts, and nothing I did or said could win more than a whispered monosyllable from her pale lips.

The following day came news that a corpse – believed to have been that of poor Jack Maugham – had been washed ashore on the Spanish coast near Tarifa. Captain Pelly journeyed there to confirm that it was indeed the remains of his dead officer that had been found. So there was a second funeral: Third Officer Maugham of the *Dolphin* was returned to the bosom of the sea that had taken his life, his flag-draped and weighted coffin taken out in a barge by his shipmates to a place beyond Europa Point, and there committed to the deep.

Next followed the ordeal of the double inquest, which was held the day after. I gave my evidence on the events leading up to the disappearance of Jack Maugham. Acutely conscious all the time that the quizzical eye of the police inspector was being directed at me from the back of the court, I repeated my original statement, leaving nothing out – and adding nothing, since I was by then thoroughly convinced that any expression of my fanciful suspicions could only bring needless trouble in its train. The coroner thanked me for my evidence; if he shared the inspector's doubts about my reasons for attempting to keep the midnight rendezvous with Maugham, he kept them discreetly to himself, and declared a verdict of Accidental Death. The unfortunate officer, he said, must have missed his footing on the darkened deck and tumbled over the side. I remember thinking at the time how unlikely an explanation it sounded.

Jason was called into the witness box to give an account of the circumstances surrounding Oriana's end. This he did with a calm gravity that won the silent respect of everyone in the crowded courtroom – and set my own heart beating more swiftly. In measured tones, he told the coroner what all the members of that fateful picnic party knew : that everyone, passengers and crew alike, had been too taken up with the tremendous spectacle of the passing Fleet to notice the exact comings-and-goings of everyone in the party. It was to be supposed, added Jason in reply to a question from the coroner, that Miss Topsham had moved towards the wall at the southern end of the plateau when the leading ships of the line had begun to turn round the end of Europa Point, since it was from there that she would have had the best view of the manoeuvre. In answer to the further question of whether Commander Saltram deemed it likely that the deceased lady had stood up on top of the wall, the better to improve her view, Jason was quite adamant : from his certain knowledge, Miss Topsham had had a strong aversion to heights and would certainly not have attempted such a feat.

The coroner thanked Jason for his lucid testimony, and unhesitatingly gave another verdict of Accidental Death, adding a comment upon the tragic workings of Fate, where, by an awful coincidence, two persons from the same shipboard community had perished within days of each other, both of them by tragic accident and both in the full flowering of their youth.

Later, over a gloomy luncheon in the *Dolphin*'s saloon – when all present were awkwardly conscious of the places that the Topshams had occupied – Jason Saltram, who had been helping himself to the claret decanter with more than his usual attentiveness, curtly announced that the *Dolphin* would be leaving 'the accursed Rock', as he put it, first thing in the morning – from which it was to be inferred that, deaths or no deaths, Melloney was not to be denied her last season of sunshine, but that the *Dolphin* summer would continue as if nothing had happened.

However, the ill fate that had haunted the yacht ever since she had steamed close to the portals of the Pillars of Hercules had still one more shock in store for us before we left Gibraltar.

I had been sitting with Melloney all afternoon, and Nanny Bagley had just come to take her back to her cabin for a nap and an early supper. Something – perhaps my patient efforts at cheerful conversation, or more likely the prospect of leaving the shadow of the glowering Rock in the morning – had lifted the depression from Melloney's mind, and we parted company with something of a note of her usual lightheartedness. Scarcely had Able Seaman Flack retreated with his tender burden than John Bennett came nimbly down the companionway to the poop deck.

'My dear, you look to me like a girl who's in need of a change of scenery,' he informed me. 'So I'm taking you ashore for supper this evening. And I'll not accept no for an answer.'

'But, John – Melloney might want me to be with her later.'

He shook his head firmly. 'I've fixed it with Melloney,' he declared. 'She won't be needing you again today, and hopes the both of us have a splendid evening. I'll be waiting for you at about a quarter of eight.'

'But' – searching desperately for a pretext – 'I've nothing to wear, John.'

'The gown you wore last evening will suit again real fine,' he said. 'See you at a quarter of eight.' And without waiting for any more of my excuses, he twinkled a brilliant grin at me and darted back up to the boat deck.

I made my toilette, putting on the old maroon-coloured velvet that served me for a dinner gown; and piling up my intractable hair with a battery of pins. A Paisley shawl – a legacy from my dead half-sister – set the maroon off nicely, and I was not totally unpleased with the result that my mirror offered. Nor was my face completely lacking in interest: it seemed to have lost some of its over-healthy fullness and become more fine-drawn, in a pale and interesting kind of way.

Women in love, I had read somewhere, tend to grow in beauty ...

The thought lasted me till I joined John by the gangway, and he took my hand and told me I looked a picture. He helped me into the carriage, which was driven by none other than our old friend Arthur Mendoza, who bowed low and presented me with a posy of jasmine.

The thought was still there when, looking back towards the *Dolphin*, I noted the lights in the cabin portholes under the bridge where I knew *he* would be at that hour, seated at his desk, his dark head bent over some work or other, or perhaps a letter; the lean, capable hands moving swiftly across the paper ...

My companion was addressing me.

'I – I'm sorry, John. What did you say?'

'That we shall be in for some pretty lively weather at sea in the next few days,' he said. 'There's an easterly wind blowing up right now – what they call locally a "levanter". I guess you must have noticed the beginnings of it when we were on the crest of the Rock the other day. Darn it, Annabel. I shouldn't have brought that up.'

'It doesn't matter,' I told him. 'It's no use pretending it didn't happen.' There was silence between us for a few moments, as we clattered through the archway and into the lamplit Main Street. Then I said: 'So we are in for some bad weather, John?'

'Captain Pelly has advised Saltram that we should remain here till the levanter blows itself out,' he replied, 'but Jason will have none of it. Speaking, he says, as an old Mediterranean hand, he pours scorn on Pelly's gloomy prophecies and is confident we shall make Oran and beyond without any trouble. I hope he's right.'

'It's for Melloney's sake,' I told him. 'After what's happened, he can't wait to get Melloney away from this place. You saw him at luncheon.'

'I sure hope that, by rushing away from Gib, Saltram doesn't run his precious little invalid into a bad storm at sea,' said John, adding wryly, 'not to mention yours truly and friend.'

We both laughed. Laughing still, we entered a courtyard off Main Street, where a string of Chinese lanterns revealed the white front of a tall and narrow house whose flat roof was bathed in a warm glow of light against the night sky.

'It's up there we have our supper,' John informed me.

The way up was by a spiral staircase at the rear of the house; and on our arrival, we were met by our host and hostess of the establishment: a stout and swarthy couple who greeted us with flashing smiles and amusingly fractured English, waving us to a table set with dazzling white napery and candlelight, under an awning of latticed vines. There were no other customers; the establishment was all ours. From somewhere out of the gloom came the tuneful thrumming of a mandolin.

'The place was recommended to me by Captain Pelly,' explained my companion. 'The menu won't be up to the standard of the *Dolphin*'s, I regret. Catering as it mostly does for coarse, cheap food for the common sailors, Gibraltar doesn't have a great culinary tradition. But Pelly tells me they do good, simple Spanish cooking here.'

'It's delightful,' I told him.

'You're not finding it too chilly in the open, I hope? We're mostly sheltered from the levanter by the lie of the Rock and the buildings around us.' Indeed, the buildings at the far side of the courtyard loomed higher than where we were sitting, and contributed to the sense of being warm and enclosed; a candlelit island in the sub-tropical night.

The menu was simplicity itself: a spiced soup, a delicious Spanish omelette with a fresh salad, a flask of a light and slightly effervescent wine. We talked as we ate, and John was the most entertaining of hosts. I asked him about his own life back in the United States of America.

'Mostly composed of hard work,' he said ruefully. 'Coming from self-made stock, with none of the traditions of the European leisured classes, I've always had my nose held pretty firmly against the grindstone.'

'Not much gadding about in luxury yachts?' I asked him.

'We – that's to say my old man – don't own a luxury yacht,' he said. 'Now, my Uncle Josh, he runs the New York end of the business, has a fast yacht in which he travels daily to and from his place on Long Island Sound, and has incidentally gotten himself caught up in an internecine rivalry of a most fiendish kind.'

'Do tell,' I asked, amused. 'Who are the rivals?'

'Uncle Josh's fellow Yacht Club members,' said John. 'Morning and evening, when these fellows quit work, Hudson River and Long Island Sound present a sight like a stampede of buffalo, as several hundred million dollars' worth of steam-driven seagoing hardware jockey for the dubious honour of being first to the winning post.'

'It sounds dangerous.'

'It's certainly expensive. Being determined to carry off all honours, Uncle Josh had a new yacht built – secretly, in Narragansett – that, on account of stripping away everything that wasn't strictly contributing to the object of being first past the winning post, and that included the bath tub, was able to raise the speed of over twenty miles an hour.'

'And did it win?' I asked. 'Was all that trouble and expense rewarded?'

'It certainly did. Much to the chagrin of Uncle Josh's principal rival, who nearly died of an apoplexy when he saw Uncle Josh's stern vanish in the haze ahead. But New York tycoons are not easily put down. Turning to address his captain, this old fellow cried: "Go straight past the Yacht Club landing and continue to Seabury's yard, so that I can order myself a yacht that will be faster than that confounded Josh Bennett's!" '

I shook my head in amused wonderment. My upbringing in the poverty of mid-Cornwall had rendered me totally unprepared for, and almost incapable of believing, the evidence of boundless wealth and power that had surrounded me ever since I first set foot aboard the *Dolphin*. I mentioned as much to my companion.

'I've never really recovered from the experience of the Commander ordering an express train by telephone,' I told him.

'In the higher echelons of Boston society,' remarked John, 'that would be considered to be excessively penny-pinching. In the higher echelons of Boston society, we call for our own private railway car, which lies in a siding to await our pleasure.'

'Do *you* have a private railway car?'

He laid a hand across his heart in an extravagant gesture of mock-humility. 'Lady, I have to walk to my office every day.' Then he added : 'But my old man has a private railway car.'

'John Bennett,' I told him severely, 'You're trying to impress me.'

'Yes, I am,' he admitted. 'Will you marry me, Annabel?'

I had not been aware of the proprietor covertly watching us from a serving table in the shadows beyond the candlelight. He came fussing, napkin in hand.

'Madam has spilled her wine! Pay no regard to the humble tablecloth; it is Madam's so lovely gown that is being my only concern, isn't it?' He dabbed expertly at the pink pool that lay beneath my hands. I continued to stare disbelievingly at John Bennett.

And when the proprietor had gone, I whispered : 'How could you be so unkind as to make mock of me like that? I have feelings, just like everybody else – even if my father never owned a private railway car.' I was really quite angry with John Bennett, and meant him to know it.

'I was not mocking you,' he snapped, also crossly. 'The

possession in the family of a private railway car does not blind a person to the normal decencies of existence. I was asking you to marry me – in all sincerity.'

I stared at him long and hard. 'I really believe you're telling the truth,' I cried wonderingly.

'You bet your life I am,' he said, his crossness vanishing in the good-humoured grin that was his most endearing stock-in-trade. He gestured about him. 'Why else the candlelit supper?' he demanded. 'Tête-à-tête, mark you – and this with the Mediterranean Fleet in port, when – as Captain Pelly assured me – this highly-favoured restaurant would normally be crammed with the more discerning of Her Britannic Majesty's naval officers.'

'You – you booked *every* table in the restaurant!' I cried.

'That I did,' he replied. 'For let me tell you, ma'am, I number myself among the glorious company of the Go-Getters – a body of men greatly esteemed in my native land. When I propose to a lady, it must have the ingredients for success. Hence the solitude . . . the candlelight' – he gestured towards the distant music – 'the mandolin!'

'You've convinced me of your sincerity,' I told him. 'And I'm tremendously touched and grateful.'

His gesturing hand paused in mid-air; fell forlornly to his side. 'But – no sale?' he asked. 'As we say in the retail drapery business: "the cash register does not go ting" – am I right?'

'I'm sorry, John,' I told him, reaching out my hand to lay it on his. 'I think you're a splendid person: one of the sweetest and kindest men I've ever met in my life.'

'You like me a lot,' he supplied, with a self-mocking grin, 'but not enough to commit yourself to seeing this face of mine across the breakfast table every morning.'

'Something like that, John.'

The grin grew broader. 'Not even – not even in the family's private railway car?'

'Nor yet even in Uncle Josh's yacht. By the way, did the rival gentleman's vessel regain supremacy?'

He shook his head. 'The boiler blew up.'

It will be all right, I told myself. It may well be that this man – this kind and good man – loves me; but he will not suffer on that account. There are massive reserves of inner strength beneath that gay and brash exterior. John Bennett will get over Annabel Trewella. Why, even the wry and resigned way with which he's now pouring himself another glass of wine carries an overtone of relief; the role of a good friend suits John so much better than that of romantic lover ...

'Guess I've notched up yet another failure,' he said with commendable cheerfulness. 'First the deal with Jason Saltram, and now ...' He hunched his shoulders in a gesture of resignation.

'I'm sure,' I told him, 'I'm quite, quite sure, John, that your – what do you call it – Go-Getting? – will be more than a match for the Commander, who's only a simple sailor at heart; who took on Lumley's only because it was willed on him, and whose only real wish is to return to the Navy.' And I thought of the look on Jason's face – the pride and the dedication with which he had gazed down upon his former comrades and ships of the Mediterranean Fleet.

John looked at me with some surprise. 'Annabel, Annabel,' he said, 'you've got it all wrong about Saltram, I do assure you. A sailor he may be. In that capacity, he may feel free to display a certain simplicity of heart and a lack of deviousness that is properly consistent with an officer and gentleman who follows the ennobling persuasion of the seafarer. In matters of business, I am telling you that the gallant Commander displays the slippery cunning and iron-hard ruthlessness of a street Arab. He is also a confounded good general merchant.'

'Is he really?' There seemed no end to the many-faced character of the man to whom my wayward heart had decided to attach itself. 'But that, surely, was because he was pitchforked into the business. He had to make the best of it.'

John drained his glass, and said: 'If that were the case, Annabel, the world would be full of second-generation successes, and this I can tell you is far from the case. From everything I've heard and seen at first hand, Saltram could have made himself a fortune in commerce at any time, with or without the backing of Lumley's.' He squeezed my hand, which was still in his. 'Annabel, is something the matter?

Have I said something to scare you? You look as if you've seen a ghost.'

It had just happened to me – I had seen it – while John was speaking. From out of the corner of my eyes, at first; but confirmed by a swift sideways glance. Keeping my voice as steady as I was able, I whispered to him ...

'Don't look now, John. Keep your gaze on me. On the roof of the building opposite, across the courtyard. I saw – I've just seen – someone looking across at us. A man. Silhouetted – in a wide-brimmed hat and, I think, a cloak.'

John took the information without so much as a flicker of an eyebrow.

'Did he remain watching us?' he murmured.

'No. That's the disturbing part. As soon as I turned my head slightly, he ducked down out of sight behind the balustrade of the flat roof. I think he's still there. I feel it. And I think he may have reappeared again.'

'Keep looking ahead,' said John, squeezing my hand again. 'Smile as if at something I'm telling you. That's fine ... fine. If your fellow's still peeking at us, I'll catch him in the act. Talk to me now. Say something – anything.'

'John, I'm frightened,' I whispered, remembering to keep the fixed, false smile upon my lips. 'There was something about the way he stood there. A menace ...'

'Nothing to be scared of,' replied John. He threw back his head and gave a short laugh, as if I had just delivered a shaft of astonishing wit. 'There's no law against folks looking at folks. It's just that we want to be quite sure that ...' I saw his gaze flash to one side, across the courtyard, to the roof opposite. Close as I was to him, I was witness to the sudden flaring of his eyes, the explosion of fury.

'John ...' I began.

He leapt to his feet. His angry voice echoed loudly across the open space of the courtyard; his accusing finger pointed dramatically.

'*You, there! What's your game, hey?*'

I followed his staring eyes; in time to see the silhouetted figure of the watcher as it recoiled from the parapet opposite, turned and fled from sight into the shadows of the flat roof.

A moment later the sound of a banging door came across the void. Then – silence.

Our host came running; demanding to know what was the matter with the lady and gentleman. When John explained to him what had happened, he made it known to us that the building opposite was an empty hulk, formerly a warehouse, and that no one in his right mind would wish to wander around in it at that hour of the night. As he made this comment, he cast a covert glance at the level of the wine in the flask on our table.

I shivered and drew my shawl more closely about my shoulders. 'John, if you don't mind, I should like to go back to the *Dolphin*,' I whispered.

John made no demur; he must have realized that there was nothing to be salvaged from the evening that he had prepared with such obvious care. Poor John – had he really believed that the two of us would return to the yacht with the news that we were engaged to be married? Despite my great unease, I had it in my heart to pity him. Instead of joy and laughter, there was now – fear.

We walked some of the way back, in a mutual silence that hung between us like a pall, through the thronged Main Street; past the crowded bars and cafés; past oriental bazaars, where dark-skinned Indians gently haggled with Jack Tars over cheap souvenirs; under the lamplit lime trees, with music jangling all about us and tipsy voices raised in song.

And there was not a brightly-lit doorway, a garish emporium, a shadowy corner, nor an empty window where I did not imagine the sinister figure of our late watcher to be gazing out at us.

Near the arch at the end of the street, John hailed a carriage. When we were settled in our seat, he said: 'You've let this thing get under your skin, Annabel. This fellow who was watching us – he was just another fellow.'

I stared at him. His face, shadowed by the awning of the carriage, told me nothing. 'Do you honestly believe that, John?' I demanded.

'Oh come, Annabel,' he replied with a touch of exasperation. 'You're not really suggesting...'

'The last time we had this conversation,' I broke in, 'you thoroughly convinced me that my fears were the product of my lurid imagination. That was less than a week ago. Since then, other things have happened – no, don't interrupt me – there's been another death, a death that was no more satisfactorily explained than the one which went before. And now, tonight . . .'

'Stop it!' His sharp command made our driver's head whip round in astonishment. John took no heed. Seizing my wrist, he shook me roughly. 'Stop that talk, do you hear me? Don't even think things like that, Annabel. That way lies . . . *madness*!'

'Let me alone – take your hand off me!' I hissed, shaking myself free. I had a sudden revulsion against him: for his calm acceptance of the situation, for the bland assurance that came with his family wealth and power, for his very maleless that seemed like an affront.

'Annabel, I'm sorry. Please forgive me,' he pleaded.

I looked out across the looming shapes of the great ships lying by the dark quays, with the pinpoints of lighted portholes spangling their sheer sides. And a huge moon hung over all. A treacherous tear of anger lay on my cheek, already drying in the night warmth. Without looking towards him, I felt for his hand and gave it a reassuring squeeze.

We did not speak again till we came to the *Dolphin*. There was no sound aboard her, and I realized that it was later than I had supposed. We parted near the steps leading down to my cabin. He took me gently by the shoulders and planted a brotherly kiss on my cheek.

'Tonight turned out different from the way I'd planned,' he murmured. 'But I'm giving you due notice that I still haven't abandoned all hope of you changing your mind. Good night, Annabel.'

'Good night, John. Thank you for supper.'

'And you'll not worry about . . . you know?'

'I'll try not to,' I told him, without any real conviction.

I went down the steps, and heard his footsteps moving along the boat deck above. Reaching my cabin door, I was fumbling in my reticule for the key when his footsteps returned back along the deck. And he was running.

'Annabel!' he cried out from the top of the steps. 'Annabel, come quickly. Something terrible's happened – to Melloney!'

'Melloney?' I dropped the reticule, key and all, and was half-way up the steps when I saw that he was not alone.

Slumped like a broken puppet in his arms, her flaxen tresses unbound and half-concealing her ashen face, barefoot and clad only in a nightshift, was Melloney. Her head lolled limply.

'I found her lying in the corridor,' cried John. 'And that isn't all.' His face was strained with shock. 'We must get her to Weems at once.'

But I could not bring myself to move an inch without knowing what state she was in. I took hold of her limp hand. It was cool and dry.

She gave a feeble moan. Her eyes flickered open and stared at me – at first with shock, and then with the relief of recognition.

'Annabel,' she whispered.

'Melloney, what happened?' I cried.

'He – he came to my cabin,' she breathed, so quietly that I had to bring my ear close to her cheek. 'I woke up. He was standing there. Before I could cry out, his hand was over my mouth. Then he picked me up. He was carrying me out, towards the deck . . . when Flack came running . . .'

'Who was it, Melloney?' I cried. 'Who came to your cabin?'

No reply. She had swooned away.

'Flack's lying over by her cabin door,' said John. 'I think he's badly hurt. Go see to him, Annabel. I'll take her to the sick bay and send someone to help you with Flack.'

He set off down the deck, Melloney's hair trailing in the night breeze. I made my way quickly to the corridor close by the saloon, where the principal cabins lay. It was dark there. The electric lamps had been extinguished, and I could find no switch for putting them on again. I moved forward, reaching with hands to touch the walls at either side.

Then I heard a groan: it came from close by my feet. By now, my eyes had become accustomed to the faint illumination that came through the skylight above my head: by the dim rays of the moon, I picked out the shape of a prostrate man in a white duck suit that was stained with ominous dark patches.

'Flack!' I dropped to my knees beside him. When I touched the dark patch on his shoulder, my hand came away damp. He gave another groan. By then, my cry had roused others in the cabins along the corridor. A door opened close by me, throwing a revealing shaft of light across the injured man.

There was a piercing scream. Nanny Bagley stood in the doorway, her hair piled up under a nightcap, bare feet protruding from under the hem of a coarse cotton gown.

'There's been an intruder in Melloney's cabin,' I told her. 'She's all right, I think. Mr Bennett's taken her along to the sick bay. Can you help me with ... ?'

'My darling girl!' cried the woman, brushing past me. 'What have they done to her?' And she was gone, without sparing a glance for the unfortunate Flack.

Dr Weems joined me soon after. With the help of one of the officers, he managed to raise the half-conscious seaman to his feet.

'We'll get him to the sick bay and tend that nasty-looking shoulder,' he said. 'I'd be obliged for your assistance as nurse, Miss Trewella – if the sight of blood doesn't upset you, that is.'

'I'm not over-squeamish,' I told him. 'But what about Melloney?'

'Nurse Bagley's looking after her,' he replied. 'She's suffering from shock and a slight bump on her head where she fell – that's all. She'll soon be as right as rain. Let's get this fellow attended to. Easy with him, now. My, he's a weight and no mistake. Come, Miss Trewella.'

They brought the giant seaman to the sick bay, where he was laid on a metal-topped table under a strong electric light that showed up the deathly pallor of his powerfully-moulded head and neck. He lay there, now unconscious, breathing in a shallow and laboured manner.

'We'll clean up the shoulder,' said the doctor. 'Just hold this tray of instruments close to my hand, will you, please.

Mmm, the poor wretch has lost a lot of blood and is very weak. We'll cut away his tunic, which has already been slashed by the weapon that was directed against him – an edged and pointed knife, I'd say. What shoulders, eh? What a powerful fellow! His opponent must have been both quick and resolute to have scored such a mark on Flack. See the depth of that slash, Miss Trewella, right across the deltoid muscle. Ah, and there's the cephalic vein laid bare; another fraction of an inch and our patient would have bled to death by now. Now we'll sew him up.'

The *Dolphin*'s surgeon took needle and thread and deftly sewed together the edges of the deep and dangerous-looking wound, till nothing showed but a tight black line of stitching across the marbled white of the big shoulder. And when he had finished, Dr Weems looked down at his patient's still face and shook his head.

'It won't do,' he said gravely. 'It won't do at all.'

'He looks ... dreadfully ill,' I ventured.

'That he does, Miss Trewella. That he does.'

I looked along the metal-topped table.

'I think he's still losing blood, Doctor,' I said.

'I think you are right, Miss Trewella.'

Together, we turned the unconscious man on his left side, and the doctor rolled up the seaman's tunic from the waist, as high as the lower ribs.

'His attacker struck twice!' said Dr Weems.

A thin stream of blood oozed from a puncture in the back, low on the left side. I recoiled with shock, and all but knocked the tray of instruments on to the floor as my hands went involuntarily to my lips to stifle a scream of horror.

'Doctor ... is he ... ?' I whispered.

'He is very gravely hurt, Miss Trewella,' said my companion. 'The scoundrel who did it was altogether quicker and more resolute than we at first thought. It may well be that this gallant fellow's splendid defence of his mistress will cost him his life before morning.'

Able Seaman Flack did **not** die that night. When the morning's mist rolled up the steep slope of the great Rock, an ambulance from the naval sick bay ashore came to take him away. Dr Weems and I had watched over him all night, and had been rewarded by his return to consciousness. Too weak to give any account of the previous night's occurrence, he nevertheless found the strength to treat us to a heart-warming smile of gratitude, before his honest eyes closed again. The doctor and I stood at the top of the gangway and watched the ambulance rattle away across the quay.

'Will he survive?' I asked.

'I think so,' said Dr Weems. 'There are internal injuries, but he has mountainous strength to pull him through. The fellows ashore here are excellent, and can call upon the finest surgeons in the Fleet.' He looked at me. Behind the spectacles, his mild eyes seemed no more sleepy than usual, despite the long night's vigil. 'You've performed miracles of support and endurance, Miss Trewella. Now you must go and rest.'

'I must thank you for all you've done, Miss Trewella.'

I never heard Jason Saltram's approach; his voice made my heart lurch. I turned, and he was looking straight into my eyes. Surely he must see my secret written large there, I told myself – and lowered my gaze.

'It – it was nothing,' I whispered.

'It was very considerable help that Miss Trewella gave me,' declared Dr Weems. 'That Flack survived the night's crisis is due in a very large part to her nursing.'

'How is Melloney, Commander?' I asked, as much to change the subject as to reassure myself of what I already knew – having peeped in several times during the night, to see her peacefully asleep in a sick bay cot, with Nanny keeping tireless guard over her beloved.

'Nurse Bagley reports that she is none the worse for her ordeal,' replied Jason. 'By heaven, it is fortunate that Flack came upon the scene when he did.'

'What is your view of the occurrence, sir?' asked Dr Weems softly, head on one side, eyes mild and enquiring. 'What do you suppose happened last night?'

Jason flashed him a surprised glance. 'Why, I would have thought it was plain enough,' he replied coldly. 'An intruder came aboard with the intention of stealing something of value. Finding a helpless young woman, the brute took it into his head to kidnap her for ransom – but was fortunately thwarted in his design by Flack.'

'You think it was someone from ashore, then?' I blurted out.

Jason again looked surprised. 'Naturally,' he said. 'Who else? I know every man of the *Dolphin*'s crew and they're all as faithful as Flack.'

Another question was on my lips – but I let it remain there.

'What sort of scoundrel would do such a thing?' asked Dr Weems.

'There are plenty such,' said Jason. 'The Rock is teeming with foreigners of all complexions, and boats put in here from all over the Mediterranean. It's not beyond the bounds of probability that an Arab felucca from Morocco dropped anchor outside the mole after dark and put a party of cut-throat robbers ashore. Melloney will no doubt be able to describe her assailant when she recovers. Not that it will signify anything; the fellow will never be found. I have reported the matter to the authorities, but I don't expect any results – even if we were here to be told of any.'

'Then we're still leaving as planned, Commander?' asked Dr Weems.

'Of course, Doctor!' said Jason sharply. 'Last night's business only confirms me in my resolution to leave this accursed Rock, which has brought nothing but disaster to this cruise.' He turned his gaze to me. 'Nothing must be allowed to mar the *Dolphin* summer!' he cried. 'Nothing!'

We steamed out of Gibraltar at ten o'clock that morning, rounding Europa Point and meeting the full force of the easterly levanter that came tearing at us out of the wide Mediterranean. The big yacht dipped her sharp prow into the white-flecked blueness, gathered up a great load of it and tossed it skywards in a million jewelled droplets. Not a spot of water sullied the snowy decks. The *Dolphin* had the measure of levanters.

As we rounded the Point, I could not but drag my reluctant

gaze towards the heights above: in particular to the plateau from which the beautiful, cold and uncharitable Oriana Topsham had fallen to her death. And a shudder ran through me, as if I had gazed upon the scene of my own end.

I had not rested. My mind was tired – but over-tired with countless unanswered questions belabouring it and rendering any relaxation impossible. So I remained on deck and stayed awake. And while I looked about me, at the sprawling vistas of sea, sky and coastline, I put the questions to myself, one by one. And came no nearer to the answers.

Not till the great Rock was a finger of faded greyness behind us and the *Dolphin* was ploughing through a waste of emptiness, did my eyes, lacking anything substantial upon which to focus their gaze, begin to grow heavy. A defeating weariness followed immediately after. I was probably more asleep than awake when I stumbled down to my cabin and threw myself, fully dressed, upon the bunk. It was late afternoon when I opened my eyes again, and as soon as I had bathed and changed, I went to find out how Melloney was faring.

She seemed in fine spirits. I rejoiced to see this, and not only for her sake. I knew that I was capable of dealing with almost all the questions that had come crowding in on my life; but there was one thing bearing heavily upon my mind whose burden I could lessen by the simple act of telling Melloney about it.

I found her in her deck-chair, wrapped in her furs, on the poop deck. Glass screens had been erected along the sides of the deck, further to extend the sheltered area. The levanter blew and buffeted in vain; all was snug and warm on the poop. Melloney cried out with pleasure to see me and held out a hand for me to take. John Bennett was with her; he rose to his feet at my approach.

'Annabel!' cried Melloney. 'John's been telling me how wonderfully you coped last night. How lucky I am, to be surrounded by such friends...' and turning to John: 'Now you must let Annabel and me have a private talk about things. And please tell Nanny not to come fussing. I've been in bed all day, and I mean to stay up for dinner in the saloon – weather permitting.'

'By all accounts, we'll not see the worst of the levanter till tomorrow,' said John. 'And by that time, we shall be well on our way to Oran.' He nodded to both of us. 'I hope to see you ladies at dinner.'

When he had gone, Melloney said: 'Annabel, I know you want to quiz me about what happened last night. Everyone does. But I'd much sooner not talk about it, if you don't mind.' She turned away and my heart went to her. After a moment she continued, in a faint voice: 'When I think of that man prowling about my cabin while I slept, prying among my belongings, and then, when I awoke... to seize hold of me... oh!' She buried her face in her hands.

'Don't speak of it any more, Melloney,' I cried, reaching out to her. 'You must put it from your mind, the whole dreadful episode. It is all over, and thanks to Flack, you are safe and well.'

She dabbed her eyes. 'Poor Flack,' she said. 'I should have insisted on being taken ashore, to see him in the naval hospital – just to thank him for what he did for me. But Jason wouldn't hear of it. Oh, I pray that he lives. He has a young wife back in Falmouth, and two of the sweetest babes you ever saw. What will happen to them? Oh, Annabel – what misery I've brought upon that little family.'

'Don't!' I begged her. 'It wasn't your fault, and Flack was doing his duty. What's more, Dr Weems is quite confident that, with his great strength of constitution, he's going to make a good recovery.'

'Oh, I pray that he does,' cried Melloney. 'And that he's safely returned to us, so that I can thank him from the very bottom of my heart.'

A long silence, and her eyelids flashed open. The ghost of a smile played across her lips.

She squeezed my hands. 'You're so good for me, Annabel,' she said. 'You are my dear Harriet all over again. Before you came, no one was ever able to restore my downcast spirits the way that dear Harriet could.'

'I rejoice to hear you say it,' I told her. And, my mind returning to the tremendous secret that I had decided to share with her, I added: 'And now, because we have such a perfect understanding, there's something I have to tell someone with a sympathetic heart, or I think it will drive me out of my mind.'

Her eyes danced with excitement. 'Annabel darling, you're in love!' she cried. 'How stupid of you to think I hadn't noticed. Why, it's written all over your face!'

A fitful blaze of sunshine came from behind one of the massed cloudbanks above. It seemed to illuminate my whole world with a new splendour.

'You ... *know?*' I breathed.

'I've suspected it for quite a while,' she said. 'And I've always known that he fell in love with you at first sight.'

A seagull, wheeling above the speeding yacht, mast-high, let out a piercing screech. To me, it could have been the call of a nightingale.

'He ... loves *me?*' was all I could say.

'Of course he does, dear. Hadn't you guessed? Everyone else aboard the *Dolphin* realized from the first. It was so plain that he doted on you. Even that poor, stupid Oriana realized and was quite furious. But wouldn't you have expected it of her?' She took my hands again, held me out at arms' length and swept me with the dazzling gaze of her brilliant eyes. 'And now, it's plain that the very best has happened, and that you love him in return. Oh, Annabel, I'm so happy for you both – you and John.'

'Me and ... *John* ... ?' my voice trailed away.

Melloney was unaware of my change of expression, because she was looking down at her hands – pensively, as if assembling something in her mind. It took her some moments, during which time I continued to stare at her irresolutely, not knowing what to say. Presently, without looking up, she said: 'And now, dear Annabel, I've decided to repay confidence with confidence, and tell you *my* secret.'

'Yours?' I whispered faintly.

'I'm in love too, Annabel,' she murmured. 'I'm not in your happy position, because he doesn't love me in return. Although I sometimes wake in the night and tell myself that it cannot be mere duty that binds him to me so devotedly.'

The seagull cried again, and was echoed by one of its companions. They sounded like the cawing of carrion crows in the high trees above a graveyard.

'Who ... who is he?' I breathed, knowing with a dreadful certainty what the answer must be.

'Need you ask?' she replied. 'Didn't you guess, at that first luncheon in Falmouth, when I was faced with the prospect of Jason selling Lumley's and going back into the Navy – where I'd scarcely ever see him?'

'I remember,' I said. I remembered well enough; but I had placed a different construction upon it at the time: had thought that it was the frantic possessiveness of an invalid, and not the desperation of a hopeless lover, that had been her guiding force on that occasion.

As my mind struggled to take it in, a worse blow fell.

'But, though he doesn't love me,' said Melloney, 'as I love him, he esteems me very highly, and desperately wants to make me happy. So we shall be married. Some time during the *Dolphin* summer, with Captain Pelly officiating. And you, my dear Annabel, shall be my bridesmaid.'

'But – I don't understand,' I faltered. 'The ring that Lady Topsham brought from London. I thought ... we all thought ...'

'That Jason had ordered it for poor Oriana?' There was a note of compassion in her voice when she uttered the name of the dead woman who had spoken of her so cruelly in the hearing of both of us. 'Oh no, Annabel. You were all quite, quite wrong. And so was Oriana. Jason bought the engagement ring for me. He gave it to me on the night we left England. We are secretly engaged – and it's a secret that you now share.'

Somehow, I found the bitter-tasting words: 'I wish you – both – every happiness.'

I blessed the good fate that inspired her to embrace me, so that I could hide the treacherous tears against her shoulder.

'I so want to make him happy,' she whispered. 'My only wish in life is to be cured, so that I can be everything to him.

Nothing else matters save that — nothing! I want to be whole and strong again, so that I can be more than a wife in name only. So that I can be his right hand and his comforter. The sharer of his joys and sorrows. Mother of his children...'

I heard it all through the agony, and looking out through the tears that half-blinded me, I quietened my heart with the vow that my secret must now remain forever locked within me. For how — by thought, word or deed — could I place in jeopardy the slender fabric upon which this dying girl was pinning all her hopes of happiness?

It was approaching six o'clock in the late afternoon and I was still sitting in the shelter of the poop deck, alone now. Despite her protests, Melloney had been made by Nanny to take a nap in her cabin before dinner, and the replacement for the unfortunate Flack — another able seaman of scarcely less impressive bulk — had borne her off.

To divert my mind, I took from my reticule a letter that had arrived on board shortly before sailing. It had come by way of a ship newly arrived from England, in a packet of mail addressed to the *Dolphin*. It was from Mrs Penbury. The unconscious irony that lay behind her attempts to push me into a splendid marriage made me smile despite myself.

> The School House,
> St Finn,
> Cornwall
> 21 October, 1897

Dear Annabel,
I trust that you have comfortably established yourself aboard Cdr Saltram's yacht and are MAKING THE MOST OF YOUR UNIQUE OPPORTUNITIES. I beg you to remember always that GENTILITY and REFINEMENT begin in the MIND, and that yours has been well-tutored in these particulars. You are well-capable, my dear Annabel, of HOLDING YOUR OWN in any company and need have no fear on the score of appearing to be of INFERIOR ATTAINMENTS.

Who are the PASSENGERS aboard the yacht? Send me, do, a list of their names & titles (the latter is particularly IMPORTANT, for many a fine-sounding title may prove on inspection to be HOLLOW, while the heir to a DUKEDOM might yet be a humble 'Mr'), and I will reply by return and ADVISE you as to the suitability of PURSUING this or that acquaintance ...

My amusement died from lack of nourishment. I stared out across the passing wave tops: to a blue-grey, wrinkled line of mountain crests that stood faintly above the southern horizon – the edge of the vast African continent.

No more tears, I told myself. I could not afford the risk of weeping: in future, it must all be done within my heart. And I knew that this new pact with myself would call for a degree of watchfulness that I would have to maintain, day and night, while ever Melloney lived.

While ever she lived. I did not dare to think beyond that awful point ...

Staring still, I must have drifted into an uneasy sleep. There, I had dreams that were made of grotesque images – as I was pursued through long and echoing corridors by faceless phantoms bent on my destruction. And the harder I ran, the slower became my progress, so that my would-be destroyers rapidly gained upon me, till I could hear their frenzied breathing and feel their questing fingertips as they reached out to take hold of me.

Blessedly, I was aroused by what seemed to have been a sharp noise close by my ear. In fact, the sound appeared to be fading off into receding footsteps when my eyelids flickered open and I remembered my whereabouts: the poop deck, veiled in the gathering shadows of the coming night. And I was still alone.

The motion of the yacht had increased, and the levanter keened loudly in the rigging. When I got to my feet, I had to steady myself against the glass screen that protected the poop.

In doing so, my eyes fell upon a message written with a fingertip on a mist patch that bloomed in the centre of the pane of glass. I felt my skin crawl with the shock of recognition, for I had trodden this path before.

The message from the tormented soul was more rounded-

out than his previous heart-cry. And it opened a vista of un-
imaginable terrors:

FORGET YOUR SISTER'S SIN.
IT WILL BRING YOU NOTHING
BUT TROUBLE.

I was still staring at the words when they faded and died.

chapter six

The wind increased in fury, and the *Dolphin* no longer rode the rising wavecrests, but dipped her sharp prow deeply and gathered a great weight of water with every descent. From where I sat, in my lonely cabin, I could both hear and feel the heavy pounding of incoming water on the forward deck.

The telephone rang. Rising, I unsteadily crossed the heeling floor and answered it.

'Chief Steward speaking, ma'am.'

'Yes?'

The man sounded much put out. 'It is with much regret that I must inform ma'am that the present conditions preclude the serving of dinner in the saloon tonight. The motion of the vessel ... cooking is impossible. But, for those ladies and gentlemen who wish it, a cold collation is available for service in the cabins. I'm terribly sorry, ma'am. I really am ...'

'That's perfectly all right, Dacres,' I reassured him. 'It's not your fault.'

'Ma'am is very kind. Will ma'am be requiring a collation?'

'No, thank you, Dacres,' I told him.

'Very well, ma'am.' He sounded relieved. Perhaps he felt sick.

I was not hungry – though not from sea-sickness; but the cancellation of dinner meant that I had lost my best chance of a meeting and a quiet word with John Bennett. And I had to see him that night; the thought of laying my head on the pillow without confiding in him about the latest development in the chain of shocking events in which I had become enmeshed was something I could not bear to contemplate. Decidedly, I had to see John. But where and how? I had only a vague idea of the location of his cabin – and in any event, the impropriety of my visiting him there put such an idea beyond the pale. And the telephone was only connected to the Chief Steward's pantry.

Only one course remained. Throwing my shawl over my head and shoulders and knotting it tightly, I left the cabin –

locking it as usual – and set off to search for my friend.

It was quite dark outside, and the wind tore at my skirts and teased long strands of loose hair out from under my shawl. On the way down to the saloon, I met my reflection in a gilded mirror and thought how like a mad witch I looked: wild-eyed, unkempt.

John was not in the saloon; only Dr Weems. The yacht's surgeon was lying asleep on a sofa, his booted feet resting on one of the arms. An empty rummer lay upturned on the Persian carpet near his limp hand, rolling with every motion of the vessel. When I reached down to pick up the fallen glass, I caught the heavy aroma of alcoholic spirits. The doctor was breathing heavily. His necktie was loose and his hair awry. It seemed to me that he was much the worse for drink.

I retraced my steps up on to the boat deck, and met the full force of the levanter again. Clinging to the rails, I gazed forward to the bridge: a dark citadel crowned with a glow of light, where a group of silhouetted figures tended to the task of directing the *Dolphin* to a safe haven beyond the storm. Perhaps John was up there with them. I went to look.

The lower steps of the companionway leading up to Captain Pelly's holy of holies brought me within earshot of those up there. I heard the Captain's deep voice – and that of Jason.

'I have been proved wrong, Captain. For the sake of the ladies' comfort, we should have postponed our sailing for a day.'

'Not so, sir,' came Captain Pelly's stout response. 'Another few hours will see the end of this. You were right to insist on sailing as we did. By four bells of the middle, Alboran Island will be abeam, and I wager that the sea will be a millpond by first light. These levanters roar through the Strait of Gibraltar as if through the open doors of a threshing shed, and it may be even worse here tomorrow, but we'll be out of it. By the morning, we'll be sheltered in the lee of the Algerian coast.'

'I shall remain on the bridge with you till then, Captain.'

'It will be my pleasure, sir.'

Craning my neck, I could see Jason: his hawk-like profile dramatically illuminated from below by the light of a compass bowl; peering out, narrow-eyed, against the teeth of the levanter. *Dolphin*'s owner had one hand upon the helm, and the yacht would find her safe haven for sure. On top of all my secret terrors, there had been the nagging fear of the unknown, of the angry elements. That fear, at least, was gone.

I went back on to the boat deck, for John was not on the bridge with the others. Passing the closed door of Jason Saltram's cabin, I noticed that the lights were on behind the curtained portholes – which was quite normal. It was only when I saw a shadow flicker briefly across one of the curtains that I paused in my stride. Given any other time, any other circumstance, and I would have dismissed it with the thought that one of the stewards was tidying up, or perhaps laying a solitary supper for the owner; but this was not an ordinary time, and the episode of the second message on the glass had charged my nerves to snapping point. I was immediately suspicious – of anything.

The curtain behind the porthole glass was not quite drawn: a sliver of space provided my peering eye with a view of part of the cabin's interior. I saw Jason's desk – and the back view of a man stooping over it.

A tall man, broad-shouldered and lean. By the colour of his hair and the set of his head, I knew him at once.

I told myself that he was obviously within his rights to be there: Jason had mentioned to him to call in and pick up a book or something of the sort.

I did not convince myself with this explanation, but remained to watch. I was still there when something – an unusual creak of the cabin panelling, perhaps – made him give a start. I clearly saw the sudden look of alertness in his face when he turned his head, ears cocked, listening.

I was right. It was John Bennett.

Whatever it was that had caught his attention was sufficient to bring his business in Jason's cabin to a close. He put something into his breast pocket – it looked like a notebook – and stepped swiftly out of my line of vision. I had scarcely time to slip out of sight behind a large ventilator on the deck before the cabin door was stealthily opened to emit the dark figure of the intruder. I watched him go down the companionway leading to the block of cabins adjacent to the saloon. A thief in the night.

While the *Dolphin* fought her way into the teeth of the levanter, I lay sleepless in my bunk, staring up at the dark ceiling and turning things over in my mind.

The latest message from my strange confidant – what could it mean? What sin had my sister been guilty of? It seemed inconceivable that she could have committed any but the most trivial of wrongs.

I assembled all my memories of Harriet: of the occasion when she had come into my room to say goodbye to me for the last time. Some heightening of my perceptiveness sparked an image of a pale and homely face; firm-jawed and grey-eyed; hair scooped up neatly under a black bonnet trimmed with a green cockade. I seemed to hear her voice again: matter-of-fact, with the Cornish burr that had never deserted her through all her years of service with 'the gentry' ...

'Good night, lovey ... 'tis almost certain that I'll be able to come and see you at Christmas.'

She had never come at Christmas; by then, poor Harriet was in her grave.

'Forget your sister's sin. It will bring you nothing but trouble.'

It was monstrous; ridiculous!

But I had to do something about it.

In whom could I confide?

Not in John Bennett, certainly. After what I had seen him at, there could no longer be any trust remaining between us. Why, his conduct might even be connected with the strange events that had dogged my existence ever since I had set foot aboard the *Dolphin*. Indeed, was almost certainly connected.

Not Melloney. The last person to be drawn into my private fears must be Melloney.

Not Jason. No matter how much I yearned to lay my burden there, I did not dare. My love had not yet cast out the fear and awe in which I stood of him. Nor could I forget the terror of his fury – as when I had dropped the teacup and saucer on the floor of his cabin, and he had reviled me for the clumsy, common creature that I was. I shuddered anew at the memory.

Who, then?

Only one person remained...

Sleep caught me unawares. It was broad daylight, and hot sun streamed in through my porthole when I woke. I flung it wide, and breathed in the tangy, salt air, revelling in the hiss of the wake, glorying in the colour of the sea, sky-blue and calm as a millpond as far as the eye could see. Captain Pelly had been right: the levanter had passed us – or we the levanter – and we were sailing through near-tropic waters under the shelter of Africa's shore that showed its high mountain-tops to the south.

The calm seas echoed a new calmness in my mind. Having made a decision before going to sleep, I was ready to pursue it, no matter what, and looked forward to the ordeal with some eagerness, telling myself that I would not flinch from whatever came of it.

Captain Pelly's usual daily report with my breakfast tray confirmed that we had indeed passed beyond the levanter and were cruising at a speed of ten knots towards the port of Oran, where we should arrive at about eight o'clock in the evening. By the time we reached Oran, I told myself, I should know the truth.

Prompted by a sense of occasion, I dressed myself with more than my usual care. The sub-tropic clime of the Mediterranean in October accorded with the best of my slender wardrobe, since I was pretty well supplied with shirts and blouses, skirts and petticoats – village schoolma'am's costume. Instead of pinning my hair up, I gathered it in a simple chignon (in imitation of Melloney, perhaps), and went out to keep my appointment with a kind of destiny.

The corridor near the saloon – where the principal cabins were, including Melloney's – looked quite different with the morning's sun streaming down through the ornamental skylight in the roof. With a shudder, I hastily quenched a wayward memory of the last time I had been there: on the night of the attack on Melloney and the faithful Flack.

No sound came from Melloney's cabin, and I knew that she usually slept till past ten o'clock – which was why I was abroad on my mission so early.

I tapped gently on Nurse Bagley's door.

'Who is it?' came from within.

'It's Annabel, Nanny,' I said. 'Can I speak to you for a few moments, please? It's rather important.'

'Of course. Come in, miss.'

The nurse was sitting in a basket chair, her breakfast tray set before her on an occasional table. She was dressed in a gown of grey wool over her night-clothes, and her grey-flecked hair lay in a plait over her shoulder. As I entered, she lowered her coffee-cup and treated me to an expressionless glance from head to foot from her button-black eyes.

'Good morning, Nanny,' I said brightly, trying to hide the nervousness that was building up within me.

'Good morning, miss,' she replied in her despairing voice. 'Take a seat, do. What was it you wanted to say to me, then?'

I looked down at my hands: to my surprise, they were trembling slightly. Lest the other woman should notice this and infer my state of mind, I folded my arms. To achieve my object, it seemed to me that I must be in control of the situation. She must guess nothing of what was coming.

'Well, miss?' repeated Nanny Bagley. 'You said it was something important.'

'Yes, it concerns' – I began, watching her eyes closely, for signs of any emotion that my words might evoke – 'it concerns my half-sister, Harriet Cadge.'

'Harriet Cadge!' she exclaimed.

I was not disappointed in the result of my statement: the sombre dark eyes flared wide with sudden shock. And there was something else . . . alarm?

'I think you knew her quite well, Nanny,' I continued calmly. 'Leastways, when we first met, you made a very complimentary remark about my late sister: you said something to the effect that a finer woman never drew breath.'

The woman nodded and pursed her lips. 'It was just a manner of speaking,' she said with a touch of reluctance.

'But must have had some basis on fact.'

'I don't understand you, miss,' replied the other truculently. 'I'm only a humble nurse. Not one of your educated sort, like you and Harriet Cadge.'

I ignored the gibe – if a gibe was intended. 'I mean, you must have had some reason for making the remark, even if it was – as you say – only a manner of speaking. You could have paid her the compliment of having been pretty, or generous, or a good governess to Melloney. But you made a particular point about her. "Fine," you said. "A finer woman never drew breath." '

The nurse shrugged. 'Well, she was a fine sort of person,' she admitted. 'Or so she struck me.'

At that moment, the *Dolphin* rode over a small wave, which caused her to roll slightly, so that the both of us gently inclined first one way, then the other, in time. And the cabin panelling gave a discreet creak.

I took a deep breath, and said: 'Then tell me how this fine woman of whom you speak could have committed such a ...*sin?*'

My shock tactics did not fail me.

'You – you *know?*' cried Nanny Bagley.

I nodded, searching her face for every telltale sign of her emotions. But, after a brief moment, she averted her eyes from me. The top of her grey-flecked head told me nothing. And her hands were still. I rose from the chair and crossed over to the porthole. Looking out, I idly registered that the African mountains were drawing perceptibly nearer.

The shock tactics having drawn first blood, I should now have to rely on guile to learn the truth.

'One thing I'm not quite clear about, Nanny,' I said coolly, 'is when it happened. Now, Harriet passed away shortly before Christmas of eighteen eighty-eight, at St Errol House. And, by the way, what did she die of – was it the consumption?'

A short pause, and then the woman's head flicked up sharply, so that she was looking at me. The dark eyes were narrowed with an expression of something like cunning.

'You know nothing about it!' she exclaimed. 'You come in here badgering me with your questions, trying to trick me into saying something I shouldn't, and all the time you know nothing about what Harriet Cadge did!'

I was nonplussed. Something I had said – or some unguarded inflection of my voice – had betrayed the slenderness of my knowledge. The woman had the answer to all my questions, but – as I had known instinctively before even coming to see her – was not for telling me, or she would surely have done so long before. Guile would no longer serve me any purpose; I would have to rely on pleas. Perhaps... threats.

'It's true, Nanny,' I admitted. 'I've been told that my half-sister did something...something awful. But I've no idea what.'

'Who told you?' she snapped.

'I don't know that either. Someone – some unknown person – left me a message, which I no longer have. I was told to forget what my sister had done – which implies that this person believed that I knew, or guessed, what she had done. And I was also advised that the knowledge would bring me trouble.'

Her eyes narrowed. 'Not trouble,' she said. 'I wouldn't say it would bring you any trouble. But it would cause you a lot of upset. Best you stay in ignorance, miss. You know what they say: "Where ignorance is bliss, 'tis folly to be wise." Never were truer words spoken.' And she smiled at me; she seemed to have recovered her composure.

'Nanny,' I said, 'I am not to be put off by platitudes. I want the whole story from your lips, and I want it now. If I don't get it, I shall go elsewhere.'

'Elsewhere?' Once more, her eyes flared wide with alarm.

'I shall go to Commander Saltram, tell him of the message I received, tell him that you insist on keeping me in ignorance about some action on the part of my late sister, and beg him to tell me. Or, if he doesn't know, to order you to give me the information. Is that quite clear?'

In the long silence that lay between us, I heard the shrill call of a bosun's pipe and the swift pattering of sailors' bare feet on the deck above our heads.

Presently, she said: 'I must give it some thought, miss. Other people's feelings are involved. I can't be too hasty. I've got to think it over.'

'I mean to know before we reach Oran,' I replied firmly. 'Depending on what you tell me, I may decide to leave the *Dolphin* and make my own passage back to England.'

'Oh, that won't be necessary, miss!' she cried.

'I hope not, Nanny. But I must know in time. Think it over by all means. Then, before the end of the afternoon watch – before four o'clock – come and seek me out, and tell me all about my late half-sister's terrible sin.'

I spent the rest of the morning on the boat deck, from where I was able to spy the distant coastline through a pair of binoculars that the First Officer brought down to me from the bridge. He stayed a while to instruct me about the various mountain ranges of Morocco and Algeria – for we were about abreast of the junction between those two lands – that dominated the skyline; and directed my attention to towns and villages of the coastal plains, whose white-walled buildings showed plainly through the glasses.

At about midday I was joined by John Bennett. I responded very briefly to his greeting, and returned to my sightseeing.

'Is anything the matter, Annabel?' he asked me.

'Should anything be the matter?' I replied.

'Then something is the matter,' he said. 'Never mind, I won't probe. Since you've decided to take umbrage with me for no reason at all, I take the optimistic view that I shall return to your good books by the same easy means. I'll leave you now, but be sure to be present for lunch in the saloon. I understand it's to be a rather special affair, to celebrate our successful passage through last night's levanter – and, by the way, did you pass a comfortable night, my dear? Don't bother to answer that!

'What was I saying? Oh yes, luncheon. Very special affair. Hope to see you there. *Au revoir*.' From the corner of my eye, I saw him tip his straw boater, but I made no response, and he walked away down the deck.

John Bennett's quizzical grin was the first thing to greet me when I descended into the saloon, with the sound of the luncheon gong still reverberating about the richly-appointed compartment. Ignoring him – and noting, with an unworthy sense of satisfaction, that his face fell with disappointment – I went straight to Melloney, who was reclining on the pink sofa. As always, she looked like a delicately-fashioned doll; dressed in the informal manner that she favoured, and bubbling over with lightness and vitality. She took my hand and pulled me close to her.

'You are deliberately cutting poor John,' she whispered in my ear. 'What's happened – a lovers' tiff?'

Confused, I could only murmur: 'Something like that. But I'd rather not talk about it just now.'

'Don't be too hard on the poor dear,' she whispered. 'He really is hopelessly in love with you, Annabel...' Her voice broke off. I was looking directly into her flawless blue eyes, so I was able to see, at close hand, how their sparkling gaiety suddenly softened. Her lips parted, and her hand tensed in mine.

'Are we all assembled?' The voice of Jason Saltram stilled all conversation. 'Good day to you, Melloney, and to you, Miss Trewella. Bennett, good day. Doctor Weems...Captain Pelly. Shall we all be seated?'

Melloney smiled weakly at me. 'Does it show terribly?' she whispered. 'Does the whole world know how much I love him?'

I could not bring myself to reply; but only squeezed her hand before relinquishing it, and lowered my eyes.

We took our places: Melloney was carried to her seat at one end of the table, and Jason took the other end. To my consternation, he gestured to me to sit at his right hand, and for John Bennett to be on his left. Dr Weems was next to me, on Melloney's left, with the Captain on the other side.

The stewards filled our glasses with champagne, and Jason raised his, addressing us. 'The toast remains "The *Dolphin* summer",' he said. 'Coupled with the health and happiness of all who sail in her. Ladies and gentlemen, I give you "The *Dolphin* summer!"'

Save Melloney, we all rose. 'The *Dolphin* summer!'

'*Your* summer, my dear,' said Jason, inclining his glass towards Melloney.

I echoed the toast with the rest; and as I repeated the phrase, I seemed to see the dead Jack Maugham drifting, sightless-eyed, near the sea-bottom; and Oriana Topsham – she who dreaded heights – lying at the foot of the sheer cliff, fingers scrabbling at the warm rock.

'The health and happiness of all who sail in her...' I shuddered.

When we had seated ourselves again, Captain Pelly said: 'Sir, I am happy to report that my estimated time of arrival may be taken as exact. Eight o'clock on the dot. Unless it is your wish to increase speed and arrive before nightfall.'

'Eight o'clock will be capital,' replied Jason. 'As you know, Captain, the topography of Oran – built as it is upon a series of natural terraces – provides a splendid landfall when approached after dark, with the lights strung out from the shoreline to the highest point of the town.' He glanced encouragingly round the table. 'I can promise you a most impressive sight, ladies and gentlemen.'

There was a concerted murmur of appreciation, and John Bennett said: 'Is your friend, the gallant Commandant de Belleisle, aware of our coming, Saltram?'

'Indeed he is, Bennett,' came the reply. 'I sent a letter on ahead from Gibraltar as soon as we put in there, by a French naval frigate which was leaving for Oran, warning de Belleisle to keep watch for the *Dolphin*. Knowing him, I should not be surprised if there is a Foreign Legion guard and band drawn up on the Quai du Sénégal, to greet us on the morning after our arrival.'

Melloney clapped her hands like an excited child.

Jason threw her an indulgent smile, then directed his gaze to John Bennett. 'Speaking of letters, my dear Bennett, I should tell you that I received a certain communication from England on the morning we left Gibraltar.'

The American carefully chewed and swallowed a mouthful of food before replying. I had the distinct impression that he found need of those few moments to compose his reply –

though his reply was brief enough in all conscience.

'Indeed, sir?' was all he said

Jason gave him a tight, inscrutable smile. 'Are you not curious as to who sent me this letter, and about its contents?'

The other returned his smile. 'Indeed I am, sir. Might one ask ...?'

'Before leaving England,' said Jason, 'I sent a memorandum to my fellow-members of the Board of Directors of Lumley's, asking for their views on your proposition: your offer on behalf of Charles Bennett and Sons for the purchase of Lumley's. Now, what do you think of that?'

I had the feeling that Jason was playing with the American: teasing him, leading him on. But John Bennett continued to smile his guileless, carefree smile; and only the nervous tapping of his finger on the side of his wine glass betrayed his inner feelings.

'I hope they turned the offer down flat!' was Melloney's interjection. And there was an angry spot of colour on each of her delicate cheekbones.

'Oh, indeed I hope not,' said John Bennett mildly.

'The directors sent me a round robin by return,' said Jason. 'You will be interested to hear that they were completely unanimous in their view of the proposition. Now, that's something, isn't it?'

John nodded affably. 'Indeed it is, sir.'

A long silence hung in the air. One of the stewards made to take up Jason's empty dish, but Chief Steward Dacres – the perfect servant, attuned to every nuance of atmosphere – checked his underling with a frown and a gesture.

Presently, Jason said: 'However, as Chairman of the Board and major shareholder, I do not feel bound in any way by the views of my directors; but I do take account of their informed advice and opinion. Their views will certainly influence the final decision, which will be mine. and mine alone' – his dark and intensely mobile countenance, which had worn an expression of gravity, was tightened by a bright grin that would have charmed away the heart of any woman and sent cowards to die heroes' deaths in battle – 'Which is why, my dear Bennett, I am not going to divulge to you the contents of the round robin. Not yet. Not till I have made up my mind.'

I shot a glance at John Bennett: a suspicion was hardening in my mind ...

'As you will, Commander,' he said carelessly.

'Later,' said Jason. 'In a few days' time, when I have turned their counsel over in my mind, I will give you my answer.'

'I shall look forward to that, sir,' said John Bennett.

I knew then, for certain, what had taken Bennett to Jason's cabin during the dark hours of the previous night's storm. While the *Dolphin*'s owner was keeping watch on the bridge with the Captain, that sly and despicable creature – that brash and hateful Go-Getter, as he was proud to call himself – had so far abused his host's hospitality as to sneak into his quarters and search for the letter that he must have guessed had arrived from the people at Lumley's.

Small wonder he was so calm about Jason's decision to keep him waiting several more days for his answer: the underhand wretch already knew of the advice which was going to influence Jason's decision. It was all copied down in his notebook!

I could have thrown my bread roll at John Bennett; instead, I tackled my Lobster Thermidor with an unaccustomed fury, slicing it to fragments on my plate – but eating next to nothing, for I had no appetite.

And my anger with John Bennett soon evaporated, being based on what had turned out to be such a mean and trivial matter compared with the agonies that were uppermost in my mind.

From time to time, my glance strayed towards the splendid ormolu clock that ticked over the ornate, false chimney-piece at one end of the saloon. It was past one o'clock: in less than three hours, Nanny Bagley – unless she defied my ultimatum – would reveal the secret connected with my dead sister.

And when I was not looking at the clock, my envious eyes wandered towards Melloney, sitting at the opposite end of the table from the man we both loved – and towards whom her eyes for ever strayed.

I could not bring myself to see how he returned her looks.

The *Dolphin* had now shaped a course to bring her closer to the African shore. Melloney was asleep in her deck-chair. I, restless and pent-up, could not settle anywhere for more than a few moments on end, but moved from side to side of the poop deck, under the awning's shade, diverting myself by scanning the barren shoreline for signs of life and habitation.

Half past three o'clock. Nanny Bagley had not shown herself throughout the afternoon. A casual enquiry of Melloney had given me the information that the woman was resting in her cabin with a headache.

White seabirds were skimming low over the smooth wake behind us. I watched them as they drifted near on the light airs, slender legs held close to their smooth bodies, unwinking, bright eyes fixed on me. In Cornwall, they say that the souls of drowned sailors inhabit the bodies of seabirds.

At a quarter to four, I decided to go down to Nanny's cabin and wrest the story from her. Melloney showed no signs of stirring: I covered her knees with her fur cape and made her pillow more comfortable. Then I went up on to the boat deck.

'Good afternoon, Miss Trewella.' I gave a start of surprise, as Dr Weems stepped out from behind a lifeboat, where he had been standing at the rail, looking out towards the shore. He raised his hat and smiled. His gentle, sleepy eyes met mine and dropped away.

'Hello, Doctor,' I said, barely pausing in my stride.

'Could I ... ?' he began, and seemed to change his mind in mid-sentence.

'Yes, Doctor?' I asked him. 'Was there something, and if so, can it wait? I'm on my way to see ...'

'Nurse Bagley,' he broke in. 'Yes, I know. It's about that I ...'

I stared at him closely, remembering that almost the last time I had seen the surgeon of the *Dolphin* he had clearly been very much the worse for strong drink. Could it be that he had been supplementing his lunchtime champagne? He certainly looked somewhat ill at ease.

'Yes, Doctor?' I prompted him. 'You were saying?'

'Nurse Bagley,' he said. 'The matter about which you spoke to her early this morning. She asked me – Nurse Bagley asked me – to provide you with the information you require.'

'About . . . my sister?'

He nodded. 'Yes, I know the whole story. And I will tell it to you' – he looked about him, up and down the boat deck, which was deserted but for the two of us – 'but not here – down in the sick bay. Come.'

We walked together down the companionway and through the door into the corridor leading to the sick quarters, the first compartment of which was decorated with a desk and chairs, bookcase and glass-fronted medicine cupboard. He motioned me to a chair and took his own place behind the desk.

He seemed nervous and ill at ease. 'Would you like me to telephone for a pot of tea?' he asked.

'No, thank you, Doctor.'

'Er – something a little stronger, perhaps?'

I shook my head. 'You were going to give me the information I require about my sister,' I told him.

'Er – quite so, Miss Trewella,' he said. 'Nurse Bagley was most insistent . . . that is to say, she felt that I should be better able to explain the background, the clinical background, to the . . . unhappy occurrence.' And he lowered his eyes.

'Please go on,' I said implacably. One thing was quite plain: Dr Weems may have accepted Nanny Bagley's commission, but he was far from happy with it. I should not hear about my late half-sister's mysterious sin either soon or without some prompting – not from his lips.

'We are speaking of a time, some eleven years ago, when Sir David Lumley was still alive,' he said. 'When Melloney was a girl of sixteen, Commander Saltram was a junior officer who only occasionally visited St Errol House when on leave from his ship, and I was in practice in the district and attended as the Lumley's family physician. Do I make the situation plain, Miss Trewella?'

I nodded. 'Yes, Doctor. And Harriet Cadge was in the employ of Sir David, as governess to his adopted daughter.'

'That is correct. Hem!'

'Please go on,' I prompted him.

'We come,' he said, 'to the tragic circumstance of Melloney's being thrown from her horse...'

I stared at him, and felt my skin crawl with a sudden dread.

'Melloney's accident?' I breathed. 'Are you going to tell me that Harriet was in some way responsible for Melloney's accident?'

He made a dismissive gesture. 'Oh no, Miss Trewella. How could that possibly be? Melloney was riding out on her own when it happened, with the full knowledge and approval of Sir David. She was a thoroughly competent, not to say expert, horsewoman. And Harriet Cadge was not present – indeed no one else was present – at the scene of the accident. The first we knew of it was when a travelling tinker, having found the unconscious girl lying in one of the rides through St Errol wood, brought her to my surgery in his cart. She soon recovered consciousness. I examined her. There were indications of a slight displacement of vertebrae in the lower part of the spine, but no fractures. No internal lesions. I was not greatly disturbed about her condition, you understand?'

'Commander Saltram told me,' I said, remembering, 'that her injuries were not thought to have been serious at the time, but that her disability increased as she grew older.'

Again, Dr Weems's timid eyes slid away from my gaze. 'One could put it that way,' he replied. 'Yes, certainly, the progress of Melloney's disability followed that pattern – superficially.'

Again, I felt that sense of dread at the proximity of an unknown horror.

'You mean – it wasn't like that at all?' I breathed.

'Melloney made a fairly good initial recovery from the fall,' he said. 'Then there was a slight relapse. Despite careful nursing, a serious complication set in. Pneumonia. Yet, still, I had few doubts that her excellent constitution would pull her through.'

'But – what happened?' I heard myself ask.

'It happened at night,' he said. 'The crisis of the disease

was near at hand, and Melloney was in a delirium. Nurse Bagley, who had not left the patient's bedside for two days and a night, had been with some difficulty persuaded to lie down on a sofa in an adjoining room. I was attending an accouchement at a house not far distant, and had planned to return to St Errol House at dawn, when I rightly gauged that the crisis would be at its height. And Harriet Cadge – your sister – was watching over Melloney.'

'Yes, Doctor. Please go on.' I was all afire to hear the rest, though half of my mind was screaming to me to turn and run, or to stop up my ears.

'I don't know the exact details of the incident,' he said. 'No one will ever know. What is certain is that, in her delirium, Melloney made an attempt to rise up from her bed and go down the stairs . . .'

'Yes – yes?'

'And that attempt was not prevented by the person who should have prevented it!'

'Why?'

'Because Harriet Cadge was asleep!'

'Asleep?'

'Drugged.'

'*Drugged?*'

He took off his glasses and passed his hand wearily across his short-sighted eyes. 'Harriet Cadge was in the habit of dosing herself with a proprietary brand of cough linctus – not prescribed by me – which contains a large amount of laudanum and other opiates.'

'For her cough, you say – she was a consumptive?'

He nodded. 'I suspected as much for some time before her death, but she would never let me examine her. With the fatal optimism of the consumptive – in itself a classic symptom of that dreadful disease which is the major scourge of our modern world – she would not have it that she was suffering from anything worse than what she called "a bit of a cough and catarrh that a spoonful of the linctus won't ease". I think it would be true to say that, by the time of the incident of which we are speaking, Harriet Cadge was, to some degree, addicted to the opiates which she had been ingesting.'

I shuddered and said: 'She drugged herself – and wasn't able to prevent Melloney from doing harm to herself! Is that it, Doctor?'

He nodded unhappily. 'Though I think it can be said that she took a large dose of the linctus in order not to disturb the patient with her coughing...'

'And, as a result, Melloney did harm to herself?' I persisted.

He nodded. 'Melloney managed to get out of bed and take a few faltering paces towards the door before she fell. In falling, she completed the damage that her accident had already begun. There was no progress after that. She recovered from the pneumonia, as I had predicted. But the irreversible damage to the spine, to the central nervous system...'

'Please, Doctor,' I cried out. 'Stop! I can't bear to hear any more.'

He got up and crossed over to the medicine cupboard. I heard a chink of glass on glass, and the sound of pouring. Soft-footed, he returned to the desk, and I saw a tumbler of amber liquid being laid at my elbow. Dabbing my eyes, I took it up and drank gratefully. The neat spirit burned my throat and made me cough. But it shocked me back to immediate reality.

'Don't stop crying,' he said gently. 'The effect is invariably beneficial.'

One thing, above all, I had to know...

'Was Melloney ever told,' I asked him, 'that it was because of my sister that...?'

'No.' He shrugged his shoulders. 'What profit would there have been in telling her? Harriet Cadge's devotion to Melloney was only matched by Nurse Bagley's. She was truly remorseful, and begged us – Nurse Bagley and me – not to report her action to Sir David, but make it possible for her to remain in his employment and – as she put it – "work out her salvation".'

'And you agreed to this?' I demanded. 'You allowed this woman, who had totally failed in a moment of crisis, and had been directly responsible for ruining the life of that girl...' I could not go on, but buried my face in my hands and gave way to my emotions.

After a while, he said: 'Don't be too hard on your sister's memory. I must tell you that, after agreeing to her plea – with much heart-searching, you may be sure – Nurse Bagley and I never had cause to regret it. Your sister almost literally slaved herself to death for Melloney, and died with her name on her lips. In truth, she "worked out her salvation".'

'So, if Melloney was never told, nor Sir David – what of Commander Saltram?' I asked.

'We have never told him either,' replied Dr Weems. 'The sole recipients of Harriet Cadge's secret were Nurse Bagley and myself – and now you, Miss Trewella. Just the three of us.'

Just the three of us?

But at least one other person knew: the person who wrote the message on the glass; the one whom I had come to know in my own mind as 'the unknown prisoner'.

But I said nothing of this to Dr Weems.

So that was Harriet's sin. It was bad enough in all conscience.

The blow was softened, for me, because I had never had any real love for my half-sister, only a deep respect for her good qualities, and nothing that Dr Weems had told me would change that; that Harriet had died 'working out her salvation' was all of a piece with the letter she had written to me from her death bed.

No tears, then, for poor Harriet; my tears were only for Melloney.

Tears – and an even greater determination to live up to the solemn vow I had made with Jason Saltram: to fill the brief time left to her with happiness.

Even if she were to find her happiness with the man I loved.

chapter seven

When it grew dark and we drew near to Oran, a buffet supper of cold meats, salads and chilled wines was served on the poop deck, under the snowy awnings, all lit by fairy lamps in the night's blissful coolness.

Jason presided, handsome as a corsair captain in a white mess jacket, with a row of medals glittering on his breast. I had deliberately to force myself not to stare at him all the time, while being agonizingly aware that Melloney's eyes followed his every move.

She was looking very beautiful. She had abandoned her usual plain, Greek-style gown for a many-coloured creation adorned with a green feather boa wound about her slender neck and shoulders. And a plume of bird of paradise feathers was set in the burnished platinum of her hair. On almost any other woman – and certainly on me – the effect would have been too extravagant for words, absurd even; on Melloney it was just another aspect of her dazzling beauty.

The approach to Oran was unpromising: nothing but the tumbled mountain peaks silhouetted against the shore, and only an occasional light winking in the blackness.

All at once, however, it was as if a curtain had been drawn aside to reveal a scene of fairyland. A high headland, towards which the yacht was steering, proved to be the gateway of a wide bay that enclosed countless diamond points of dancing light, stretching from shoreline to sky, and right across the bay. As Jason had promised us, Oran at night presented an unforgettable sight. Melloney cried out for joy.

'Oh, dearest Annabel,' she cried. 'Now I really do feel that the *Dolphin* summer has truly begun!'

There was a change in the rhythm of the yacht's engine, and the backdrop of lights began slowly to revolve about us.

'Captain Pelly is turning to approach the harbour mouth,' said Jason. 'May I suggest, ladies, that we go on the bridge, which will command a fine view of the anchorage and the town.'

The burly seaman appeared from nowhere and gathered up

Melloney in his arms. I followed after, and Jason himself gave me his hand to assist me up the companionway to the boat deck. The nearness of him, the fleeting scrutiny of his deep brown eyes, tore at the hastily-improvised defences that I had lately thrown about my heart. In vain, I repeated to myself that to love Jason, even in my thoughts, was to steal something from Melloney. But it was no use; I loved him still.

We reached the bridge just as *Dolphin*'s sharp stem and gilded figurehead passed between the winking beacons that marked the entrance to the harbour. We saw dark figures on the harbour wall, and a cheerful voice called out to us in French. I caught the sweet, half-rotten smell of the shore line – of seaweed and shellfish and the tangy breath of salt water; and beyond all that, another smell: a new smell that came out of the velvet night, dry in the nostrils and overlaid with the pollen of a million small herbs, warm with the warmth of a long day's blistering run: the scent of the great desert that began just beyond the lights of civilization and stretched out into the heart of Africa.

Captain Pelly's reckoning had been correct: within a few minutes of eight o'clock a cry went up: 'Drop anchor!' and there was a splash from the prow, followed by the rattling of a heavy chain as it sped across the deck. Then an officer's voice came up out of the shadows: 'Anchored in six fathoms, sir.'

We were in Africa.

Boats were approaching from the shore. Native sailboats bearing fruits and vegetables, silverware, leather goods, long rifles chased with silver and seed pearls. And a white steam launch with the French tricolor painted on its side. 'This will be the harbourmaster,' said Captain Pelly.

The launch joined the other craft that lay in the pool of light surrounding the Dolphin, importantly jostled its way through them and came to rest against the yacht's ladder, up which soon trotted a stout little man in a braided képi and a blue uniform heavy with faded gold lace. He came up on to the bridge, saluted Captain Pelly and twirled his waxed and pointed moustaches when he saw Melloney and me – particularly Melloney, who smiled sweetly at him.

'I am Monsieur Cambronne,' he said in heavily-accented

English, to no one in particular. 'Harbourmaster of Oran, at your service, *mesdames et messieurs*. Do I 'ave the honour of addressing Monsieur le Commandaire Saltram?'

'I am Saltram,' said Jason, extending his hand to the official. 'Good evening to you, monsieur. From the promptness of your appearance aboard the *Dolphin*, am I to assume that you were anticipating our arrival?'

Monsieur Cambronne inclined his head in assent. 'Commandant de Belleisle informed me, sir. He is asking me, as a personal favour, to greet you on arrival and to escort you to your berth alongside the *quai*.'

Jason frowned and shook his head. 'The *Dolphin* will remain at anchor out here,' he said flatly.

'But, Commandaire . . .'

'Out here,' repeated Jason. 'As far from the *quais* as possible, for so long as we are in Oran.'

The little Frenchman spread his hands in despair. 'But, Commandaire,' he cried, 'for your sake, and as a mark of the very personal favour, I 'ave caused the removal of a P & O liner from the most favoured berth on the Quai du Sénégal, right in front of the Château-Neuf. Many peoples has been put to the inconvenience. The P & O will be furious.'

'I am sorry.' Jason was adamant. 'The *Dolphin* will remain at the anchorage.' He nodded to Captain Pelly. 'I will leave you gentlemen to complete the usual formalities connected with our arrival.' He turned to Melloney and me. 'May I escort you down to the saloon, ladies? The night air is beginning to turn a trifle chill and I should not wish you to catch a fever.'

Down in the saloon, when the big seaman had laid Melloney upon the sofa and I had taken a seat beside her, Jason poured us both champagne, and a rummer of spirit for himself. His face was grave, but Melloney was eyeing him with a light, teasing smile that would surely have melted the heart of any man.

'You were very short with that perfectly delightful little Frenchman, Jason,' she said. 'Why ever did you do it?'

He shrugged. 'Yes, I was,' he said. 'And I will send him a note of apology first thing tomorrow. The fact is' – he looked out of the porthole, towards the necklace of lights strung along the shore-line – 'the fact is, I do not intend to risk a similar occurrence to that dastardly outrage in Gibraltar. Thanks to the presence of the Foreign Legion, Oran is a law-abiding port as ports go. But while we remain here, the *Dolphin* will ride to anchor in deep water, with an armed guard on the gangway to repel any intruders.'

'Dear Jason,' smiled Melloney. 'You fuss too much. Does he not, Annabel? But I'm sure we shall all feel safer in our beds, in consequence.'

Safer in our beds? – I asked myself that. Was it any use to bolt and bar the doors against an intruder?

What if the thing that menaced us was not from without? In that case, Jason's action would be like locking us in with the menace.

I was awakened by the silvery notes of a trumpet. It came from some way off, from the shore, and sketched out a lively march. I reached the porthole in time to see a tricolor rising on a flagstaff above the tall keep of a large and impressive castle that dominated the centre of the white-walled town. Some distance further to the east, and on higher ground, was another fortress. So marvellously clear was the morning air that I could discern yet another splash of colour ascending there.

It was early – five o'clock – but the port and town seemed to be well awake. White-clad figures strolled along the quays, and the harbour was dotted with small sailing craft, flitting like mayflies in the morning air, in and out among the craft that lay at anchor. The harbour was crowded with shipping. There was a huge vessel (it might have been the P & O liner of which the harbourmaster had spoken) not far from us, her tall funnels pouring black smoke high into the azure blueness, and a cloud of seabirds massed about her, screaming.

I was enchanted. It was so alien, other-worldly, so utterly entrancing. My fears, my secret heartache were put out of my mind by the keenness of the experience. The sudden aware-ness of the strange and exotic. The magic of the unaccustomed.

A native sailboat came close by, sliding past my porthole and out of sight again. There was a wizened old man with a coloured scarf wound about his head, and he was leaning on a great steering oar. A small boy, naked as the day he was born, and a dirty white dog walked side by side down the heeling deck of the boat. The boy pulled on a rope, and a kipper-brown sail the size of a windmill flapped lazily and swung over to the other side of the mast, obedient to the naked boy's touch. The old man saw me and waved. Then they were gone.

A breath of wind ruffled the surface of the water. There was a creak of woodwork and rigging, and the *Dolphin* seemed to sigh with contentment and swing lazily at her anchor chain. The nearest part of shoreline slid slowly into my view. I gave a gasp of wonder and delight.

Quite near – in the clear light, it seemed so near that I could almost reach out and touch it – the shore rose steeply from the beach in rocky terraces. A handsome villa was set on the uppermost terrace, splendid in the morning sun, with white stone walls and columned arcades that were all over-hung with wistaria, jasmine and oleander. As I gazed, a man in a saffron-coloured gown and a scarlet fez was slowly descending a flight of steps that led from the uppermost terrace to the gardens that stretched, one below the other, to the beach. In his descent, he passed sunlit lawns of startling green-ness and the shadows of sentinel cypresses and dramatic palms, where marble statuary gestured in secret bowers of bougain-villaea and rhododendron, and tall fountains rose in crystal droplets. The man – I took him to be a gardener – paused from time to time to examine a clump of blossoms here and touch a piece of trailing shubbery there, all with an air of quiet pride. At the lowest terrace, he clapped his hands, and a pair of turtle doves rose from the balustrade and soared upwards till they reached the highest part of the villa's russet-tiled roof, where they settled. The gardener looked up at them, seemed to smile, and resumed his descent.

I wondered who owned that beautiful palace. Perhaps some French colonial official, or a powerful native sheikh. How I envied that person ...

Time wore on, all unnoticed by me, till the steward's tap on my cabin door told me that it must be eight bells and breakfast. After breakfast, I took stock of my wardrobe and decided that, now the *Dolphin* summer was really with us, I should have to spend some of my salary on clothes suited to the sub-tropical climate of North Africa. I needed a couple of light linen frocks and a summer coat. Such garments were presumably obtainable in the town. I would seize my first opportunity for a shopping expedition.

At about nine-thirty, bathed and dressed in the lightest and coolest things I had, I went up on to the boat deck. I had scarcely gone half-way up the steps before the sound of cheering came from the deck above. This was immediately followed by the sudden blare of a brass band.

The First Officer greeted me when I came out into the sunshine. He gestured towards the rail, where the *Dolphin*'s sailors were crowded, waving out across the water to – what?

'The Foreign Legion has arrived, ma'am,' he informed me with a grin. 'Band and all! I've just informed the Commander and the other passengers.'

I rushed to the rail. Coming towards the *Dolphin* was a trim steam launch with a polished brass funnel and an enormous tricolor fluttering over her stern. Under a canvas awning that stretched the length of her deck, a military band of at least thirty men were blowing and drumming for all they were worth. The tune – 'Rule, Britannia!'

'A generous compliment to the British flag,' drawled an amused voice at my shoulder. Turning, I saw John Bennett standing beside me. He raised his boater and smiled good-humouredly. 'Good morning, Annabel. How are you today?'

'Quite well, thank you,' I replied primly. Let John Bennett be as agreeable as he pleased. I would be perfectly civil in return; but after what I had seen the other night there was no longer any question of warmth and friendship existing between us.

He seemed unaware of my veiled snub. 'It seems,' he said, 'that Saltram's friend Commandant de Belleisle, taking a leaf from the book of the Prophet, has decided that, the mountain being disinclined to come to him, he must go to the mountain. I take it that that must be de Belleisle: the gentleman with the group of officers in the stern there, the one with the handsome beard and the four rows of braid on his cuffs and his képi.'

I followed his directions and picked out the tall, commanding figure standing beneath the tricolor. I had an impression of a bronzed countenance, piercing eyes, and a moustache and beard of fearsome proportions. Meeting my glance, he raised a white-gloved hand in a smart salute. And the band broke into a tune which I knew – from hearing it played by the Bodmin Boys' Brigade Bugle Band on fête and market days – to be the French National Anthem, the *Marseillaise*.

Jason Saltram welcomed his friend aboard, together with the other Legion officers, accepting, without discernible embarrassment, a kiss on both cheeks from the whiskered Commandant. The band remained on the launch, and played selections from Gilbert and Sullivan throughout the proceedings that followed.

'Miss Annabel Trewella, may I present Commandant Armand de Belleisle? Armand, Miss Trewella is a very dear friend of Melloney's, and her company on this cruise has been a great delight to us all.'

I whispered a silent prayer that I was not blushing before Jason Saltram's formal compliments as he introduced me.

'*Enchanté*, Miss Trewella.' The Frenchman bowed low over my hand. Since he was now hatless, I was able to see that his thick thatch of raven hair was streaked with grey. Grey, also, were his eyes – and watchfully good-humoured, like those of an amiable eagle. I liked Armand de Belleisle on sight.

'And this, of course, is Melloney. Melloney, my dear, may I present ...?'

At an instant's notice, we were holding a semi-formal reception under the poop deck awning. Chief Steward Dacres had arranged it all, with the practised smoothness that informed every social gathering which took place aboard the great yacht. Coffee, both hot and iced, appeared at once. Magnums of chilled champagne were brought forward. While the morning sun climbed higher in the azure blueness, corks popped and compliments flew in two languages. And the

Legion band blew triumphantly on, through *HMS Pinafore* to *The Pirates of Penzance* and on to *The Mikado*. And Melloney – lovely as a picture in one of her simple Grecian frocks – was the heart of the gathering and the object of every eye.

'Mademoiselle Melloney,' cried de Belleisle, 'you and Miss Trewella may consider yourselves as honorary officers of the Legion. While you are in Oran, the entire garrison is at your service. This afternoon, when the sun has gone down, I will personally conduct you round the sights of the town. This evening, you will all be guests at our mess in Château-Neuf, where we will dine in state with the Legion trophies on display. And tomorrow ... tomorrow, mesdames and messieurs, we will go to Sidi-bel-Abbès.'

'A night ride?' cried Melloney, with delight. 'Across the desert?'

'Just so, Mademoiselle Melloney,' assented de Belleisle. 'I will have the battalion carpenter construct for you a de luxe litter, which will be slung between two horses. You will ride in state to Sidi-bel-Abbès! It is an experience that will live with you for ever.'

An experience that would live with her for ever ... As I looked down at Melloney's eager face, I think I would gladly have willed her ten years of my own youth at that moment. My looks almost betrayed me, for she turned to flash me a smile, saw my expression, and her eyes clouded with sudden anxiety.

'Do you ride, mademoiselle?' one of the officers was addressing me, and the moment passed. By the time I had composed a reply, Melloney was again facing her battery of admirers. All de Belleisle's officers were young and – apparently – susceptible.

Jason's voice rose above the hubbub nearby, and I felt a tingle of excitement at the sound.

'I must apologize, Armand,' he said. 'For my own peace of mind as much as for everyone's safety, I must insist on the *Dolphin* remaining out at the anchorage. You are not offended?'

'How could I be so, *mon ami*?' his friend replied. 'It will not be quite so convenient to visit you as it would be if you were at the Quai du Sénégal; but, at least, I have you literally at the bottom of my garden, and can row over for the occasional *apéritif*. And you can do the same.'

'Indeed I will, Armand,' said Jason. 'I cherish the memories of many happy hours at the Villa La Blanca in the old days.'

They were both looking out across the water, towards the near shore. And both heard my small gasp of surprise and awe, for they turned to regard me.

'Commandant, is that lovely villa really your home?' I asked him.

'It is, mademoiselle,' replied de Belleisle, smiling. 'I trust the Villa La Blanca has the honour to give you pleasure.'

'I think,' I said with heartfelt sincerity, 'that it is the most beautiful house I have ever seen in my life. And that ...' I checked myself, feeling myself getting rather over-emotional.

'And what, mademoiselle?' he asked. 'I hang breathless on your words. What other delicious compliment are you going to offer to the Villa La Blanca?'

'Well, it occurred to me,' I said, 'when I first set eyes on it early this morning, that no one who lived in such beautiful surroundings could possibly know a moment's unhappiness there.'

The searching eagle's eyes grew very soft. 'Now that is perhaps very true, mademoiselle,' he said. 'Without knowing the history of the villa – and I presume you do not know its history – you have made a very remarkable observation. Do you not think so, Jason?'

But Jason was not listening; instead, his dark eyes were turned towards the slight figure reclining on the sofa, with the adoring Legion officers surrounding her, each one vying for a smile or a glance.

Despite all my brave resolutions, it cut me to the heart to be reminded that Melloney was never far from his thoughts.

The reception extended through to a protracted buffet lunch, and the Legion did not make its departure till mid-afternoon. This was the hour, we were assured, when all Algeria finds a cool and shady spot and goes to sleep; and, indeed, the afternoon's heat was so overpowering that I was glad to go down to my cabin and – after carefully locking my door as usual – lie down on the bunk in only my chemise. It was six o'clock when I was awakened by the steward's knock, when he came to inform me that the French gentlemen had come to take us sightseeing.

We went ashore in the Legion launch – all save Jason, who said, to my disappointment, that he had urgent business letters to write and send off to England. John Bennett came; but I was relieved to hear him make an arrangement with one of the French officers who was taking him and Dr Weems to see the Legion barracks – an invitation to which male abode was, properly, not extended to Melloney and me.

Commandant de Belleisle appointed himself our guide. An open landau drawn by four matched bays was waiting at the quay, together with an escort of native cavalry – Spahis – in a glory of white cloaks and scarlet fezes. The Commandant sat with us in the carriage, képi jauntily aslant, beard gleaming with new pomade. In this manner, I was introduced to the colour and excitement, the squalor and the smells of the romantic and mysterious East.

Oran owes its existence – as our guide pointed out – to continuous occupation by different warring peoples; Arabs, Spaniards, Turks and lately the French have ruled there; and the different styles of buildings bear testimony to the tastes of the various warriors whose writ has extended over the arid, scrub-covered hills surrounding the shimmering waters of the bay.

The Château-Neuf, once the palace of the Arab beys and now the French army headquarters, carried me back to the stories of King Arthur and his knights, to Sir Walter Scott's *Ivanhoe* and *The Talisman*. The narrow, dark and winding alleys of the native quarter were pure *Thousand-and-One Nights*. But the wide, tree-lined boulevards that spanned the newer parts of the town, with their fashionable shops and smart cafés – they were Paris. Just as I had always imagined her to be.

Melloney, cheerfully announcing herself to be a complete philistine and not one bit interested in dusty old buildings, demanded to be carried into a de luxe dressmaker's where, perched in state upon a sofa, she charmed the proprietor – a fearsome lady with the rudiments of a very fine moustache – into calling forth a train of pretty young assistants all wearing the creations of the establishment, for her delectation. Yes, Melloney said, she would have that one. And that one. Then, turning to me, she asked me if I agreed that the dinner gown of white organdie was just the ticket for me to wear at the Legion dinner tonight? I replied laughingly – for it was painfully obvious that such a gown was quite outside my ambitions, let alone my pocket. Then I must try it on, she told me. In case any alterations needed to be made.

Bemused, I allowed the chattering French girls to dress me in the white organdie, furnish me with long white gloves and an ostrich feather fan, and scrape my hair up in the fashionable tight manner that poor Oriana Topsham had favoured. They then ushered me out into the showroom, where Melloney and Commandant de Belleisle awaited.

I had no say in the matter. The Commandant – the complete Frenchman, as I had come to expect Frenchmen from novels – showed his unashamed admiration by saying 'ma foi' and twirling his moustaches, and Melloney simply said: 'We'll have it.'

There was no use in protesting. It was a present, she told me. And she hugged me, with the sweet and direct way she had, and told me I looked beautiful.

We wended our way back to the quay, politely admiring the things that the Commandant pointed out to us, such as the new Town Hall, completed only three years previously in what he called 'the Renaissance manner' (I thought it looked a little overpowering, and Melloney stifled a yawn); the sun had gone behind the citadel of Santa Cruz on its high hill by the time we re-embarked in the Legion launch and were taken back to the *Dolphin*, to dress for the gala dinner.

On our way through the crowded anchorage, I said to Melloney: 'I never thought to own such a beautiful gown in all my life. You are generous to me. I don't know how to begin to thank you.'

'It was nothing,' she replied carelessly.

'It was by no means nothing, Melloney,' I told her. 'It was an absurdly extravagant gesture.'

She squeezed my hand. 'He'll adore you in it,' she said.

I had a sudden vision of Jason's regarding eyes turned upon me with an expression of favour. Then I remembered who she must mean ...

'I ... I hope so,' I murmured. 'Melloney, is that why you bought it for me?'

She nodded. 'I know you two have had some kind of a quarrel,' she said. 'You've been so downcast these last few days. Almost since the time you told me your wonderful secret. And I caught the look of absolute misery in your face during the reception this morning.'

'I remember.' It had been when Commandant de Belleisle had made the remark that Melloney would remember her night ride to Sidi-bel-Abbès for ever.

'So I've decided that I must lend Romance a hand,' she said. 'Hence the gown. And that isn't all –' she glanced towards the tall figure of our guide and host, who stood up in the prow of the launch – 'I've had a few discreet words with the Commandant.'

'Melloney!' I cried. 'You haven't told him ...?'

'Nothing that could cause you the slightest embarrassment, my dear,' she assured me. 'I haven't told him of your feelings, but just lightly indicated that John admires you greatly, and would he see to it that you two are seated together at the dinner tonight, and that the lady on his other hand shall be either plain, or elderly – preferably both.'

'Melloney!'

'You're not angry with me?' Her smile was faltering, and her eyes showing the beginnings of hurt.

'Of course not. How could anyone be angry with *you*?'

The sunlight came out from behind the clouds, and she was her own gay, adorable self again. Impulsively, I embraced her. And when I laid my cheek against hers, there was no holding back the tears.

'Don't cry, Annabel,' she whispered. 'It's going to be all right, I promise you. Your love will be rewarded.'

My love rewarded – what chance of that? Yet it was not my hopeless love that hurt me at that moment. But a new and more pressing awareness of the loveliness that would go out of my life when the light of Melloney's brilliant spirit passed into the shadows.

The night was scented with honeysuckle and overlaid with a million stars. We were taken by carriage from the quay to the Château-Neuf, with native cavalrymen our jingling escort; over the wide drawbridge and past the legionnaire sentries and their long bayonets; into the echoing courtyard, where Armand de Belleisle and his officers waited for us, sashed, bemedalled and incredibly dashing.

Melloney was in a gown the colour of old gold, with no jewellery or ornament whatever. When the able seaman carried her up the wide steps and into the vast reception hall, with its lofty Moorish arches, she was like some pagan princess being borne into her palace.

The menfolk from the *Dolphin* were all in tail-coats. Jason's dark handsomeness won him many glances from the wives of the French officials who were our fellow-guests of the Legion that night. My head was up in the stars when he paused by me and murmured a formal compliment about my appearance; but I suffered a swift return to earth when I overheard him deliver exactly the same elegance to the stout and overdressed lady of, I believe, the Inspector of Waterworks.

Champagne was served to us in the huge hall, the walls of which were hung with tricolor banners bearing the names of ancient battles. I read: *Constantine, Solferino, Magenta, Sebastopol, Alma, Camarone* ...

'Camarone, ma'am, was our greatest victory,' came a voice at my elbow. 'When a handful of legionnaires stood firm against an army, and fought to the last bullet and the last man.' He was very young and nice-looking, and spoke without a trace of accent. 'May I introduce myself, since I was on duty this morning and unable to come aboard the *Dolphin*. Lieutenant Jobling.'

'You're English!'

He smiled. 'Contrary to the popular novels, there aren't many of us in the Legion, and I'm the only English officer in the battalion. I didn't join the Legion to forget, and the gentlemen of Great Scotland Yard are not seeking me, nor am I the runaway scion of a noble family. So I disappoint you, Miss Trewella? You see, I know your name. My comrades – those who were fortunate enough to make your acquaintance this morning – told me all about you.'

His eyes were flirtatious, and reminded me forcibly of poor Jack Maugham. I firmly refrained from asking what his comrades had told him about me, and said: 'Then why *did* you join the Legion, Mr Jobling?'

He looked disappointed with my reaction. 'When I passed out from Sandhurst, it seemed an amusing alternative to following a family tradition and going into the Indian Army,' he said. 'You look perfectly fizzing in that gown, Miss Trewella.'

'Good evening, Annabel. I believe I have the honour of escorting you in to dinner.' John Bennett's usually good-humoured eyes were strangely pensive, and I wondered if he had put two and two together and realized that I had been the unwitting observer of his sly deception on the night of the levanter.

'That will be nice,' I said, suiting the lame comment with a nervous smile, for I had no wish to be accused of spying on him.

'And I have the honour to be placed on your left,' said Lieutenant Jobling cheerfully.

I introduced the two of them, and noted with some wry amusement how they sized each other up, each eyeing the other, then shooting a speculative glance at me. Never having received male admiration before joining the *Dolphin*, I found their mutual jealousy a refreshing tonic. Being in love – particularly love of the unrequited sort – is no bar to the enjoyment of admiration. The thought brought my mind to Jason and Melloney. I was looking round the company for sign of them when a pair of enormous doors at the end of the hall were flung open, and a magnificent negro in regimentals appeared, saluted the Commandant and announced dinner.

John Bennett offered me his arm, and we followed the others through into another vast and candelabra-hung hall containing a single long table set for dinner with gleaming silver and dazzlingly white napery: silver dishes, epergnes filled with flame-coloured blooms of peony and rhododendron, silver statuary of soldiers and horse – all under the suave candle-light. On a dais at the far end of the stone-flagged floor, a regimental string orchestra was playing 'The Blue Danube'.

Solemn grace before meat was intoned by a cassocked priest, and the first courses were brought in by a line of legionnaires with long aprons over their blue tunics and white pantaloons.

After the soup, John Bennett coughed slightly and inclined his head towards me. 'How this reminds me of our first luncheon together aboard the *Dolphin*,' he murmured. 'Except that, on this occasion, I'm very much afraid that our worst fears are going to be realized, and not a pickled herring in sight.'

'You don't mean,' I whispered, alarmed, 'that we really are going to have frogs' legs this time?'

'Worse,' he replied. 'Snails!'

'Do you like *les escargots*, Miss Trewella?' asked Lieutenant Jobling later, while I addressed myself grimly to the task of spearing one of the twisted scraps of rubbery meat from out of its shell, as I had observed the lady opposite doing with every appearance of delight.

' – I adore them,' I replied fervently, closed my eyes and popped the thing into my mouth.

'I wish you well of the confounded brutes,' said the Lieutenant, making a dismissive gesture to the waiter and breaking himself a morsel of bread. 'And I shall, as usual, forgo this course. While perfectly willing to fight and die for the Legion, I have steadfastly set my face against the wilder eccentricities of the French cuisine.'

'Enjoying your escargots?' asked John Bennett.

'If the other five are no worse than the first, I shall get through them,' I told him. And took a deep draught of wine.

'Château-Neuf is very fine,' said Lieutenant Jobling, breaking more bread on my left, 'but it is not the Legion. Oran is not the Legion. The heart of every legionnaire, his only true home-land, is Sidi-bel-Abbès, which we built with our own hands on a small mound rising up out of the barren plain. It would be my great delight to show you Bel-Abbès, Miss Trewella.'

'You are very kind,' I said.

'Melloney is looking very well tonight,' said John Bennett. I followed his glance. She was seated on Commandant de Belle-isle's right, with Jason opposite.

'Her marvellous spirit keeps her going,' I said. 'In her place I would be – hopeless.'

'You do yourself less than justice, Annabel,' he replied. 'I don't know her well, of course, but even from a brief acquaintance, it's clear that having you around has done a lot for Melloney.'

'Oh, that can't be so,' I said. 'I really see very little of her. She has to rest so much.'

'Nevertheless, I'm sure you've left your mark,' he persisted. 'You'll be remembered in this family after you're gone – just as your half-sister Harriet Cadge is remembered.'

Harriet! Not her – I had no wish to speak of her! I turned to the lieutenant.

'Tell me more of Sidi-bel-Abbès, Mr Jobling,' I asked him. 'You said the legionnaires built it with their own hands. That was very – er – enterprising of them.'

(*Shut out the thought of Harriet sitting there, in the small hours of the night, by the bed of the stricken girl. Her head nods, her lips grow slack. The drug is taking effect. No – shut it out!*)

'All manner of men are attracted to the Legion,' said Jobling. 'Doctors and burglars, architects, cut-throats and plumbers. Once, so the legend goes, a general in command of a detachment of French troops that had taken a town decided that a ceremonial High Mass should be celebrated in the local church. The troops paraded with banners and drums. But no town priest – he had fled with the inhabitants. In despair, the general was about to give the order to abandon the ceremony, when up spoke a legionnaire: "*Mon général*, I think it will be in order for me to celebrate the Mass, for I was once a bishop and, so far as I know, have never been unfrocked." So you see, Miss Trewella, with such a diversity of talents, it was not difficult for us to build our own vast headquarters. And this we have done – without a sou from the French government.'

'What a wonderful story,' I said.

He held my gaze. 'You have beautiful eyes, Miss Trewella,

he murmured. 'Did no man ever tell you that before?'

I was saved from having to compose a reply to this flirtatious declaration by the arrival of the next course, which looked and smelt marvellously appetizing.

'I fancy this is called couscous and that it's an Algerian or Moroccan dish,' commented John Bennett. 'Perhaps our friend on your left could clarify the point if you asked him.'

'I won't bother him just now,' I murmured flatly.

The American grinned at me. 'Do I take it that the lieutenant is being heavy-handed with his gallantry? Then, my dear Annabel, you'll have to bear with my conversation. Do you like the couscous?'

'It's excellent.'

After a while, he said: 'What will you do when the *Dolphin* summer's over and we all return to England – will you stay in Saltram's employ as companion to Melloney?'

'I suppose so,' I said. 'No one's ever told me that my position would terminate at the end of the cruise. I've come to accept that it's a permanency. At least . . .'

It is astonishing to look back and realize that this was the first time it had occurred to me that Melloney's threatened end would also mean the termination of my employment. From the moment that Jason had admitted me into the secret, to that instant during dinner with the Legion, the thought had never entered my mind.

'I guess they'll keep you on,' he said. 'I guess you've got yourself a job for life. After all, though your sister was initially employed as governess, she was kept on after Melloney left the school-room. Melloney must have been turned eighteen when your sister died.'

Again Harriet! Why should he again bring her into the conversation? I glanced at his face, but it told me nothing.

(*Fight hard not to think of it – of the moment when the feverish girl in the tousled bed opened her eyes and babbled in her delirium; tried to raise herself up . . .*)

'There is a saying,' came the voice on my left, 'that a legionnaire will thrive and grow fat where a guardsman will starve. It was in the Crimea, in fifty-four and fifty-five, when the Allies were dying like flies from exposure, cold and disease, that our three Legion battalions suffered less than any other.'

'Really – and how was that?' I asked him. 'Did they loot and steal?'

'Whenever possible, I've no doubt,' he said. 'But there was so little to be had, you see. No, the Legion survived on the articles that other soldiers threw away. From broken bits and pieces of metal they fashioned cooking stoves and ovens, stoves for heating the snug bivouacs which they built from scraps of wood and canvas. I daresay, if the war had lasted long enough, the Legion would have built a city there to rival Sebastopol itself.'

'What a wonderful spirit,' I said.

My left hand, which rested on the edge of the table by my plate, felt the pressure of his fingers. I did not snatch it away, thinking the gesture to have been accidental. The pressure persisted: it was no accidental contact.

'You are very beautiful, Miss Trewella,' said Lieutenant Jobling, his voice heavy and slurred. It was then I noticed that the decanter of red wine, which stood near his plate, was nearly empty.

'Here comes the next course,' I said brightly, withdrawing my hand.

John Bennett had spotted the incident. He rescued me. 'Have you ever been to Bristol, Annabel?' he asked.

'No,' I replied.

'My family hails from there,' he said. 'The first John Bennett, a merchant, sailed out of Bristol for the New World in the year seventeen-nineteen ...'

Protected from Lieutenant Jobling's flirtatiousness, I relaxed and let John Bennett's words wash over me. All was well – provided he did not turn to the subject of my dead half-sister, as he had done twice before (and surely that had been mere coincidence?). I was only called upon to murmur 'yes' and 'no' at intervals, which gave me the opportunity, from time to time, of glancing down the table to the hawk-faced man with the dark exciting eyes that never strayed in my direction, but sometimes rested upon Melloney with an expression that was something like sadness.

Would Jason and Melloney announce their betrothal in

Oran – perhaps this very night? He must know how desperately she longed for it to happen, and how, with so little time left for her, every day's delay cut short the small measure of happiness that she would live to enjoy.

How would I feel, to hear the announcement? If, for instance, Jason himself rose to his feet at the end of the meal and, calling for a toast for Melloney, announced her as his bride-to-be?

I was still examining my conscience and gauging the depths of my fortitude when our host, Commandant de Belleisle, signalled the end of the meal by getting up and proposing a toast to Her Majesty Queen Victoria, Empress of India, et cetera.

'Next,' said Lietenant Jobling when we sat down again, after also toasting the French Foreign Legion and the French Republic, in that order, 'next, we have the ritual of *"Boudin"*. Watch de Brassy, the lad at the bottom of the table, and the junior officer of the battalion. You will see him get up and call for the Commandant's attention.'

De Brassy was one of the young officers who had made such a tremendous fuss of Melloney aboard the *Dolphin*. By the high colour of his smooth cheeks, he appeared to have taken as much wine as Lieutenant Jobling, or possibly more. Nevertheless, he got to his feet and glared down the long table at his commanding officer.

'*Garde à vous!*' he shouted.

Gesturing to the rest of us to follow their example, Armand de Belleisle rose with his officers, all with wine glasses raised.

'*Attention à la poussière!*' bellowed de Brassy.

'Which means "look out for the dust",' murmured Jobling in my ear. 'And that's an order to drain your glass!'

I came no way near to emptying my brimming glass, but most of the others seemed to accomplish it. This done, the doors of the great hall were flung open and a cascade of sound burst upon our ears. Led by a drum major, a giant of a man with a huge black beard and a chestful of decorations, the regimental brass band – I recognized them as the same fellows who had come out to the *Dolphin* – marched slowly towards the table and began to circle it, bugles blaring, kettledrums rolling, and a big bass drum beating out a steady, stately rhythm that set my every nerve a-tingle with a strange excitement. And such a tune! The officers were singing lustily to it – and I regretted the poverty of my French that rendered me incapable of following the words.

Six times they circled the table, and then the march was ended with a clash of cymbals. The drum major saluted his commander and was given a glass of wine.

'That was "*Boudin*",' said Lieutenant Jobling. 'The famous slow march of the Legion, which we have sung on the way to battle ever since the Crimea.'

'What is "*Boudin*"?' I asked. 'Was he a Legion hero, perhaps?'

'Nothing so high-flown,' he replied. '*Boudin* is nothing more than the name of a common black sausage. *Garde à vous!* – the Commandant is going to make an announcement.'

'Ladies and gentlemen!' cried Armand de Belleisle. 'Dancing will now commence in the reception hall. I beg you to take your partners.' He repeated the announcement in his own language.

'May I have the honour, Annabel?' asked John Bennett.

'Of course,' I replied thankfully, with a glance towards Lieutenant Jobling, who wore the expression of a man who had just been narrowly forestalled.

The American gave me his arm and we followed the others to the reception hall, where the string orchestra was playing the lilting strains of a Viennese waltz.

He danced well, leading me with confidence and skill. As we circled the great Moorish chamber, I was able to see that Melloney had been established in a handsome chaise-longue that afforded her a view of the dancers. Jason was standing by her, so was Armand de Belleisle. She caught my eye and waved her hand.

'As I was saying,' commented John Bennett, neatly reversing our turn, 'I should like to pay a visit to the home city of my ancestors before I go back to the States.'

'To Bristol?'

'Yes. Given happier circumstances' – and he gave me a sad smile – 'I would have taken you with me, Annabel.'

'I'm sorry, John.' And I really felt sorry. Whatever his lack of scruples in matters of business, he had always been a kind and delightful companion. And he *was* the first man to propose to me. The music and the wine made me feel charitable towards him.

'I'm really surprised you haven't been to Bristol already,' he said. 'In view of – well, you know . . .'

'In view of what?' I asked him.

'Well, as I understood,' he said, 'isn't it true that your half-sister's buried there? I would have thought you'd have visited her grave.'

Again Harriet! I stopped dancing. We faced each other in the middle of the floor. I stared at him, uncomprehending.

'Why did you say that?' I demanded.

'About your sister – didn't you know she was buried in Bristol?'

'Well, no, I . . .'

'I guess she died at a hospital or sanatorium there, huh?'

Before I could make another comment, while I was still trying to assemble a reason for this strange and persistent interrogation – and on a dance floor of all places – about a long-dead woman whom he had never met and scarcely heard of, there was a sudden turmoil, a scuffling of feet and a man's sharp cry. The orchestra faltered on a high note, and the strings faded away into a wavering silence.

'It's Melloney!' John Bennett's voice at my elbow.

'*Melloney!*' I ran through the press of people, elbowing them aside in my frantic haste to reach her.

She was lying with her head back on a cushion, and Jason was bending over her, chafing one slender hand in his. Her eyes were closed, and her smooth cheeks were waxen.

'What happened?' I cried.

Jason turned to regard me, and my heart went out to him as I saw the anguish there. 'She collapsed without a sound,' he said. 'Without any warning. Here's Weems, thank heaven.'

Dr Weems came out of the encircling crowd of onlookers. By the set look on his face, I guessed him to be a man who had accepted the possibility that it was too late to do anything.

chapter eight

Melloney did not die – not then. They bore her back to the *Dolphin*, to the sick bay, where Nanny Bagley quickly quenched her own distress and set about tending for the needs of 'my darling girl'. Jason drew Dr Weems aside into the adjacent compartment – the same in which the doctor had told me the terrible story about Harriet – and I followed, anxious to hear the physician's verdict.

'Well, Weems?' said Jason gravely. 'Is this the end?'

'Sir, it is an indication of the manner in which the end will eventually come,' replied the doctor. 'But the acute stage has not yet been reached. Miss Melloney will suffer several more of these seizures – I had it from Professor Lindstrom in Basle, and his prognosis was confirmed in every detail by Dr Levy at St Thomas's only last month – before her agonies truly begin. She still has a year of life. Perhaps somewhat less.'

I looked at Jason. And I wanted to cry aloud to him: 'Make her your wife! Give Melloney her hour of happiness before it is too late!'

'So she will make a recovery from this seizure, Doctor?' asked Jason.

'Yes, sir. By tomorrow she will have returned to something like her normal physical condition. Within a few days, her spirits will have revived and she will be as right as she ever was, as she ever can be. Till next time.'

Till next time . . .

'Thank you, Weems,' said Jason. He nodded gravely to me. 'Good night to you, Miss Trewella. It's a great pity that this evening ended so badly, for I've never seen Melloney in a happier frame of mind. Good night, Weems.' He nodded again to us both, and went out.

'If you'll excuse me,' said Dr Weems, 'I must go and give the patient some medication. Good night, Miss Trewella.'

'Good night, Doctor,' I replied. And then – at the door – a sudden remembrance came into my mind. 'Doctor, there's something . . . I wonder if you can tell me . . . ?'

'Yes, Miss Trewella?' His eyes, behind the thick lenses, were guarded. 'What do you want to know?'

'It's about my sister . . .'

'Yes?' Did I see something like – fear – spring to life for an instant in those short-sighted, lazy eyes?

'You told me she wouldn't let you attend her. What then happened to her when she became gravely ill and about to die? Was she moved into a hospital?'

'Into a hospital – yes.' He nodded.

'Which hospital? Where was it?'

'Which hospital, let me see . . .' He bit his lip and stared across at the medicine cabinet, as if seeking inspiration from the row of bottles contained behind the glass doors. 'Now, where was it?'

'She wrote to me from what was obviously her death bed,' I said, 'and I still have the letter in a trunk of personal bits and pieces that I left behind at my old place in St Finn. There was no address in the letter, and the envelope with its postmark has long since gone. But she must have written it at the hospital.'

'Now I seem to remember,' said Dr Weems. 'It was Bristol.'

'A Bristol hospital?'

'A hospital near to Bristol,' he said. 'A hospital that deals with the diseases of the respiratory system. A chest hospital.'

'And it was there, near Bristol, that she was buried?'

'I believe that is correct.'

I wished him good night again and left him. With some difficulty Dr Weems had confirmed John Bennett's statement about the location of Harriet's resting-place. But I had got no nearer to discovering the reason for the American's strange persistence in pursuing the matter throughout the evening.

I dreamed that I was back in St Finn, in the graveyard there. It was night time. An owl was hooting down in the copse behind the school, and another was replying from the direction of the clay mountains.

I was waiting for someone.

Held there by a sense of duty, I had no other wish in my mind but to turn and run: out by the lych-gate and down the lane to the dark row of cottages, to hammer on one of those barred and bolted doors till someone took pity on me and gave me shelter from the night's perils.

Waiting ...

I heard the footsteps approaching down the lane long before I saw the one for whom I was waiting: they rang loudly on the hard-packed ruts of droughty summer. It could have been a man or a woman. Either.

I heard my own heartbeats and my own heavy breathing. They sounded unnatural to my ears.

The figure came out of the shadows of the tall yews that surround the churchyard; out into the moonlight, walking towards the lych-gate; slowly.

The figure was wearing a dark hat with a wide brim. And a long cloak that billowed with every slow step.

The lych-gate squealed its protest and closed again. My heartbeats grew louder, my breathing heavier.

The figure was coming up the path towards me, past the overhung graves, the gesturing angels, the broken columns, the dusty immortelles. Now there was urgency in its movements, and a gloved hand was stretched out towards me, as if to offer me help.

Calling to me ...

'I have come as quickly as I could, but it is no use ... I can see that I am too late!'

The gloved finger was pointing. Not to me, but to something behind me – something that had been there all the time, sharing my waiting vigil. So close to me that I had mistaken its heavy breathing and the sound of its heartbeats for my own!

I turned, my eyes shut fast. And I felt its charnel-house breath upon my face.

And I knew that Death was staring close at me, and that when I opened my eyes I should see him.

Melloney was in wonderful spirits. I found her on the poop deck, with the First and Second Officers, Dr Weems, John Bennett, and a lieutenant of the Legion – all paying court to her.

'Dearest Annabel!' she cried. 'What a late riser you are this morning. Come and sit with me. The rest of you ...' She turned to her admirers and blew them a kiss of dismissal.

'*Au revoir, mam'selle. Je suis désolé.*' The French officer bowed over her hand.

'Your servant, ma'am.' John Bennett gave a formal bow, and his eyes slid sidelong to meet my gaze. He winked at me.

When they had gone, Melloney fanned herself vigorously. Then turned anxiously to me. 'My dearest Annabel, you don't look well this morning, you really don't.'

'I didn't sleep well,' I admitted. 'I had a terrifying nightmare. But how are you, Melloney?'

'Splendid!' she cried. 'Don't I look well?'

'You do,' I had to admit.

'But,' she said, more seriously, 'Dr Weems says I must forgo the trip to Sidi-bel-Abbès, which takes place tonight. He says I simply can't stand the shaking-up, and I'm inclined to agree with him.'

'Then it will be postponed till you're better?'

Her lip trembled and she lowered her eyes. 'No, it won't be like that, Annabel. You see ... Dr Weems has more or less told me that I'm not going to get any better, not in the foreseeable future, that is. So there wouldn't be any point in postponing the Sidi-bel-Abbès journey, because I'm not going to be able to stand the shaking-up.'

'Oh, Melloney ...' My hands went out to take hers.

She met my gaze and gave me her wonderful smile. 'Best for the Sidi-bel-Abbès trip to take place as planned,' she said. 'In a few days' time, when I'm more or less back to normal, you'll be back aboard again, and I shall be able to join you in less active pursuits.'

'I'm not going without you,' I said firmly. 'I shall stay aboard and keep you company – naturally!'

'No, my dear – no!' she cried. 'It will be an experience of a lifetime. I insist on your going. And then – there's John. He'll be going. And, by the way, how are things with you two ...?'

I shrugged. 'About the same. But, Melloney ...'

'No arguments,' she said with mock severity. 'If you've no regard for the happiness of *your* beloved, please pay some regard to the happiness of *mine* . . .'

'Of yours?'

'Jason is going to some trouble to arrange this trip to Sidi-bel-Abbès, and so is Armand. I want you to go and act as châtelaine in my place. Be nice to Jason. I know you find him rather terrifying, but be as pleasant as you can to him – for my sake, Annabel.'

For her sake – the irony of it! That she, of all people, would trust me sufficiently, as to ask me to 'be nice' to the man I longed for with all my heart.

'Well . . .' I faltered.

'You *will* agree, won't you?'

Of course I agreed. How could I deny Melloney anything?

When the sun touched the edge of the craggy-crested hills on our right, we had left the outskirts of Oran behind and were passing into a desolate land of sand and rock dotted with parched scrub. The last of the sun brought the dull colours to life: its dying rays tingeing the grey pumice with mysterious purples, blues and pinks. I gave an exclamation of surprise and pleasure, and the Commandant, who was riding at my side, guessed the cause of it and told me of the fantastic sunsets to be seen in the great sand deserts of the south; whole seas of sand, he told me, with every particle seeming to take on a colour of its own in the dying day.

We were journeying to Sidi-bel-Abbès. Avoiding all roads and tracks; taking the straightest line across the hills and valleys of the Tell – the coastal part of Algeria that stretches as far as the great barrier of the Atlas Mountains which look down upon the vast Sahara. And we would so regulate the speed of our progress, Armand de Belleisle told me, as to arrive at Bel-Abbès in the dawn light.

There were sixteen of us: the Commandant, Jason, John Bennett and myself, and an escort of native Spahi cavalry. The mount with which they had provided me was a docile-looking hack – for which I was much relieved; Jason and the others were all riding spectacular-looking arabs, with wild eyes and high-stepping ways. My riding experience having been limited to the farm horses of mid-Cornwall, I was well content with the animal they had given me. Melloney had insisted on lending me one of her own costumes: a linen suit, with a sensible skirt for the saddle. And the Legion had provided me with a military riding cloak against the coldness of the desert night, and a képi with a white cover and neck-cloth such as the legionnaires wear for protection against the searing sun.

On the way to Sidi-bel-Abbès, and poor Melloney left behind aboard the *Dolphin*, with Dr Weems and Nanny Bagley to look after her, I had made a last plea to be allowed to remain with her; but she had been adamant – I must go in her place, and – most particularly – I must be 'nice to Jason'. My conscience pricked me when I recalled how glad I had been that Melloney had not changed her mind about my going.

The sun dipped behind the highest hill-crest, and we were riding through shadows. In the deepening indigo of the sky, the stars looked down upon us, and a soft breath of wind – the scented, desert breeze that I had first noticed when we dropped anchor in Oran – fanned my cheek and ruffled the neck-cloth of my Legion képi.

'Miss Trewella,' said the Commandant, 'I must go and exchange a word with the Spahi officer.' He saluted me and wheeled his horse round. His place beside me was immediately taken by John Bennett, who was also wearing a Legion cloak and képi.

'Fine night, Annabel,' he said. 'But it will be cold before morning. We're moving into winter, and they get frost on the high plateau. You're still mad at me about something. What is it?'

'I prefer not to talk about it, Mr Bennett,' I replied after a few moments' thought.

'You're resentful, among other things, because I was probing you last night. Right?'

'Probing me?'

'About your sister.'

I stared ahead of me, willing myself not to reply. My sister Harriet's life and death, her shortcomings, were no concern of this man. And I was not to be drawn out. Whatever the reason for his curiosity about poor, erring Harriet, he would get nothing from me.

He said: 'But that isn't all. You were mad at me before last night. It started the morning after the levanter, at sea. And it's gone on. Annabel – can't we lay our cards on the table, talk the whole thing through and be friends again?'

After a while I replied: 'I'm sorry – John. We can never truly be friends again. I'm in Commander Saltram's employment, and – though you may think me old-fashioned and a country bumpkin, you with your go-getting ways – I have a sense of loyalty to my employer. I can't stand by and see him being deceived, and go on calling his deceiver my friend.'

'His – *deceiver*? What are you trying to say, Annabel?'

I gazed at him steadily. His eyes, shaded in the gloom, told me nothing. 'I think you know what I mean, Mr Bennett,' I replied.

We rode in silence for a while, and then he said: 'I think I get it. On the night of the levanter, you couldn't sleep and went out on deck. Am I right?'

'You are quite correct,' I replied primly.

'And you saw – something – someone?'

I did not reply; there was no need, and my silence told him all he required to know.

He said quietly: 'What do you think I was up to in Jason Saltram's cabin at that late hour, Annabel?'

'I have no idea,' I replied.

'Oh come now, Annabel. A young lady with the ability to concoct lurid, but logical, explanations can surely do better than that.'

Stung to retort, I snapped: 'It's obvious enough, isn't it, what you were doing there?'

'I see. As I thought. You have decided that I went in there for no other reason but to spy on Saltram's correspondence; to read the round robin that he received from his directors while we were in Gibraltar. Now, tell me – how, in the astute and logical mind enshrined within that lovely head, do you figure that I knew that such a thing as the round robin existed?'

'A consignment of mail arrived aboard just before we left Gibraltar,' I said. 'I know, because there was a letter for me among it. It was obvious that there would be letters for the Commander, among which there would certainly be something from Lumley's and that it would probably concern your offer to buy the firm.'

'You should have been England's first lady detective, Annabel,' he said. 'Great Scotland Yard lost a real acquisition when you decided to become a lady's companion. And now, if you will pardon me . . .' he raised his képi, wheeled his mount and cantered back down the line of horsemen.

I had scarcely time to think back over his conversation, or to make up my mind whether John Bennett's reaction to my accusation sprang from guilty shame or injured innocence, when another horseman came riding up on my other side. For a terrifying instant, I thought it might have been Jason (who had not taken the slightest notice of me since we set off from the *Dolphin*); it was with a sense of disappointment, not unmingled with relief, when I saw it was the Commandant again.

'Miss Trewella,' he said, 'we shall soon be on the crest of the escarpment that commands a splendid view of Oran and the coastal plain behind us. I think you will find the sight alone well worth all your efforts.'

'It's no effort,' I assured him. 'Though I have to admit that I find myself very much out of practice in the saddle.'

'We ride much in the Legion,' he said. 'Not the men, for we are an infantry regiment, but most of the officers keep their own horses. One day it is to be hoped that we shall have a cavalry wing. And I would dearly love to command it.'

He spoke awhile of the Legion, which, as with all the officers I had met, was his whole life; the institution to which he gave his entire allegiance, before home, family and friends, before his own country – for a man of the Legion, he told me, swears his fealty to the Legion and not to France.

As he went on to speak of his regret that he and his command were not fighting with the First and Second Companies of the Regiment in a campaign that had been taking place in Madagascar for the previous three years, I fell to wondering what manner of man he was, this Frenchman – presumably high-born and obviously very rich, to be able to live in a palatial home such as the Villa La Blanca. Was he married? Did he have any children?

I remembered a previous conversation we had had. When next de Belleisle paused, I said: 'Commandant, I am intrigued by a remark you made concerning your lovely villa. You said that, without knowing of its history, I had made a very perceptive judgement about it – do you remember that?'

'Indeed I do, mam'selle,' he replied. 'You had made a most illuminating statement about the happiness that a person should experience by living there.'

'That's right. I said: "No one who lived in such a beautiful place could ever know unhappiness", or words to that effect. But tell me, what is the history of the Villa La Blanca that so illuminates the remark I made? A remark which, by the way, came as a flash of inspiration. Almost as if ... no, that's ridiculous ...'

'Ridiculous? *Pourquoi?* Tell me, nevertheless, I beg you, mam'selle.'

'I was going to say: *Almost as if a voice in the wind, an unseen voice, a disembodied voice, had whispered the thought in my ear.*'

We came to a narrow gully in the upward track, so that de Belleisle was obliged to urge his horse ahead into single file. In this manner we travelled some distance. Several minutes passed before the trail widened again and he was able to resume his place by my side.

'Mademoiselle Trewella,' he said gravely, 'it is clear that I must burden you with the story of the Villa La Blanca.'

'It will be no burden to me,' I assured him. 'Only a tedium for you, perhaps.'

'Above all, it will not be that,' he replied.

'Then I should love to hear the story,' I said.

'The Villa La Blanca, as the name implies,' he said, 'was built during a Spanish occupation of Oran. In the late eighteenth century, it was the private residence of the Spanish military governor, one Marqués de Riego. De Riego was young, distinguished in his profession, and a man clearly marked for the very highest office. His wife, the marquesa, complemented him in every way, being beautiful, loving and witty. Theirs was a perfect love match made in heaven – which was all the more remarkable since, as was the custom of their class and their times, the marriage of these two young people had been arranged by their respective families while they were both in their infancies.

'For a few months only, this delightful couple lived in their beautiful Villa La Blanca and tended their jasmine and their irises. A powerful Spanish garrison and fleet were more than enough to keep at bay the marauding pirates of Mers-el-Kebir, and no other perils cast the slightest cloud over the De Riegos' tranquility. Or so they thought.

'The marqués was at sea, on a punitive raid against the pirates, when news reached him of the disastrous earthquake of seventeen-ninety that destroyed one-third of Oran and killed half the inhabitants. He hastily returned to port. Faced with scenes of indescribable devastation, and with another earth tremor threatening, he ordered his ships to put back to sea again for safety. Only he went ashore. To be with his wife, be she alive or dead, and no thought for his own safety.'

'And ...?' I hung on his next words.

'De Riego found his marquesa. She had escaped the fury of the earthquake and was working to relieve the misery of the wretched, frightened, starving survivors – she who had never in her life performed any task more menial than picking a bunch of irises. Her husband joined her in this work. They were still engaged upon it when a deadly fever swept through the pitiful survivors, and the marqués himself fell a victim.'

'Oh no!' I cried.

'He died in her arms at the Villa La Blanca,' resumed the Commandant, 'and was laid to rest in the private chapel there. The Marquesa de Riego lived out the rest of her long life at the villa, during which time the Spaniards had given place to the Turks and the Turks to the French. I met her – oh, it must have been close on twenty-seven years ago – when I first came to Algiers as a newly-commissioned young officer of the Legion. An old lady of nearly a hundred years. Think of that, mam'selle – the French Revolution began before she was widowed. Do you know, she remembered her grandfather telling her that, as a baby, he had been dangled on the knee of an old man who had sailed as a cabin boy with the Great Armada against England!'

Awed by his words, which seemed to dismiss time and space, it was a while before I replied.

'What was she like, the marquesa?' I asked him.

'She carried about with her the aura of a great beauty,' he said. 'Like the memory of a lovely melody that hangs in the air after the strings of the instruments are silent. Added to that, she possessed what I can only describe as a profound tranquillity. I think I fell in love with her – and I a boy of nineteen. She indulged me, was amused by my questions, and answered them all with a simple honesty.'

'What, in particular, did you ask her?'

'As you would imagine, I asked her how she could have stayed so long in a place that must have been full of so many memories. And can you guess her reply?'

'There were no bitter memories for her at the Villa La Blanca,' I ventured. 'Only recollections of happiness.'

'Exactly!' he cried. 'She said to me – and now you will understand why I was so impressed by your remark on first seeing the villa, and by your notion that it came to you – how did you put it? – like a voice in the wind – she said: *"How could I leave the place where I have known all the happiness of my life and a love that has banished death and cast out grief? I can truly say that I have never been unhappy here."*'

' "Never been unhappy here",' I repeated.

'Her very words, mam'selle. A very few months later, my friend passed away. And she left me the legacy of the Villa La Blanca, which has been my home ever since.'

'Her spirit is still there – her happiness and her tranquillity,' I said. 'I sensed it at once. Even from afar.'

'She is everywhere,' he said. 'In every room of the villa, in the gardens. Everywhere. When we return to Oran, you must come and see the place to which my old friend gave so much of herself. You will be at home there, Mam'selle Trewella, for there is much in you that reminds me of the marquesa – as she must have been when she was young and in love.'

'In love?' I gazed at him in the darkness, but there was no telling what his expression might have been.

'You are in love, are you not, mam'selle?' he asked quietly. 'Perhaps I am more attuned to another person's inner vibrations than most rough soldiers of your acquaintance' – he laughed shortly – 'but, you see, I am the seventh son of a seventh son, and there is much in heaven and earth that, though hidden from others, is plain to such as me.'

There seemed no reason to prevaricate with this man who had seen into my inner heart. I sensed him to be of great integrity; my secret would be safe with him.

'Yes, I love someone,' I admitted. 'But ... the love is not returned.'

'You are sure of this?'

'I'm quite sure. It's out of the question.'

'Then I am sorry for you, mam'selle,' he said. 'And yet ... and yet ...'

'Yes?'

'I am puzzled. I do not sense in you a person who will go through life lacking for love. Oh no – quite the reverse. I not only feel vibrations of love and happiness coming from you, but going *towards* you.'

I smiled at him in the darkness. 'Thank you, Commandant,' I said. 'You have put my mind at ease, to know that I shall not have to end my life as an old maid.'

We both laughed. The delicate, emotive moment broke and fell away. Once again, we were two people – a soldier and a woman – riding to the top of an escarpment in Algeria, under the desert stars.

Presently, there was no more rock and dark scrub ahead of us; only the velvet sky and the myriad stars. We had reached the highest point. The Commandant and I halted our mounts to allow the others to catch up with us, and soon the whole party was gathered at the edge of a plateau: the dark-faced Spahis, the tall figures of John Bennett – and Jason ...

Commandant de Belleisle turned in his saddle and, extending his arms, took in the panorama that lay beyond and below us. With his powerful head and great, jutting beard, he looked like some Old Testament prophet about to make a pronouncement.

He pointed to the string of lights that described the whole shape of the bay of Oran, the teeming town, the busy harbour, the ships.

'Over there is Mers-el-Kebir,' he said. 'And the flashing light on the far right is from the lighthouse on Cap de l'Aiguille.'

'Magnificent!' came the deep voice of the man who owned my heart. 'And see the bright clusters of lights to seaward. The Mediterranean is a busy highway this night. See that large constellation in line with the cape? It's moving eastward. That will be one of the great passenger liners heading for the Suez Canal and India beyond. We stand regarding the thoroughfare that links east and west. The very hub of the planet. By thunder, what would I not give to be standing in this spot a century hence! What sights to behold then!'

'I'm willing to settle for eighteen ninety-eight,' said John Bennett with a cynical note to his voice that, following as it did upon Jason's stirring words, caused a most disagreeable impression. 'In less than a century, we've jumped from wooden sailing ships to steam-driven cities of steel. I reckon, if he isn't careful, the twentieth century's rate of progress is going to turn out to be more than *Homo sapiens* can chew.'

'There may be something in what you say, *mon ami*,' was Armand de Belleisle's comment.

Jason said nothing. When we set off again, he came close by me and seemed for a moment to be about to rein his mount alongside mine, as if to accompany me. Though it was too dark to see his expression, I had the distinct feeling that he was gathering himself to address some remark to me. Then the moment passed: he squared his shoulders, and, without a glance in my direction, clapped his heels against his horse's flanks and set off down the line at a smart canter. I was left alone at the tail end of the Spahis, with John Bennett and the Commandant now bringing up the rear.

And so we rode on through the night.

'Company ahead!' cried John Bennett.

We were crossing a wide plain, and sand rose beneath our mounts' hooves, so that it was necessary to make use of another item of Legion equipment with which we had been provided: a broad woollen neck-scarf which could be wrapped around the lower part of the face to protect the mouth and nostrils from the swirling, choking sand.

Narrowing my eyes against the murky darkness, I saw the flames of a camp fire ahead. It illuminated the tall shapes of palm trees and a body of men drawn up in line, as if on parade.

'It's the detachment of legionnaires come out from Sidi-bel-Abbès to meet us,' said the Commandant. 'I ordered them to make the night march and prepare camp here. We will have a rest and some good Legion coffee, my friends. And you will hear some good Legion songs.'

'*Halt!*'

The challenge rang out across the sand, and I saw the line of gleaming bayonets in the firelight. The Spahi officer raised his hand to check his men. More shouts. The Spahi officer rode forward and saluted with his drawn sabre. The salute was returned. We were accepted.

There were about forty legionnaires and an officer no older than the lad who had led the singing of the famous '*Boudin*' at Château-Neuf. The legionnaires wore capacious blue greatcoats and massive knapsacks; on their heads the képi with the Legion's white cover and neckcloth. They all looked incredibly hardy and lean-drawn.

The boy officer assisted me to dismount. He had two medals on his tunic and his face was burnt to the colour of old bronze, against which his teeth flashed whitely. He handed me a steaming tin mug.

'*Café* with cognac, madame,' he said. 'It will help to lay the dust in your throat.'

I thanked him and sipped gratefully at the bitter, aromatic brew. It tasted delicious. I stood there, warming my hands against the sides of the mug, staring into the fire, smelling the resinous wood as it hissed and oozed and crackled – and wondering all the while that I – plain, ordinary Annabel Trewella, a spinister of the parish of St Finn in the duchy of

Cornwall – should find myself in all-male company, in such a romantic and out-of-the-way corner of the globe. And at two o'clock in the morning!

Cloaks were laid on the ground about the fire and we seated ourselves. Commandant de Belleisle sat on one side of me, and young Sous-Lieutenant Marquand – for so he had introduced himself – on the other. Legionnaires, Spahis, and their guests in a circle around the campfire. Jason was almost immediately opposite me: I saw his face, in and out of the dancing flames, dark-visaged and strangely withdrawn, his eyes lowered and brooding.

'*Garde à vous!*' cried Marquand, raising his mug to the Commandant.

A roar of voices bore the sweeping cadences of '*Boudin*' into the night sky. The tune had stayed in my mind – and forever will stay – and I was able, this time, to pick up some of the words and join in . . .

Tiens, voilà du boudin,
voilà du boudin,
voilà du boudin . . .!

They followed '*Boudin*' with a gay, lilting song that must have been in some way improper, for young Marquand firmly refused to translate for me. There was another, with a title that sounded like a drum-roll: '*Rataplan*'. This, my new friend was happy to translate:

Wherever we have marched,
Wherever we have fallen,
We have sown glory.
Rataplan!

There were many other songs, and a surprising number of them were not about martial glory and the wild, male pursuit of death in battle, but told of tender and thoughtful things: as the love of womenfolk left behind, memories of home, regrets of what might have been.

As a compliment to Jason Saltram and me, Sous-Lieutenant Marquand announced a song by an Englishwoman, Caroline Norton, which had found great popularity in the Foreign

Legion. I was all interest at the sound of the name, for I had recently read of this lady and knew her to have been a poetess and novelist as well as a great fighter for the rights of women, and that her open letter addressed to the Queen had had considerable influence upon the Marriage and Divorce Act of the late fifties.

A legionnaire rose to his feet at the other side of the circle and, in a pure and sonorous tenor voice, he bridged the vast gulf in time and place, and brought Mrs Norton's words to that lonely edge of the sprawling African continent:

A soldier of the Legion lay dying in Algiers,
There was lack of woman's nursing, there was dearth of
    women's tears.
But a comrade stood beside him, while his life blood ebbed away,
And bent, with pitying glances, to hear what he might say ...

Not great poetry, some would think, perhaps. It is possible that Caroline Norton's work for the cause of women will outlive her fame as a versifier; but the sentiments were real enough for the lean and hard-bitten men about me. I had no way of knowing how many of them understood the English words, but by many a tear-misted eye they showed that the poignancy of Caroline Norton's song was not lost on them.

The impromptu pre-dawn concert ended with a dance and war-chant performed by the Spahis. These dusky warrior-sons of France's colonial empire fought side by side with the Legion and knew the Legion's ways – as evidenced by the way they had joined in the singing. When their whirling sabre dance grew wilder, the legionnaires rose to their feet and performed with the Spahis; the lighted circle about the campfire was soon alive with wildly capering figures and flashing steel, all in the lurid glance of the flames.

Suddenly, with a clash on blade, it was over. The dancers sank to the ground. Someone threw a handful of sand on the fire, and the flames wavered and declined.

'We will rest for an hour, Mam'selle Trewella,' said Armand de Belleisle, 'then resume our march to Bel-Abbès, to arrive at dawn. Come, I will lay your cloak in the palm grove over there, where you can be alone.'

Just outside the campfire's circle of light, under a palm that whispered in the night breeze, I wrapped my cloak about my shoulders and looked towards the high ceiling of stars. A footfall made me start.

'Miss Trewella. Might I have a brief word with you, please?' Jason Saltram's tall figure was sihouetted against the sky above me. I sat up, stammered some sort of reply.

'I trust you are enjoying the journey,' he said stiffly.

'Very much so,' I replied.

'It's a great pity,' he said, 'that Melloney couldn't come. You heard Weems's verdict? I thought it wise for him to break it to her that this sort of enterprise will be out of the question in future. It's best that she becomes gradually accustomed to her worsening condition, for it will make it all the easier for her to accept the full truth, when . . .'

'She took it very well,' I told him. 'But then, she's always marvellously brave. No matter how dark the shadows, Melloney can always find a touch of brightness.'

'Very true,' he said.

'Because of that, she deserves every happiness,' I said feelingly.

(Even if it means heartbreak for me – to see her married to you!)

He was silent for a few moments, and then he said: 'Your constancy to Melloney does you justice, Miss Trewella.'

It seemed to me that I had detected a strange note in his voice when he made the observation. Was it – sarcasm? I told myself that I must have been mistaken. Surely he could not doubt that I was sincere in my feelings towards Melloney.

'I shall miss her terribly when she's . . . gone,' I murmured. 'More than I would ever have believed possible for me to grieve for a friend of so short a while.'

'Everything has its end!' he said in a harsh voice. And it was then I knew that I had not been mistaken; that he was angry with me for some reason. 'If you find it painful to see her die, you are free to go.'

'But I *must* stay till the end!' I cried, appalled.

'There is no need,' he replied. 'Melloney does not lack for companionship. You need not feel that you are bound by any duty. You are free to go at any time.'

'It's not a matter of duty ...'

'The matter of the year's salary that was advanced to you – you may forget that, Miss Trewella. You have earned every penny of that already.'

I felt my eyes prickle with tears, and blessed the concealing darkness. It cut me cruelly, to realize that he thought so little of me. Not to be loved by him was unbearable enough; but suddenly to be treated as a person incapable of finer feelings was an added torment. I must make him see he was mistaken: that I was not one who would shrink from being present at a friend's death bed.

Then how was it that, given my chance to show the man I loved that I was a whole person, and not just a faceless servant, I was only able to stammer a feeble protest?

'M-Melloney might need me ...'

'Melloney will have me by her side to the end,' he replied coldly. 'As I have said, you are free to go at any time. Do not feel yourself bound in any way – save in the matter of the solemn promise that you gave me, that the truth of Melloney's condition will remain a secret while she lives.'

I could not bring myself to reply. Did he really think that I needed reminding about the sacred vow I had made?

'You must be tired after the long ride, Miss Trewella,' he said in a gentler voice. 'I apologize for troubling you at this hour and in this place. But these things ... had to be said.'

He touched the peak of his yachting cap, turned and walked back towards the campfire. I watched him go with the tears flowing, unchecked.

I must have dozed off, I remember thinking that the party had ridden on and left me behind, for a whole night seemed to have passed by, and I had been dreaming – or so I thought.

I had heard a sound. Had that been part of my dream?

It had not – for the sound came to my ears again: a gentle scuffling noise, as when someone trails the toes of a bare foot through hard-packed sand. And it came from somewhere out in the darkness beyond my palm grove. From the opposite direction to the campfire – now only a distant smudge of embers, glowing redly.

Someone was coming towards me ...

On hands and knees!

I sensed my peril before I saw its shape, and my mouth was open to scream, even though my mind could not summon up the will to direct my limbs to move.

My scream sounded hideously loud in my ears, wakening the desert's silence and reverberating through the darkness. At its sound, a shape rose from the ground nearby – no more than ten paces distant – and came bounding towards me, pell-mell. I had a vision of flying limbs, darkly swathed in native costume, one upstretched arm raised on high to strike at me. There was something in my attacker's hand – I knew with a numbing certainty that it was a knife.

He was big and powerful: I caught an image of a tallness and a barrel-chested broadness; an open mouth framed by a beard. I shrank back against the rough trunk of the palm tree and shut my eyes, waiting for the end from which I had neither the strength nor the speed to make my escape.

There came a shout from behind me. The sharp crack of a gunshot.

'À moi la Légion!' The shout was repeated: 'To me the Legion!'

I opened my eyes to see my would-be destroyer staggering back with one hand pressed against a shoulder. He stumbled and nearly fell. Then, with a harsh curse, he reeled away into the darkness. Moments later, the palm grove was alive with running men. More shots rang out.

'Are you all right, madame?' It was young Marquand, hatless, a revolver in his hand. He helped me to my feet. 'Did he hurt you?'

My reply was lost to him in the sound of drumming hooves. Some of the Spahis galloped past, drawing their sabres as they vanished in the gloom after their quarry. A line of legionnaires moved out from the palm grove, bayoneted rifles extended before them. Marquand ran to join his men.

The Spahis were soon back. Gesticulating wildly, they called out to Commandant de Belleisle in their native tongue. He nodded and snapped an order. They wheeled their horses and rode off again.

'Have they found the fellow, Armand?' came Jason's voice. He strode out of the darkness with John Bennett at his heels. Both carried revolvers.

'There were two of them,' said de Belleisle. 'The accomplice was holding the horses. I've sent half the Spahis after them, but they will lose them in minutes among the rocks and gullies.'

John Bennett came up to me. He took me by the elbow. 'Are you badly shaken up, Annabel? I heard you call out. Next thing, Marquand was shooting. I reckon you owe him your life.'

I found myself trembling all over, and did not trust myself to speak.

'Marquand is the best marksman in the battalion,' said de Belleise, 'and the holder of the Legion's silver cup for pistol-shooting. You could not have found a better protector, mam'selle.' He stooped and picked something from the ground. 'And you most certainly stood in very grave need of protection at that moment.'

I glanced at the thing he held in his hand and trembled anew. It was a native knife, with a thick, curved blade that came to a wicked point. John Bennett had struck a match the better to see it; the flame was briefly reflected along the two cruelly sharp edges of the weapon.

'It is a Berber knife,' said the Commandant. 'We have not had much trouble of this kind recently, but it will happen from time to time while ever there are tribesmen who remain unpacified.'

'You regard this as a routine attack by hostile natives then, Commandant?' demanded John Bennett.

'Why, yes,' replied de Belleisle, with a note of surprise in his voice. 'You may not be aware, monsieur, that we had a major uprising of the Arabs in the Oran Province as recently as eighty-two, and there are some who will never accept France. The attack was unusual, but by no means unique.'

Jason Saltram's deep voice intervened. 'I take it, Armand

'– but, of course, it goes without saying – that you posted sentries tonight?'

'A ring of legionnaires stood sentry-go round the camp since we arrived,' said the other stiffly.

'You will forgive my asking, Armand?' said Jason.

'But of course, *mon ami*,' replied de Belleisle. 'You had every right to enquire.'

'Some sentries!' broke in John Bennett harshly. 'They must all have been asleep, to let that fellow through and darned nearly murder Miss Trewella here!'

'Bennett, you have no right to say that!' blazed Jason. 'I demand that you withdraw the slur immediately!'

'That will not be necessary, Jason,' said Armand de Belleisle. 'The American gentleman is substantially correct. Our sentries – at least the sentry in question – fell short of the standard of vigilance demanded of a legionnaire. He allowed the enemy to see him first.'

Both men stared at the Commandant, and I sensed a cold finger of dread trailing down the length of my spine.

'The Spahis found the sentry,' said de Belleisle harshly. 'The enemy had come upon him by surprise, but the man put up a good fight.'

'And . . .'

I turned away, suddenly sickened as, after a swift glance in my direction, de Belleisle made the brusque gesture of drawing his forefinger across his throat.

We came to Sidi-bel-Abbès in the splendour of the African dawn: the line of cavalry and the marching men, and a still form draped in a greatcoat, lying across the back of a horse.

Dazed with lack of sleep, numb with shock, I saw it all with a pair of eyes that hardly seemed my own, looking out upon a scene that was as remote and insubstantial as a dream. Surely I was no part of the strange cavalcade that clattered in through great iron gates and into a vast, tree-lined space where rank upon rank of legionnaires were drawn up on parade.

A chorus of bugles shrilled out. A tricolor flag rose up a tall pole and stirred its folds lazily in the wind of the morning. As if in a dream, our cavalcade passed down those long lines of watching eyes, and came to a large building at the far end of the parade ground, beyond the trees. It was there that John Bennett reached up and handed me down from my mount. The expression of deep concern on his face jolted me back to reality. He told me I would feel better after a rest, and summoned up an encouraging smile.

I saw them lift down the shrouded figure and bear it away on a stretcher. As I followed Commandant de Belleisle up the steps to the main door of the building, I looked back and saw that the flag was already descending to half-mast. The Legion was mourning a dead comrade that morning.

The Commandant gave his own quarters over to my use. There was a sitting-room, bedroom with bathroom adjoining, all simply and sparsely furnished, as befitting the lodgings of a soldier. My only thought was for the Spartan-looking iron bedstead, on which, as soon as I was alone, I lay down and found to be more comfortable than one would have believed possible. I was asleep the instant I closed my eyes, and did not wake till the midday sun was causing a swirling heat haze to rise from the sand of the parade ground, beyond the shade of the trees outside my window.

Our baggage – enough clothing and personal possessions to suffice for the two or three days we were to stay at the Legion Depot – had been sent on ahead by road. I changed into a skirt and cool blouse for an informal luncheon, which was served in the Commandant's sitting-room next door. Present were de Belleisle, John Bennett, Jason and myself. It was a strained and awkward meal, the events of the previous night having cast a pall of tragedy over what had started as a holiday jaunt. Armand de Belleisle, particularly, seemed much affected with gloom and scarcely ate anything, but crumbled bread between his fingers and stared morosely out of the window, to where the tricolor stood against the sky. He excused himself at the dessert course, pleading duties to be performed. I was left alone with John Bennett and Jason – a circumstance which, considering the state of our relationships, held out the promise of nothing but embarrassment. I was assembling in my mind a suitable excuse for cutting short my own meal when John Bennett broke the silence by brusquely addressing the legionnaire who was waiting at table. He told him, in passable-sounding French, that we would not be requiring him any more and to leave the room.

When the door shut behind the soldier, the American got up and went over to the open window. After first looking out, one way and then the other, he carefully closed the window. Then he turned to regard the pair of us. His face was set and determined – like that of a man who had taken careful counsel in his own mind and had arrived at a painful decision.

'What in the blazes is the matter with you, man?' demanded Jason Saltram.

'I think the time has come,' replied the other, 'to lay a few cards on the table ... *before anyone else gets killed!*'

chapter nine

'Bennett, have you gone insane?'

Jason got to his feet and rasped out the words, his lean form arched across the table, dark eyes blazing at the man by the window. I had never seen him more dangerous-looking, like a panther crouched to spring.

If John Bennett was alarmed by the other's air of menace, he did not show it.

'No, Saltram,' he replied. 'I'm as sane as you are. Don't worry. I haven't caught a dose of the famous Legion *cafard* that's supposed to drive strong men to madness.'

'Then what's this talk of someone else getting killed?' demanded Jason. 'What are you trying to do? I would have thought that Miss Trewella has been through enough without having to listen to your wild talk. Explain yourself, man. Either that, or keep your overheated ideas to yourself.'

I drew a deep breath and said: 'I think I know what Mr Bennett's trying to say.'

Jason turned to stare at me, incredulity written all over his face.

'You do?' he said. 'Then perhaps you would be so good, ma'am, as to enlighten me.'

I looked across to John Bennett. 'You think, don't you,' I said, 'that there's some connection between last night's attack on me and everything that's gone before?'

He nodded gravely. 'Reluctantly and belatedly,' he said, 'I have become inclined to the point of view you first put to me in Gibraltar. The one I talked you out of.'

'You must *both* be insane!' cried Jason. 'Last night there was a senseless and random attack upon a Legion camp, of the sort that Armand de Belleisle described as "unusual, but by no means unique". What connection could there possibly be between that and – what was your expression? – everything that's gone before? To what are you referring?'

'To begin at the beginning,' said John Bennett, 'there was the unexplained death of Third Officer Maugham.'

'Maugham?' cried Jason. 'But there was no mystery about

Maugham's end. In my years at sea, I've known at first hand of at least half a dozen similar cases of men losing their bearings and falling overboard at night.'

'Oriana Topsham,' said John Bennett quietly.

Jason sat down. Without his eyes leaving the other's face, he reached out and took up a decanter of cognac that stood on the table before him. Still watching Bennett, he took out the stopper and poured himself a bumper measure.

'Please continue,' he said coldly, raising the glass to his lips.

'The attempted abduction of Melloney and the injury to the sailor Flack,' said John Bennett. 'And now the attack upon Miss Trewella.'

'You see a connection between all these events?'

'No. Any more than you see a connection. I never have. But, Saltram, these violent events, while seemingly unrelated, are loosely strung together by a series of minor incidents that simply cannot be explained away.'

'Such as?' demanded Jason.

I blurted out: 'The sobbing man. The figure that watched John and me from the roof-top in Gibraltar . . .'

'The message written upon the glass,' supplied John.

'Two messages,' I cried. 'There was another that I never told you about, on the night of the levanter.'

'Was there, by hookey?' exclaimed John. 'Then, for heaven's sake, Annabel, why didn't you tell me?'

I cast a sidelong glance to Jason, who was staring into his brandy glass; only the intensity of his gaze betrayed that he was alert and tensed as a coiled spring, and was certainly listening to, and weighing, every word that passed between John and me.

'It was the night of the levanter,' I repeated. 'I was out on deck looking for you, to tell you – when . . .'

The American's hazel-flecked eyes flared with a sudden understanding. 'Ah, yes,' he said. 'That explains a lot. You were out on the boat deck, looking for me . . .' he turned to Jason, whose head flicked up sharply when he was addressed. 'Saltram, I have a confession to make to you, sir.'

'As you please, sir,' replied Jason, with the same air of studied formality that John had used. ' "Confession" is rather a strong word. In the interests of our continued friendship do you not think it might be advisable to sleep on it, before you embark upon what you call your "confession"? We have all been through the somewhat demanding experience of an all-night ride and a murderous attack ...'

'On the night of the levanter,' interrupted John, 'while you were keeping watch on the bridge with Captain Pelly, I stole into your cabin and made a search of your papers!'

I was watching Jason when John blurted out that statement: not by so much as a flicker of an eyebrow did he display any emotion, but simply replied: 'I was aware that the contents of my desk had been disturbed, and I have to confess, Bennett, that my suspicions first flew to you.'

'Which was why you brought up the subject of the round robin at luncheon the next day?' asked John. 'You were testing me, to see how I responded to your account of the correspondence between you and your directors. Tell me – what conclusion did you come to?'

'That my suspicions were entirely unfounded,' replied Jason blandly. 'I have a little talent for this and a little talent for that' – his marvellous eyes twinkled with amusement, and my heart gave a lurch – 'but I am particularly good at distinguishing between honesty and rascality. I have thought from the first that you are an honest man. I thought so after I had tested you, and I think so now.'

'That's mighty gratifying to hear, sir,' said John, looking pointedly at me, so that I had to lower my gaze in confusion.

'Then,' said Jason, 'since you did not search my cabin for the purpose of taking a mean advantage in the business negotiations on which we are at present engaged, just what *were* you looking for?'

John, who had not taken his eyes off me, replied: 'Even after Oriana Topsham's death, I stood convinced that you were mistaken in your fears, Annabel. What we found when we returned aboard at Gibraltar made me change my mind. What's more, I sensed a pattern of danger that could encompass everyone in the yacht. For that reason, I set out to do some – spying – on my own.'

'Beginning with a search of my cabin,' said Jason dryly.

'In the twelve hours or so that elapsed between the attack on Melloney and our setting sail from Gibraltar,' said John, 'I searched every cabin that I could get into. I even tried yours, Annabel, but found it locked. I found nothing – till I came to yours, Saltram!'

Jason looked puzzled. 'I am at a loss to know what you could have found. A certain rearrangement of the papers in my desk drawers led me to think that someone had been – er – *prying*' – his smile removed any slur from the word – 'but nothing appeared to be missing.'

'What I took from your cabin did not come from the desk.'

'From where, then?'

John drew a notebook from his breast pocket. 'From the bookcase.'

'You removed a book?'

'I removed something *from* a book ... see?' And he took from the notebook a folded piece of paper, which, on being opened out, proved to be a cutting from a newspaper. He held it out to Jason.

The effect upon Jason was nothing short of catastrophic. 'Not that!' he cried. 'Heavens – I was insane to leave that thing lying about!'

'It was far from lying about,' retorted John. 'But for the fact that it was hidden at the title page of the first volume of a quite nice edition of *The Letters of Charles Dickens*, by Tauchnitz of Leipzig, the secret would have remained. But, you see, I am an avid collector of Dickensiana ... and I opened up the volume.'

'*Secret?*' I seized upon the word. 'What secret?'

They were both looking at me. And the expression on both their faces was alike: deep concern, mixed with – what?

'She must see it,' said John.

'It need never have happened,' said Jason. 'She could have gone through her whole life in happy ignorance. For heaven's sake, why did you have to dredge it up, Bennett?'

'Let Annabel be the judge of that.'

I screamed in their faces then ...

'*What are you both doing to me? What's in that piece of paper that's been hidden from me?*'

Searching their expressions, I knew then that the thing common to both was compassion. They felt sorry for me.

John handed me the newspaper cutting, and I sat down and read it to myself. It had been scissored from a paper, now yellowed with age, and bore no headlines, no illustrations. Just the stark account:

The November general sessions of the peace for the county of Somerset commenced this morning at Bristol before Mr Serjeant Rawlings, Assistant-Judge, and a full bench of magistrates. The calendar contained the names of 81 prisoners – of whom 67 were charged with felony, and 14 with misdemeanour.

In the course of the morning, several cases of petty larceny committed at Bristol docks were tried, and the prisoners sentenced to various terms of imprisonment with hard labour.

In the afternoon, Harriet Mary Cadge, aged 22, was indicted for the murder of Simon Penberthy, aged 31.

The prisoner was governess to the ward of Sir David Lumley, Kt, of St Errol in the duchy of Cornwall, and had been so for five years. She was given every third Sunday off from her duties, and it was on one of these occasions that she met the deceased, a gamekeeper, afterwards forming a liaison with him. On the night of Sunday, September 9th last, at about 8 p.m., the servants of St Errol House were summoned to Cadge's sitting-room by the sound of a cry and a heavy fall. There, they discovered the shocking sight of Penberthy breathing his last from a knife wound in the upper torso, with the prisoner bending over him, crying, 'I would not have had it happen for the world, my darling.'

Cadge acknowledged at once that she was guilty; and stated she and Penberthy had had a lovers' quarrel, during the course of which she had struck him with the knife.

The prisoner offering no evidence on her own behalf, the jury found her *Guilty*.

The prosecutor, in the most feeling manner, entreated for mercy for the prisoner. He said she had a dependent half-sister living in the care of foster parents in mid-Cornwall, that she belonged to a most excellent and worthy family, and had been a good and faithful servant for five years.

Mr Serjeant Rawlings said that, despite this truly kind appeal, none knew better than the prosecutor that the law permitted only one sentence for a person found guilty of wilful murder by the jury.

The sentence was, that Harriet Mary Cadge be hanged ...

'NO! – NO! It can't be true!'

I pressed my hands against my ears, to shut out the sound of my own cries; and I looked to them for reassurance. All I saw in their faces was compassion.

'All your sister ever wanted,' said Jason Saltram, 'all she ever spoke of, or wrote of, at the end, was that you should not know. That you would not have to live your life – as she put it – in the shadow of her shame. With this, my uncle, David Lumley, was in total agreement. He had already used his considerable influence, in order to have the venue of the trial moved away from Cornwall. Newspaper editors were persuaded, bribed, coerced, into glossing over or suppressing the reports of the case. Only this newspaper – an obscure Bath weekly – slipped through the net of Uncle David's vigilance. Scarcely anyone in Cornwall, and certainly not you, could ever have known that Harriet Cadge paid the full price for what she did.'

I stared at him, trying to come to terms with Harriet's awful end, and being unable to encompass it.

'Then she was ... was ...?'

'There was no reprieve,' said Jason quietly. 'Her last act was to write to my uncle, asking him to care for you. I'm glad to say that her appeal was not refused.'

The scales were falling from my eyes ...

'The money that paid my foster parents,' I said. 'The money that saw me through when I was an unpaid pupil-teacher at St Finn – I had always thought it came from Harriet's life savings.'

'She had had to support both you and your mother at one time,' said Jason. 'There were no savings. My uncle was glad to provide for you. And his instructions to me were – I remember well his very words – "Do something for that poor child Annabel Trewella when she comes of age." '

'Who else was in the secret?' demanded John Bennett. I gave a start at the sound of his voice; I had been so intent upon

Jason's words that I had forgotten the American's presence.

'The staff of St Errol House,' replied Jason. 'Including Nanny Bagley, of course. They were the first on the scene. As much for Melloney's sake as for Miss Trewella's, they were sworn to secrecy about Harriet's fate.'

'Melloney has never been told, then?' John asked the question that was trembling on my own lips.

'Oh no! She was already crippled beyond all help. And she was devoted to Harriet Cadge. The shock might have been fatal to her.'

It was hot and stuffy in the airless room. From beyond the closed window came the shrill notes of a lone bugle. Then silence.

I remembered something: the second message that the unknown one had left for me on the glass, and I told them about it:

FORGET YOUR SISTER'S SIN.
IT WILL BRING YOU NOTHING
BUT TROUBLE.

'"Your sister's sin!"' cried John Bennett. 'There you have it, Saltram. Find whoever wrote that and I think you will find the connecting link between all the death and violence we have known during the *Dolphin* summer.'

'I still find it difficult – no, impossible – to believe that the tragedies were all linked,' said Jason. 'What Harriet Cadge did, and the way we banded together to hush it up, all that happened nearly ten years ago. You don't really think . . . ?'

'I think nothing,' said John, 'because I know nothing! At present I can only speculate. I only have this feeling – I had it as soon as I found that newspaper cutting, and afterwards checked by quizzing Annabel that she knew nothing of her sister's crime and sentencing – that that nine-year-old murder was somehow connected with our present horrors. I may say that, if I had known of the second message at that time, my convictions would have been even stronger.'

'What was your reaction, Miss Trewella, when you received the second message?' asked Jason Saltram.

'I went to Nanny Bagley,' I replied. And I told them of my encounter with the nurse, and of the revelations I had subsequently had from the reluctant lips of Dr Weems. When I came to the account of Harriet's tragic negligence, Jason leapt to his feet and commenced to pace about the room in what seemed a great agony of mind.

'It's unspeakable!' he cried. 'Unspeakable, that I have never been told of this! By heaven, Bagley and Weems have much to answer for!'

'What do you propose we do now, Saltram?' demanded John Bennett.

Jason did not reply till his pacing brought him to the window, where he remained, looking out, his back towards us.

He said: 'I propose that we return immediately to the *Dolphin* and thrash the whole thing out with that confounded pair.'

'Bagley and Weems?' asked John.

'Who else?'

'What about de Belleisle – do we confide in him?'

Jason turned to face us. He was now entirely in control of himself and of the situation, and he reminded me of that first occasion when, in his cabin, I had covertly studied him while he was dealing with the minor crisis of Lady Topsham's train.

'We are in French territory,' he said calmly. 'Subject to French law. At present, we have only speculation to guide us. Blind speculation. If there is more than coincidence involved in the incidents we have been discussing, something more than accidental chance, if there is an infernal *design* behind it all – then the Legion is involved, for a legionnaire died out there last night.' He pointed to the window, and to the distant hills. 'No, at this stage, I think we keep our doubts and suspicions to ourselves.'

Before either John or I had the opportunity to comment upon Jason's words, the door opened and Armand de Belleisle strode into the room. His face was grave.

'*Mon ami*, I have bad news for you – from Oran,' he said, addressing Jason.

'*Melloney!*' The name sprang to my lips, all unbidden.

The Commandant nodded. 'We have just received a tele-graph from Château-Neuf,' he said. 'Mademoiselle Melloney has had a serious relapse. She is . . .'

'No! It can't be . . .'

'I much regret that your friend is dying, mam'selle!'

So we journeyed back to Oran that afternoon. Not on horse-back, as we had come, across the hills and gullies and plains; but by the quickest and most direct route: the military road, built by the Legion and maintained by the Legion. Our four-wheeled post-chaise, driven four-in-hand, covered the dist-ance in a few hours. We passed a road-gang of legionnaires on the way, who leaned on their picks and shovels and waved to us.

We travelled mostly in silence, the three of us: Jason, John Bennett and myself.

About half way to Oran, passing through a shallow valley leading to the coastal plain, where there were farmsteads and cultivated land, John broke the silence. 'When did Sir David Lumley die, Saltram?'

Jason was watching a line of men and women working in a lemon grove. Without turning his head, he replied, 'Three years ago, in ninety-four. Why do you ask?'

'Just trying to get your family situation clear in my mind. Was your uncle ailing for very long?'

'Yes, for very many years. He suffered from a heart condi-tion which greatly reduced his ability to get about towards the end. He moved into a room on the ground floor at St Errol House: a bedroom and study combined, from which he direc-ted the fortunes of Lumley's, and with considerable success. He had a telephone connection between there and our head office in Exeter, and was working on the very day he died.'

'Of a heart attack?'

'Yes, of course.' Jason looked round. 'Of a heart attack.'

'Was anyone with him at the end?' asked John. And now I knew – and Jason must have realized it also – that there was some serious purpose behind the American's persistent ques-tioning.

'No. He died alone. As a matter of fact, I discovered him

myself when I called in to see him that evening.' Jason's voice was calm, even matter-of-fact; but his eyes were fixed on his questioner with a burning intensity. 'He was lying on the floor, midway between his desk and the chimney-piece.'

'On his way to put some coal on the fire, perhaps?'

'There was no fire,' said Jason flatly. 'It was high summer and a heat-wave. The french windows were wide open. No – he was obviously crossing the room to reach his medicine, which was standing on the chimney-piece. He must have had a premonition of the attack.'

'A man in constant hazard of a heart-attack,' mused John slowly. 'Now, why didn't he keep his medicine close by him when he was working – in his desk drawer, for instance?'

'He usually did,' replied Jason. And a strange new light had come into his eyes. 'I remember we commented at the time, Weems and I, on my uncle's rotten bad luck at having left the medicine on the chimney-piece just when he needed it . . .' his voice trailed away.

'So he feels an attack coming on,' said John. 'And he spots the medicine at the other side of the room, on the chimney-piece. Why doesn't he ring for a servant to fetch it across? Surely a man in his condition would have a bell to summon help?'

A long silence. I looked at Jason. We both looked at Jason.

After a while, he said: 'You must realize that the facts of the medicine and the bell were only matters for regret at the time of my uncle's death, nothing more; they have only assumed a sinister significance in the light of what has happened recently. In answer to your question, Bennett: yes, he had a bell. That was kept on the desk too . . . *but somehow the bell had also found its way to the chimney-piece, just when he needed it most!*'

I believe that all our thoughts were alike at that moment. It was John who framed them into words.

He said: 'We'd better order this driver to whip up the horses, so that we can get to Melloney before she suffers the same fate as the others.'

The Quai du Sénégal was a kaleidoscope of vivid colour and

alive with movement. Native vendors, dancers, musicians, snake-charmers, fire-eaters were vying with each other for the attentions of a crowd of Europeans who were disembarking from ships' boats at the quay. They would be passengers from one of the great liners, on an evening's sightseeing.

Jason masterfully elbowed a way through the press, to where the *Dolphin*'s little steam launch lay waiting for us. First Officer Crane was there. He saluted us and gave me a hand to help me aboard.

'Received your telegram of acknowledgement, sir,' he said, addressing Jason. 'Didn't take you long to get back here.'

We sat down under the awning, and the launch put out from the quay; past a fleet of native boats laden down with fruits, vegetables and fish; leaving behind the cacophony of shouting voices, the jangle of bells and cymbals, the wail of the charmers' pipes.

'What's the present situation aboard *Dolphin*?' demanded Jason. 'How is Miss Melloney?'

'She's unconscious, sir,' said Crane. 'Nanny's in attendance upon her. The Captain being ashore till tomorrow, I took the liberty of requesting the French authorities to send out a doctor – which they did.'

'A doctor?' rasped Jason. 'What did you need another doctor for – what's wrong with Weems?'

'Didn't you know, sir?' said Crane. 'Didn't the French send that information when they telegraphed Sidi-bel-Abbès? Doctor Weems has disappeared!'

'*Disappeared?*'

'Yes, sir. Soon after Miss Melloney collapsed – and that was about ten-thirty this morning – Dr Weems sent for me and told me that she was very seriously ill and likely to die. And that you should be summoned to return immediately. Before I had a chance to get a message ashore, Dr Weems came up on deck in a very excitable state: clothing all awry, no hat, looked as if he'd had a fall or something. Ignoring me, he called out to one of the Arab harbour boats that hang all day about the *Dolphin* in the hope of a passenger. Told the fellow to take him ashore. I saw them heading for one of the nearest quays. Saw him get out and pay off the boatman. Then he disappeared into the crowd. And he hasn't been seen since.'

'Been gone all day?' cried John Bennett. 'Abandoned a dying patient?'

'What about the French doctor?' demanded Jason. 'You say he's seen Miss Melloney?'

'Came aboard just before midday, sir,' replied First Officer Crane. 'And stayed for an hour. Not much of a fellow, if you ask me. Hardly spoke a word of our language and demanded to be paid five English sovereigns before he'd so much as open his bag.'

'Well – what did he say about the patient?' snapped Jason.

'As far as I could make out, sir, he didn't seem to think that Miss Melloney was in any immediate danger. Kept saying that she'd been drugged.'

'Drugged? What do you mean by drugged?'

'My French isn't very good, sir,' said Crane stiffly, 'but I understood him to say that she'd been given a very heavy dose of what he called a "*drogue*".'

'By Dr Weems?'

'I suppose so, sir.'

We were approaching the western end of the harbour, near to the entrance, with the wide sweep of dazzling blue sea beyond. The Villa La Blanca crowned the nearby shoreline; below it, the *Dolphin* swung lazily at her anchor, gleaming white and gold in the late afternoon. Everything looked perfectly normal. Two sailors, lowered over the side on a wooden staging, were quite unnecessarily retouching her brilliant paintwork. As we drew near to the ladder, the ship's bell sounded the passing of the first hour of the second dog watch: seven o'clock.

I followed Jason and John up on the deck.

'Miss Melloney's in the sick bay, sir.'

We went below. The door of the sick bay was open, and screened with mosquito netting, through which, between the shoulders of the men walking before me, I could see the dark-clad form of Nanny Bagley sitting by the patient's bedside.

She got up when we entered. Her eyes were red-rimmed in her haggard, uncomely face; her hair, hanging in a single plait, clearly had not been dressed since she had got out of bed that morning. Her manner was that of someone in extreme agony of mind and spirit.

'She's going – my darling's slipping away in a coma. I've seen them go like this many a time!' The woman fell on her knees by the bed and took one of Melloney's slender wrists in her large hand.

Melloney looked like a creature already dead. The wild-rose complexion had faded to ivory, the luminous eyes were closed, the lips slightly parted and bedewed with a surrounding rime of sweat. Her hair was spread out on the pillow like a flaxen grave-cloth. Only the slight rise and fall of her breast told that she still lived.

'My darling girl!' keened Nanny. 'Don't leave me now. Not after all we've been through together. What's he done to you, my lovely – what's he done, that evil creature?'

I saw Jason's eyes meet those of John Bennett, and they nodded to each other. Jason indicated the door of the adjacent apartment. The two of them took the woman by the elbows and guided her, unresisting, out of the sick bay. I followed them, after a backward glance at Melloney's white profile.

Then began the examination of Nurse Bagley.

Jason acted as Grand Inquisitor, seated at Dr Weem's desk, with Nanny in the chair before him – where I had sat on the occasion when I had learned about my half-sister's act of neglect. John Bennett and I looked on from the side.

Nanny was in a state of near-collapse. It was as if the very life force had been drained from that large and very capable woman. I put it down to her anguish about Melloney. She appeared to have no fear of her employer, but gazed at him with streaming eyes, seemingly uncaring. Even his first shocking question did not arouse her.

'Did you have any part in the death of Third Officer Maugham?'

'No, sir.' Her reply came brokenly, in a dying voice, quite without emotion.

'Was yours the hand that pushed Miss Topsham over the edge of that cliff?[2]

Again : 'No, sir.'

'I recall to your mind the death of my uncle, Sir David Lumley, in eighteen ninety-four. You rendered such nursing as was required during his frequent attacks?'

'Yes.'

'On the occasions that you were present when he suffered from his attacks, you gave him the medicine?'

She nodded.

'The medicine was always kept close at hand?'

'Yes, sir.'

'At night, on his bedside table. During the day, on his desk. Yet when he had his last and fatal attack, the medicine – and the bell that could have summoned you or someone else within earshot – was at the far end of the room! Did *you* move them to the chimney-piece?'

'No, sir.'

Jason leaned back in the chair and regarded the woman broodingly. From first to last during that brutal and wounding questioning, Nanny had not been aroused to express so much as a start of surprise, let alone to show any resentment or fear. To me, at least, it seemed that her fears about Melloney's present condition had cast a protective wall about her mind – a wall upon which Jason would hammer in vain.

I was mistaken; his next question struck home with visible force.

'What has Dr Weems done to Melloney?'

'That evil creature!' Nanny raised her head, and her tear-swollen eyes flared with a sudden passion. 'That drunken, wicked thing! He fed something to my darling. Told me it would soothe her nerves. Soothe her nerves! Kill her more like!'

'Where is Weems now, Nanny?' asked Jason, in more gentle tones.

'Ran away! Gone to drink himself into a stupor, I don't doubt. Left my darling here to die!' She buried her face in her hands and sobbed brokenly.

'But,' said Jason, 'the French doctor who came aboard at midday said that Melloney was in no immediate danger. In other words, so I take it, the effects of the drug that Weems gave her will wear off. Weems, it appears, was mistaken in his diagnosis, and Melloney is not about to die.'

'That foreign fellow!' cried Nanny. 'That Frenchy who came. Call him a doctor? Dirty fingernails and smelling of garlic. Touching my darling with his dirty hands. What does he know? I tell you she's dying' – her voice rose to a wavering speech – 'dying!'

'Calm yourself, woman!' cried Jason.

Nanny Bagley was on her feet. 'What do you care?' she screamed at him. 'You're only waiting for her to die, then you can go off and forget about her. Very convenient, my fine gentleman, to have my darling safely dead and buried.'

'Will you be silent?' blazed Jason.

But the distraught creature was not to be quietened. She pointed to Jason; screamed into his face like someone demented.

'You've always treated her like a burden, for all that you've pretended to be her loving guardian! Loving guardian indeed! It's my belief you want her dead!'

'How can you say that – how dare you?' It was I who cried out – for nothing on earth could have prevented me from springing to Jason's defence against the woman's evil and lying accusation. 'Commander Saltram's only wish is for Melloney's good. He's already sacrificed much for her sake. His naval career –'

'Thank you, Miss Trewella, that will be quite sufficient.' Jason's cold voice cut me short.

Nanny Bagley was no longer attending to Jason; her hate-filled eyes were now directed against me; and her vehemence also.

'You!' she mouthed. 'I've had my fill of you, wench! I've known your sort of old – creeping up out of the servants' hall to take your place at the master's table. Putting on your fine airs and graces, when you're no better than a scullery maid – a common skivvy. Worming your way into my darling's good graces, making out you're a friend when all the time you're only feathering your own nest. You're another who doesn't care a fig if my darling lives or dies!'

'That's not true!' I cried. 'Oh, I don't care what you think of me, you evil-tongued woman. I'm only a paid servant, like you, and I don't care who knows it. But I'm as concerned with Melloney's well-being as you are!'

'Miss Trewella ... Bagley ... this discussion will cease!' Jason stepped forward between us, his dark countenance set with fury. But Nanny Bagley thrust aside his restraining arm and, pointing to the door behind which Melloney lay, she returned to the attack on me.

'I tell you my darling's dying in there! That Weems killed her with his potions, the drunken wretch. She's in a coma – and she may never awaken! And you – who boast of being her friend – where are your tears, hey?' She pointed to her own ruined face, her swollen, red-rimmed eyes. 'That's what real grief looks like, wench! That's true heartbreak for you!'

My anger evaporated before the extremity of her agony. It was useless and selfish, I then realized, to try to explain the depth of my own sorrow for Melloney's state; the compassionate course was to try and lessen hers. And in this I made my fatal error.

'We shall all grieve together if she doesn't awake from the coma, Nanny,' I said gently, laying a hand on her arm. 'But how much better this way – to die peacefully and without pain. Better than suffering another year of increasing agony and then dying hideously – the way the doctors have predicted.'

In the following silence, I quickly realized what I had done. I had no way of telling, from Nanny's face, whether my words had given her comfort or not. It scarcely mattered.

I had forgotten that there was a fourth person in the room: John Bennett, who had not, till that moment, been a party to the terrible secret concerning Melloney.

John was staring at me in sudden shock; but I had eyes only for Jason Saltram, as he cut me to the heart with his furious denunciation.

'*By heaven, woman! Do you have no respect for your sacred vow?*'

Even as Jason glared at me, his anger became overlaid with a fresh emotion. His lips opened to utter a cry; but the sound died in impotence.

He was looking past me, beyond me ...

I turned, and I think that part of me died in that instant.

Half-standing, half-swooning, the slight figure of Melloney Lumley clung to the jamb of the part-open door, one leg bent beneath her, and already slipping away, so that she fell heavily before we could rush forward and catch hold of her.

Falling, her eyes never left my face. And I knew that she had heard my every word.

When the sun died, I heard the thin cry of a *muezzin* calling the Faithful to prayer from one of the minarets of the old city, and the men on a passing native boat prostrated themselves on the deck in obedience. The last rays turned the white walls of the Villa La Blanca to a glowing red, rivalling the hibiscus flowers that overhung them; and I yearned to be there, among the cool fountains and the sentinel cypresses, so that the shade of that wise old lady, the Marquesa de Riego, would hear me and understand.

How I longed for the counsel of a loving friend: one who would not shrink from the knowledge that my half-sister, a convicted murderess, had also committed the scarcely lesser crime of condemning a gay and lovely child to a terrible fate; a friend who would not turn away, on hearing that I had broken a most solemn and holy vow to preserve that poor creature from the truth about herself. How had Jason put it? — 'the ultimate agony: the agony of hopeless despair'. Because of me, that agony would now be Melloney's.

And Jason . . .

How he must have hated and despised me at that moment. I shrank from the recollection — but forced myself to suffer the pain — of the glance he had thrown me when he stooped to pick up Melloney's unconscious form, limp and ethereal in its flowing shift.

'*Madam — will you please get out of my sight!*' — those had been his words, and they had sent me, blinded with bitter tears, to hide behind the locked door of my cabin.

First Harriet . . . and now me. As if in a conspiracy, we had banded together to destroy Melloney.

What now? I asked myself.

To stay — or to leave? Though, surely, the choice would

not be offered to me; surely, at the earliest opportunity – perhaps even that very night – Jason Saltram would demand my removal from the *Dolphin* and my return to England. He might even – awful thought – send someone else to perform the task: his secretary Robbins, or the First Officer, perhaps even John Bennett. I decided that that would be the last straw: not to see him again. Better by far, despite the hurt, to be summoned to his cabin and be told by him to leave. To shut my ears to the words; make believe that he was speaking of a love that I had only dared to contemplate in the twilight places between dreams and waking . . .

A knock on the cabin door snatched me from my reverie.

'Annabel, are you there? It's John. May I come in, please?'

'John! Just a moment.'

I ran to the mirror. My eyes and face were beyond all mending. I contented myself by dabbing a little powder on my nose and patting my chignon into place. Nothing could hide the fact that I had been crying my heart out for over an hour.

Opening the door to him, I dropped my gaze before his look of sympathy.

'I came to tell you,' he said, 'that Melloney's sleeping peacefully. She must have recovered from the effects of the drug – which was some kind of soporific, I guess – and crawled to the door when she heard voices beyond' – he took hold of my chin, gently but firmly, and directed my gaze to meet his – 'and it's my belief that she didn't hear what you said, or if she did, was too woozy to take it in.'

'She heard every word,' I told him flatly. 'I *know* she heard. It's kind of you, John, to try to put my mind at ease, but quite useless. I know she heard . . . and so does Jason Saltram.'

'Jason Saltram,' he repeated. 'Second only to the hurt you think you've done Melloney, that's what's destroying you, isn't it – the thought that you may have earned his anger?'

'I could bear his anger,' I whispered against the palms of my hands. 'What I can't bear is for him to . . . shut me out for ever.'

He took my hands away from my face, fingers gentle about my wrists. 'He means all that much to you, Annabel?'

I nodded miserably. 'Surely it must show,' I said. 'I'm not

very good at concealing my feelings, and I've almost given up caring about hiding them – now.'

Suddenly his arms were very comforting, and his shoulder a very broad and reassuring place upon which to lay my cheek.

'Cry away,' he said. 'I think this must be my true role in life: to fall for girls, and end up being best friend and confident. Call me Uncle John.'

'John, you're a dear, kind man,' I said. 'And I never apologized for misjudging you, after I saw you in Jason's cabin.'

'Nor you did,' he said with mock-severity. 'And now that I seem to have you at a disadvantage, may I play the complete cad – and ask you again to marry me?'

I smiled at him through the tears that welled afresh. 'You can't believe what a tonic it is to be asked that, John,' I told him. 'Feeling as wretched and unwanted as I do. You make me almost believe in myself again; believe that I shall be able to carry on tomorrow ...'

'Then?' he cried, holding me out at arm's length. 'You accept?'

'No, my dear,' I told him. 'It wouldn't be fair to you, to bind you to a woman who, no matter how much she admires you – and might even grow to love you – will always be a half-person because of ...'

'Because of him – of Jason?'

I nodded.

'Your feelings towards him will never change?'

'No matter how much he reviles me,' I said. 'No matter how hopeless it is, my feelings towards him will remain the same. I know it with a certainty that almost frightens me.'

He touched my cheek with his fingertip, wiping away a tear that lay there. 'You poor kid,' he said. 'I sure wish there was some way I could help you.'

'You must never tell him!' I cried. 'Promise me that, John: never to speak a word about what I've told you to Jason. It wouldn't be any use, you see? I'm nothing to him; but, at least, he doesn't have any cause to feel sorry for me. I couldn't bear for him to feel sorry for me.'

'I promise,' he agreed. 'And now, Annabel, I've got to go.

One of the reasons I came to see you – apart from bringing you the news on Melloney – was to tell you that we've had a message from Commandant de Belleisle. They've found the Arab who tried to kill you the other night.'

'Found him?' I shuddered.

'That's right. The Spahis ran him to earth in the hills, and he's talked. We were right: this fellow and his companion were paid to kill you.'

'Paid – to kill me?' That someone in the world hated me enough to want me dead – and was willing to pay out money to bring about my destruction – was the most terrible sensation that I had ever experienced, comparable only to the moment of living nightmare when I had turned to see Melloney by the open door.

'Sure,' said John. 'But it's all right now. Whoever's behind it all has just about come to the end of his tether. The trail leads right back to Oran, de Belleisle says. He's over there now, at the Villa La Blanca, awaiting further news from the police who're making enquiries in the town. He's sent for us to come to the villa – Jason and me – to be there when they catch our villain.'

'Who do you think it is, John?' I whispered.

'Weems,' he said without hesitation.

'But . . . why?'

He shrugged. 'Why should anyone want to kill you, or Meloney, or Oriana Topsham, not to mention Third Officer Maugham and poor Flack? There has to be some reason, some logic, behind it all. I can't see what it is from where I'm standing, but that doesn't alter anything; by tomorrow morning, the reason will be plain.'

'Is he mad?'

'He kills with the merciless single-mindedness of a madman,' mused John. 'But I think we shall find that there's more to it than that. I think we shall find that he's driven by some hard and pressing reason.'

'They'll find him?'

'I understand that the police, both civil and military, as well as the army, are combing Oran,' said John. 'Weems won't be at large for long. They've probably arrested him by now.'

I shuddered, as if someone had walked over my grave. 'I hope so,' I murmured.

'Good night, Annabel,' said John. 'Don't worry about a thing. And remember what I told you: despite what you think, Melloney didn't hear, or didn't take in, what you said. Lock your cabin door and have a good night's sleep. Everything's going to be different tomorrow, you'll see.'

'Good night, John.' I kissed his cheek.

'Mind you lock the door,' he said, going out.

'John!' I called after him.

'Yes?'

'Did Jason say anything ... anything about me, after he sent me away? Please tell me, whatever it was. Don't spare my feelings.'

'He said nothing about you,' replied John. 'Neither good nor ill. Good night, Annabel.'

I heard the motor launch leave from the companionway, and I imagined it carrying Jason and John across to the landing-stage below the Villa La Blanca; but I was unable to see them from the porthole because the *Dolphin* had swung at her anchor and was pointing in such a direction – towards the shore – that I was unable to see the villa from either my sleeping cabin or the bathroom. Half an hour later the launch came back. It was quite dark, with no moon. And it was hot, with a dry and dusty heat that was quite unlike any weather we had so far experienced in the Mediterranean.

I heard the shrill call of a bosun's pipe and a homely West Country voice calling the duty hands. This was followed by a patter of bare feet on the deck above my head – a curiously commonplace sound that drove away the feeling of lurking unease that seemed to have crept into every corner of my locked and brightly-lit cabin. It was half past eight. I decided to go up on deck and get a breath of fresh air before attempting sleep.

It was no cooler out in the night air. A million small insects swarmed about the lights that were strung the length of the foredeck under the canvas awnings. I went there because it commanded a view of the shore, towards which the great yacht was pointing. I stood right up in the 'eyes' of the vessel, above the gilded figurehead of the lovely sea creature from which she took her name, and looked out across the intervening space that separated me from the object of my hopeless love. As I did so, the full moon came out from behind a bank of clouds and showed the Villa La Blanca clearly against the skyline above. A single light burned in an upper window. Closing my eyes, I could imagine the circle of men seated round a table – Jason among them – with their eyes fixed, perhaps, upon a telephone instrument set in the middle of the table; an atmosphere of nerve-searing suspense as they waited for the news that the monster of the *Dolphin* had been apprehended.

As I stood there, the yacht seemed to give a sigh. The anchor chain creaked, and there was a perceptible movement. At the same moment, I felt a slight breeze disturbing my hair. And, as if the doors of some giant furnace had been opened out there in the darkness of the desert, the night grew suddenly hotter. I felt the touch of a new and unreasoning fear that could only have sprung from the garnered memories of my primitive ancestors : the fear of Nature and her elements.

Something was going to happen, something large and terrifying – I sensed it as surely as the deer who sniffs the innocent air and stands poised to flee.

A footfall on the deck behind me : it was the Second Officer, a bearded young man named Thomas, with whom I had barely exchanged a word since joining the *Dolphin*. He picked his way towards me, past the anchor chains and other pieces of nautical gear that littered the foredeck.

'Good evening to you, ma'am,' he said, saluting. 'I'm afraid we're going to be in for a bit of a blow.'

'A storm?' Even as I put the question, a gust of wind teased out a strand of my hair and fluttered it against my cheek.

'I could scarcely believe it when I looked at the barometer just now,' he said. 'Thought someone had been trying to play a trick on me. The bottom's dropped right out of the glass. Never seen anything like it.'

My unease deepened, for it seemed to me that Second

Officer Thomas was in a state of some anxiety. His next re-mark confirmed my impression.

'I've called the duty watch on deck. No point in taking any chances, for you get some funny weather in these parts, and there's only a quarter of the crew aboard tonight, and me the only watchkeeping officer.' He peered down the deck. 'Here come the bosun's mate and the duty engineer.'

The engineer was a dour Scot in greasy overalls, who for-ever wiped his hands on a piece of rag. He appeared to hold Second Officer Thomas in some contempt, a feeling that seemed to be shared by the young and rather bumptious bosun's mate.

It was the latter who opened the conversation, addressing Thomas. 'I've carried out your orders,' he said. 'All the loose gear on the upper deck's been secured and the hands are taking down the awnings now. It's going to be a bother, put-ting 'em up again in the morning. The skipper's not going to like it.'

'When you speak to me, you'll call me "sir",' said Thomas in a tight voice. 'And I'm not interested in your views on Captain Pelly.' He turned to the engineer. 'Macintosh, you'll raise steam for the main engine. How long will it take you?'

Macintosh wiped his hands anew. 'Ah'll be needin' that order in writing, meester,' he said.

Second Officer Thomas snorted. 'Don't bandy words with me, man! How long?'

'An hour,' said the other reluctantly. 'Mebbe a wee bit less.'

'Get on with it then!'

'Aye.' Macintosh turned and ambled slowly back the way he had come.

'Hurry, man!' shouted Second Officer Thomas. 'I don't want to get caught out in a gale in an open anchorage!'

The Scottish engineer did not perceptibly hasten his step.

Thomas whirled on the bosun's mate. 'You! Get the hands for'ard and clear away the second anchor in case of an emergency.'

The other raised a languid eyebrow. 'Now?' he demanded. 'Or after the lads have taken down the awnings, like you ordered?'

'*Sir!*' cried Thomas shrilly.

'Like you ordered – sir!'

'Do the anchor first!'

'Can't – sir!' said the other smugly. 'No steam to the capstan.'

'Tell Macintosh to get steam on deck!' shrieked Thomas. 'Do I have to think of everything?'

'Aye, aye – sir!' The young bosun's mate gave me something near to a wink and went.

Second Officer Thomas took off his cap and mopped his brow with a handkerchief. 'Nothing to get alarmed about I assure you, ma'am,' he said. 'Just the normal precautions, in case this hot southerly breeze develops into a sirocco – which is the name they give southerly gales in these parts.'

'I'm not in the least alarmed, Mr Thomas,' I told him, with more conviction than I felt. 'I'm sure you will be able to cope with an emergency.'

The sirocco struck Oran at a few minutes to nine, barely half an hour after I had gone up on deck, when there had been nothing but a fitful breeze to announce the cataclysm which was to come.

At a few minutes to nine, back in my cabin, I was suddenly catapulted from my dressing-table and across the floor, to land with my head against a chest of drawers, rendering myself dazed for some moments. When I got up, the *Dolphin* seemed to be lying on her side. I half-fell, half-clawed my way to the porthole and looked out at a small boat that was being carried past on the crest of a monstrous wave, its sail streaming in rags.

On deck – though I was not to know it – fatal disaster had already struck. While fighting to prepare the second anchor for lowering, both Second Officer Thomas and the young bosun's mate were swept overboard by the giant wave that I had see through the porthole. This same wave also tore the *Dolphin*'s anchor from its hold and carried her towards the harbour entrance and the open sea. With no steam for the engine and no hand at the wheel, the yacht was simply a plaything for the elements – and we in her the helpless victims.

I found my way to the top of the ladder leading to the boat deck and saw a trio of sailors gathered round one of the lifeboats, which they were trying to lower. I called to them, but the cry was snatched from my lips on the screaming wind. Next instant, the vessel heeled over more sharply and the men were immersed in foaming waters up to their waists; struggling, clawing, fighting to remain alive and on their feet, they bravely persisted in their task. Somehow, I knew, the miracle would come to pass: they would lower the lifeboat.

Escape . . . rescue . . .

The theme ran through my mind. With it came the memory of the weak and helpless creature who lay sleeping or unconscious in the sick bay. Melloney – I must go to Melloney. Then, either by my own strength, or with Nanny's help (and she must surely be with her darling), I would carry her up on to the boat deck before the lifeboat left the doomed yacht.

I set off, clawing my way from handhold to handhold, while the *Dolphin* pitched and rolled, first one way and then the other. The night was jet black. No stars. The air was all sound and fury; torrid wind and choking sand.

Below, it was quieter. The electric lamps still burned. The rich carpets underfoot gave a lie to the imminence of disaster. Nor was the motion so violent. It occurred to me that the worst of the sirocco might have gone past, and the sailors must surely now be able quite easily to lower the boat. I must hurry.

I came to the door of the sick bay, open as before. The mosquito curtain had been looped back, revealing the dimly-lit interior. One shaded lamp alone burned near the bed – which was empty and tousled.

'Melloney! – Melloney!'

I called out to her, a breathless panic rising in my throat, threatening to choke away the cries. I rushed into the adjoining compartment. The glass door of Dr Weems's medicine cabinet swung idly with every movement of the vessel, and an empty tumbler slowly rolled from one end of the floor to the other.

Melloney had gone. Had she, then, been saved? Had Nanny

got her on deck in time, perhaps, to be rescued in another lifeboat? Had they left the *Dolphin*! If so, it was likely that I was the last person still on board – I and the sailors who were labouring to float the lifeboat.

But – what if they had done it already, and departed? That would mean, in truth, that I was the only person on a foundering yacht which was being driven out to heaven knows what perils on the hot breath of the sirocco!

I retraced my steps, calling out as I stumbled along the empty corridors and companionways. Reaching the boat deck again, I saw that my worst fears had not been unfounded: the lifeboat had gone, and the sailors with it. I was alone in the abandoned vessel!

Clinging there, against the sickening motion of the sweeping combers, with the sand-filled wind tearing at my hair and searing my skin, I took stock of the peril I was in: the *Dolphin* was being swept in a direction that was roughly parallel with the coast, across the wide bay, with her port side presented to the force of the gale, so that she moved crabwise, inclining her decks steeply to starboard. I had no way of telling what lay ahead, but the shoreline seemed temptingly near, and though I am not a great swimmer, I nevertheless felt that, given the support of some floating object, I might reach dry land.

It was then I remembered the life-jacket that hung in the wardrobe in my cabin ...

I was half way down the companionway when I heard, above the howl of the gale in the rigging, the sound of footfalls on the deck above my head, and then a voice calling out my name.

'Miss Trewella! ... Annabel Trewella, where are you?'

It sent me racing down the long corridor towards my cabin door, my whole body shrinking against the anticipation of a hand reaching out to take me – for I knew by his voice that my companion aboard the *Dolphin* was Dr Weems.

chapter ten

The waking nightmare began: a nightmare that I have re-
lived a hundred times in the dark hours, with a hundred
variations of detail. In the reality, he was at the door and
forcing his way in before I had time to close it and turn the
key in the lock, or to bar the door with a piece of furniture;
I had to rely upon my own puny strength, while knowing that
I was pitting myself against a madman.

'Let me in! I want to come in!' His voice rose above the
wind that sounded in the companionway beyond, as inch by
inch he opened the gap. Presently his hand appeared round the
side of the door: muscular, capable-looking. My citadel was
breached.

'Please!' I pleaded. 'I've done nothing to you. Why should
you want to hurt me?'

'Hurt you?'

The intolerable pressure suddenly eased. I found myself
able to close the gap, till only his fingertips prevented me from
shutting the door and locking it.

'You think I would hurt you, Annabel?' He said this with
a break in his voice.

Silence for a moment, and then – the inexplicable, the unbelievable . . .

He began to weep.

Long-drawn-out and choking sobs, telling of a misery of
heart and mind that must have been quite insupportable.

I had heard it before, in that very place, coming to me
through the night, by devious ways, through the length of
the great yacht.

He – Weems – was the one I had named in my mind 'The
Secret Prisoner'.

There was no resistance to my pressure, and his hand fell
away. I could have closed the door; instead, I opened it and
looked upon the creature who stood there, his head bowed,
one hand pressed against his streaming eyes.

Was this, I asked myself, the monster of the *Dolphin*? Was
it possible that the creature cowering before me could be the

demented killer for whom the entire police and army in Oran were at present searching?

The yacht gave a violent lurch, and he almost fell into my arms. I backed away – but with less alarm than I would have believed possible a few moments before; and I was able to watch with almost a cool detachment as he swayed across the cabin and slumped into an armchair, where he gave himself up to a new paroxysm of grief.

'Dr Weems!' I cried. 'I demand that you tell me what this is all about.'

'You think I would hurt you?' His tear-streaked face looked up at me. 'You, whom I esteem so highly . . . whom I would have saved . . .'

'Saved?' I echoed. 'Saved from what?'

The mild eyes – peering at me in a pitifully short-sighted manner without the spectacles he normally wore – removed the last vestige of fear from my mind. Here was a creature who would not, could not, willingly hurt a fly. Or so I believed . . .

'You should have heeded my warning when there was still time. You shouldn't have pried so deeply into your sister's end. Now there's only one way in which I can save you . . .'

I felt my skin prickle with terror as Dr Weems put his hand in his coat pocket and took out a pistol.

'No!' I cried.

The mild eyes were glazed with sadness. 'There's no other way, Annabel,' he said. 'It has to be done, don't you see? Or you will never be happy. Trust me, Annabel. Believe me when I tell you I'm doing it for your benefit, my dear.'

I backed away against the dressing-table, and my hand fell upon a silver-mounted looking-glass that was part of the rich furnishings of the cabin. I had a wild notion to hurl it across at him in the hope of striking the weapon from his hand, and then to duck and flee – out into the night of storm, to take my chance in the raging seas.

'Forgive me,' he pleaded. 'Forgive me for what I have to do, Annabel. I've no alternative, for I'm in it too deeply. The people ashore – the French authorities – know what I've done and are searching for me. I had to bribe a native boatman with

every penny I had to smuggle me back aboard. Annabel ...'
He tried to focus his gaze more clearly upon me.

'You're insane!' I cried. 'Insane!'

'Not insane!' he hurled back at me. 'I have been driven to it, by forces stronger than myself. When I tell you how ...' He lowered his head, choking with fresh sobs, and the pistol wavered in his hand.

Now was my chance to escape. I turned my head, to measure the distance to the door – and found myself looking at Melloney.

It was a repetition of the vision that had met my gaze earlier that evening: Melloney clinging to the side of the door, her flimsy shift draped about her like a grave-cloth, her lovely eyes staring.

'Go away, Melloney!' I screamed. 'He's got a gun, and he's insane!'

She made no move, but continued to cling there, swaying with the motion of the storm, her gaze fixed on the man in the chair.

Weems raised his pistol, unsteadily took aim. I saw his lips tremble as he stared down the barrel.

'The last of the deaths!' he cried. 'The settlement of the score!'

'Melloney!' I screamed. 'Throw yourself aside!'

Weems's pistol was aimed directly at her breast.

I had the impulse to throw myself forward and take the bullet intended for her, but she must have sensed my intention, because she raised one slim hand and waved me aside.

'Stay where you are!' she cried. 'He won't pull the trigger!' And she laughed ...

I was still staring at her, trying to tell myself that I was not hearing what I was hearing, nor seeing what I was seeing, when Weems's pistol thudded to the floor and he sank to his knees beside the chair, face buried in hands.

'What did I tell you, my dear?' sneered Melloney Lumley.

And before my dumbfounded gaze, she let go of the door with which she had been steadying herself against the motion of the vessel – and walked with swift, elegant and long-legged strides across to where Weems's pistol lay.

She stooped and picked it up.

'Surprised, Annabel darling?' she asked. And aimed the dark muzzle of the pistol at me.

Melloney said we should all go down to the saloon for farewell champagne – as she put it. Dr Weems and I went ahead, she following with the levelled pistol.

Down the boat deck, where the spindrift rose high over our heads and the sirocco, undiminished, lashed the *Dolphin* ever onwards; down the carpeted staircase, past the pagan girl and her dolphin, with the pure fountain still gushing – though rank sea-water poured down the plum-coloured carpeting and ran in puddles across the mosaic floor below; down into the saloon, where Nanny Bagley brought a foaming bottle of champagne and filled four glasses.

'A funeral libation for four,' cried Melloney, with a strange madness in her too-perfect eyes.

Her hair was unbound and floating free. Under the crisp light of the chandeliers, I saw tiny lines about her eyes and a coarsening of the skin at her neck that I had never noticed before; and I remembered how she had never presented herself to my gaze in full light, but only in the shadow of a parasol, an awning, or by suave candlelight. I wondered how it was that I had always looked upon her as a girl, younger than I. Here was a woman whose decaying beauty would soon need hours of attention before she could show herself; a whole palette of cosmetics.

She must have noticed my critical gaze, because she tossed her head in defiance.

'You are not drinking, my dear Annabel,' she said.

'You're not crippled at all,' I whispered. 'It was all a sham!'

'It began as a necessity,' she said, amused. 'And ended up as a caprice, almost as a dedicated mode of existence. A "professional invalid", as that absurd Oriana Topsham very shrewdly dubbed me – that is what I became. My adoptive father – that mealy-mouthed draper who bought himself a knighthood by lavishing free soup on the deserving poor – caught me one day torturing a kitten and realized that little Melloney, whom he had taken from a foundlings' home and

made his own daughter, was not *quite* the paragon of girl-
hood that he had imagined. He threatened to send me away
to school. A particularly strict school. The following day, I
contrived my ... accident.'

'But ...' I began. 'Harriet's part in it ...'

She laughed and held out her glass to the indulgent Nanny
Bagley, who topped it up. 'Poor darling Harriet,' she said. 'As
a result of my lying out in that wood, in the rain, waiting to
be found, I really did catch pneumonia, and Harriet decidedly
was insensible from the effects of her appalling cough linctus
when I tried to get up out of bed. It was after I had chained
poor Harriet to me with bonds of deathless devotion that I
developed a taste for power – the power of the professional
invalid. I also had another reason, as you will presently hear.'

'I don't understand ...' I glanced towards Dr Weems, who
was slumped in a chair, staring at the woman with fascination
mixed with loathing. 'The doctors' verdicts ... the specialists
whom you visited all over Europe?'

She laughed. 'We certainly travelled far and wide, and a
very amusing time we had – but the only physician who ever
set eyes on me was darling Trevor Weems, who did as I told
him for love of me, didn't you, darling?'

'She-devil!' hissed Weems. 'You defile the state of woman-
hood! But for you, I – I could have been the most brilliant
practitioner of my generation ... it was predicted of me at
medical school ...'

'A prediction,' retorted Melloney tartly, 'which obviously
did not take into account your addiction to the bottle, and
sundry other small vices we will not go into on this occasion.'

Weems groaned and buried his face in his hands once more.

Light was dawning in the innermost recesses of my mind,
and unanswered questions teemed and jostled to be expressed.
One question – one monstrous accusation – needed to be
levelled against the lovely, depraved creature who reclined
on the sofa opposite, a champagne glass in one hand, a pistol
in the other, regarding me with her amused contemptuous eyes.

'You let my sister go to her grave,' I cried, 'believing that
she destroyed your life. You let her go on believing it, so that
she would remain your slave.'

Her eyes danced with a strange ecstasy. 'How true,' she murmured. 'You express it very well, my dear. Poor Harriet was, in every way, my "slave". She wanted to die for me, to placate her silly conscience. And in the end she did ... just that.'

'*Died* for you?'

'Yes,' she said calmly. 'That vulgar, handsome creature who used to walk out with her – that gamekeeper whom she wanted to marry – they hanged her for killing him, you know. And she took it upon herself, with all the passion of a saint embracing martyrdom.'

'You mean' – I stared at her in disbelief – 'she was *innocent*?'

Melloney shrugged. 'What is innocence? If this yacht continues drifting all the way to Greece or Turkey, we may yet have time to discuss the question. But – no, poor Harriet didn't kill her big handsome swain. I did.'

'You?'

'He was – very silly!' She wrinkled her nose disdainfully. 'I amused myself by being slightly flirtatious with him when Harriet was not about. One day, the stupid, ignorant brute took me seriously and tried to ... embrace me. I had the paper-knife with me on the table. So I ...'

'You killed him in Harriet's sitting-room,' I cried. 'When the others came in, they found Harriet alone with the dying man, and she was speaking to him. She said: "*I would not have had it happen for the world, my darling.*"'

'To *me*,' said Melloney with a touch of smugness. 'She was saying it to me. I was behind the curtain, where she had carried me, to be out of sight when the others came.'

I stared at her, appalled by the blandness of an evil that – save for a slight hardening about the eyes – had left unmarked that vision of beauty and innocence.

'You let my sister sacrifice herself for you!' I cried. 'In all the years between, haven't you known one single pang of conscience?'

'No, my dear,' she said briskly. 'Why should I?' Then accompanied by the patient smile of a teacher putting a simple point to a particularly stupid child, she added: 'The silly

221

woman died happy in the belief that she had made amends for crippling me. I presented her with a rather splendid martyrdom.'

More champagne had been opened. Nanny Bagley was the worse for drink and spilling more than she poured. The motion of the yacht had increased, and ankle-deep water sluiced back and forth across the great saloon. Everything that could fall had fallen: a jumble of broken glassware and china, mixed with silver and gilt items, wax fruits, smaller pieces of statuary, moved to and fro with the passage of the sea-water across the ruined carpet. Pictures hung at drunken angles from all the walls. Most of the electric lamps had gone out.

Melloney sat in the flattering glow of half-light. Still bland and smiling, still guiding the conversation: the presiding hostess at a nightmare soirée.

She was addressing me. 'Given that you knew nothing of all this when you came aboard, dear Annabel, you really have learned quite a lot. Much too much for your own good.'

'She knew nothing when she came,' confirmed Nurse Bagley, unsteadily refilling her glass. 'You sent me and Weems to search her cabin, but we found nothing.'

'Soiling my hands with such work!' cried Dr Weems. 'I who could have been the leading practitioner of my generation. I was so ashamed . . . I cried out for help.'

'I saw your cry for help,' I told him. I swung round to face Nurse Bagley. 'Someone came to my cabin on an earlier occasion,' I cried, 'and killed my little bird!'

'She did that at my order,' said Melloney. 'You had the impertinence to make cow's eyes at Jason Saltram over lunch. It was when he described his ride across the desert to Sidi-bel-Abbès. Do you remember?'

I remembered very well: how our eyes had met and I had looked away, suddenly confused.

Melloney was speaking again. 'Before the *Dolphin* summer was even mooted,' she said, 'Jason sent for Weems and asked him, in strictest confidence, if Melloney could – as he put it – "bear the strain of marriage". Upon being told that she could, Jason began to make his arrangements. These he made discreetly, tactfully, even secretly – after his own manner. He didn't even inform me.

'I knew, when he brought that ring aboard – had that silly old woman collect it in London – that it was to be *my* engagement ring. I laughed at them, because they thought it was for Oriana. That night, I couldn't trust myself to face you all at dinner. I was so elated that I wanted to dance and sing. I stayed in my cabin, didn't I, Nanny? We drank champagne, didn't we? We made our plans: once I was Jason's wife, my condition would suddenly improve; Weems would announce the possibility of a near-miraculous cure – later to be confirmed by the great specialists of Europe. What plans we made!'

'And the champagne we drank!' sniggered Nanny, rocking herself backwards and forwards in her chair, so that the wine spilt over her hands and down her skirts.

'But Jason didn't give me the ring!' grated Melloney, suddenly harsh. 'So I sent Weems to see him. That was in Gibralter.'

I remembered. 'I was with Jason – with the Commander – when Dr Weems came in,' I supplied. 'He said he had something to discuss that concerned you. Then I joined you on the poop deck.'

'Yes,' she said. 'We were talking about John Bennett.'

'You asked me if he had tried to flirt with me when we were ashore.'

Melloney said: 'As soon as I saw Weems coming back, I knew from his face that something had gone terribly wrong.'

'You had some kind of seizure,' I said.

'For once,' she replied flatly, 'it was genuine. And for this reason: when Weems asked Jason what had happened to his plans to marry me, his reply had been that he had changed his mind. His words were "My heart is elsewhere"!'

'Oriana!' I cried. 'And so . . .'

'And so,' said Melloney, 'Oriana had to die.'

Some fluke of the driving winds had brought the *Dolphin* round, so that the drifting vessel pointed her sharp prow the way she was going. This eased the dreadful rolling, but caused a new and alarming motion in the other direction. Only by clinging tightly to my chair (which was attached to the deck) was I able to prevent myself from being thrown forward the whole length of the saloon every time the yacht buried her prow deeply into the tortured seas.

My three companions of the living nightmare had not moved. Weems remained staring at the woman who had destroyed him; Nanny Bagley was slumped in a chair, her head lolling, and every so often she laughed aloud at some secret thought passing through her befuddled mind. Only Melloney remained cool, poised and unchanged.

Melloney said, very seriously: 'You must remember, my dear Annabel, that I love Jason Saltram, that I have always loved him – ever since I was a little girl and he a smooth-cheeked midshipman – and that I shall love him through death and beyond. Given that great truth' – she treated me to one of her most brilliant and engaging smiles – 'you will understand why I had no hesitation in removing a contemptible obstacle like Oriana Topsham.'

'Does he – does Jason – love you in return?' I asked her. It was something I had to know once and for all.

'Frankly – no,' she replied. 'Nor does he realize the intensity of my feelings for him. He thinks I have an ... infatuation for him. Because of that he is – was – willing to indulge me by making me his wife for what he believed to be the last few months of my life.'

'It would've ... would've been a lovely wedding,' wailed Nanny. 'My darling girl all in white!' She began to cry.

'It was so easy,' said Melloney. 'While you were all watching those silly battleships, I got up from my litter. Half a dozen swift paces towards poor Oriana ... a push in the middle of her back at the moment that the *Dolphin*'s sailors were giving three cheers. You never heard her scream. I did. It proved an admirable descant to the cheering.'

'You're evil!' I cried. 'Evil! To have destroyed an innocent life ...'

'Innocent – that's good!' Throwing back her head, she laughed, and Bagley joined her in a hideous cackle. 'Did you hear that, Nanny? Dear Annabel has all unknowingly stumbled upon the cream of the jest.'

'Heh! S'funny, all right,' confirmed Bagley, and she winked at me. 'S'funny when you know the joke!'

'You can joke about a woman's murder!' I cried.

Melloney raised a pale, slender hand to silence her nurse. Then she turned to me, and her face was a mask of calm and gravity. I sensed that what she was about to say lay at the very heart of all her actions that dreadful night.

She said: 'When Jason didn't give me the ring, soon after we left England, I assumed that his change of plan was due to the fact that he had fallen for Oriana Topsham, that she was the creature who had – to paraphrase his own remark – directed his heart elsewhere. For that, I killed her. But I was wrong.'

'I don't understand you,' I said, puzzled.

'I was wrong,' she repeated. 'We were all wrong. He bought the ring for me – yes. But he hesitated to give it . . . after . . .'

'After what?' I demanded.

'After he had set eyes on . . . *you!*'

Swept on through the night. With Melloney's hate-filled voice dinning in my ears, and a great glory spreading like a rich cloak about me . . .

'I loved him,' said Melloney. 'And I love him still. To utter distraction. I tried every way to win him. I was Diana the Huntress on my splendid horse. I was the belle of every ball.

'When all that failed, I tried to bind him to me with bonds of compassion. Harriet presented me with the idea of becoming a tragic invalid. I was content with his sympathy, his pity – anything. I am a proud person, but I would have crawled on my hands and knees through the mire to win a loving glance from Jason Saltram. But no use . . . no use . . .

'Along comes some coarse country-bred wench with rough hands and a thin veneer of gentility that she picked up at third hand from heaven knows where . . . you have only to look at him once, he has only to set eyes on you (great heaven – you were not aboard a day and a night before he had changed his mind about marrying me!) and he's yours! Yours!

'*Can you understand why I hate you so much!*'

She finished with a scream that cracked and broke in the end. She raised the pistol and pointed it at me, so that I thought she was going to kill me there and then. And I desperately didn't want to die – not then. Especially not then!

'Why – why did you kill Jack Maugham?' I threw at her.

The muzzle of the pistol wavered slightly, but did not drop.

'In the dark hours of the night,' she said, 'I am – was – in the habit of creeping out on deck, unseen, for some exercise, to stretch my limbs. One night, Maugham saw me. I think he was going to confide in you – indeed, I saw you go to keep your rendezvous with him.'

'You passed me in the dark corridor leading to the poop,' I murmured, horrified, remembering.

'I had just assisted him to a watery grave,' she said. 'I'm very strong, and it's the easiest thing imaginable, to creep up behind an unsuspecting person ...'

I could bear to hear no more, so I interrupted her, still to keep her talking, to make her forget the weapon in her hand, aimed at me ...

'Who was it who followed John and me ashore at Gibraltar?' I asked her. 'Was it Dr Weems?'

'Weems?' She almost spat the word, and threw the wretched man a glance that made him flinch. 'No, it was me. I knew John was going to propose marriage to you. Would you believe it, my dear Annabel – John confided in me? And I gave the project my blessing. It was your last chance of life, Annabel. If you had accepted John Bennett, I know that Jason would have abandoned his unspoken hope that – one day when I was dead and gone – he would be able to marry you. For the irony is that, in presenting Jason with the idea that he must marry me to make my last days happy, I also gave him the knowledge that he would soon be free to marry you without hurting me.'

'But I refused John – and you must have realized that, because you were watching from the roof opposite!'

'From that moment,' she said viciously, 'you were condemned to die! And that would have happened before now, but for Weems's constant interference, his arrant *treachery*!'

'Locked her cabin door on my darling that night, he did!' broke in Nanny Bagley. 'And her wandering about at dead of night in seaman's clothes.'

'I warned you time and time again!' cried Weems brokenly. 'I told you that there must be no more killing, but you wouldn't listen, so I locked the door, so that they'd discover you – and all my torments would have been over!'

'I stripped off the seaman's clothes,' said Melloney, looking at me, as if for approval of her astuteness. 'I was wearing my shift underneath. All I had to do then was to call out for Flack, who always slept in a hammock slung in the corridor, within earshot. I waited for him in the shadows. I carried a knife with me always when I was out at night. And I struck at him – twice!'

'We found you, and John carried you to the sick bay!' I cried.

'Where I confronted my faithful Weems,' snapped Melloney, with another vicious glance at the tormented man. 'And told him to go and unlock my cabin door immediately.'

'I should have refused you then,' wailed that wretched creature. 'A hundred times, in the dark hours of the night, I have cursed myself for my weakness then.'

Melloney reviled him with a contemptuous epithet, but I was not listening to her. While she, Weems and Nanny Bagley went into a grotesque quarrel, my mind was trying to encompass the beauty that was filling the whole world about me and shutting out all else.

Jason loved me. He had fallen in love with me on sight.

Perhaps, even, while I was defying him to take my hansom cab in Falmouth railway station yard – and me in my battered straw with the bedraggled feather – he was already choosing me from out of all the women in the world to be his own. The glory of it warmed my heart.

Perhaps, when I went to his cabin and was shocked to learn who he was, the magic had already taken place; so that, even while he was pretending to deal with a small emergency on the telephone, he was rejoicing to have found me again.

And later, when the knowledge of my love for him had burst upon me, high on the Pillar of Hercules, we had joined hands without knowing of the other's feelings.

From this thought stemmed another: Jason would never know of my love for him, not while I still lived – for John Bennett would feel bound to keep my secret till he heard of my death. And I knew that Melloney Lumley had no intention of my surviving that night of tempest. The sea would have me – or she would.

I must live at all costs!

I was searching my mind for some means by which I could accomplish this, when the *Dolphin* struck the rocks.

The first impact was like the tearing of a great bolt of coarse calico, followed by the shattering of all the glass on earth. The *Dolphin* was brought up sharply in her onward plunging with a jar that pitched me to the heeling deck. I rolled on to the thick carpet and a wave of foul-smelling sea-water and debris sluiced over me. When I regained my breath and looked round the lights had gone out – save one above the sofa upon which Melloney still reclined, the upholstered back-rest having held her in place during the impact.

The electric lamp picked out the burnished lights of her flaxen hair and showed up the magnolia whiteness of her face and shoulders. The revolver hung limply in her right hand. Her eyes were shadowed and inscrutable.

After the impact, the *Dolphin* remained for a while on a more even keel, while waves cascaded down upon the decks above us. The yacht seemed to be held in the grip of the rock fangs that had penetrated her – but not for long. There came another tearing and rending. The floor lurched and slid beneath my feet as the vessel parted company from the rocks and became once again the plaything of the sea and the wind. But she was not the same *Dolphin* as before; mortally wounded by the rocks, her movements were sluggish from the weight of water that was pouring into her.

Looking down, I saw, with a shock of horror, that the water in the saloon was rising fast and plucking at my skirts.

We were sinking!

'Melloney, my darling girl!' Nurse Bagley's voice rose in a screech as she splashed forward into the lamplight and reached out for the figure on the sofa. 'Don't stay here and die. Come with Nanny. Nanny will see you safe. Up on deck, lovey ... we'll find a way.'

'No one leaves this saloon,' came the implacable reply. 'No one – we all perish together!'

But not Annabel Trewella, I told myself – not the Annabel who is loved, and loves in return. She will fight for her life.

Keeping my gaze firmly fixed upon the hand that limply held the gun, I backed slowly away; towards the shadows beyond the ring of lamplight, towards the saloon door and the staircase.

'Stay where you are!' rasped Melloney. The hand tensed. The black muzzle swung towards me.

'Don't harm her – let her go, for pity's sake!' Dr Weems came through the swirling water towards the sofa, staggering with every step, steadying himself against pieces of furniture. 'Melloney, for all that I've done for you in the past, for the sins I've committed for you – I beg you to give her a chance to get out of here.'

'Do you think I would give her a chance in a million to become ... *his*?' She lifted her head, so that I could see the hatred in her eyes.

Meeting her stare, I did not see Weems when he leapt for her – not till his hand closed about her right wrist. He almost had the revolver from her grasp, when a lurch of the vessel sent him toppling across her. Another lurch brought him upright again, and he was still holding her wrist.

There was a flash in the half-darkness, and the revolver went off with a deafening report.

The weapon, wrenched from Melloney's hand when Weems reeled back, fell into the swirling black water. Weems, clutching at his chest, waded a couple of unsteady paces towards me. I went to meet him, stretching out my hands to support him.

Together, we edged our way slowly down the sloping deck

towards the door and the staircase beyond, where the water touched my waist. It had not reached so high in the middle of the saloon, but the level was rising fast.

One last backward glance ...

Melloney Lumley was just as I had seen her when I first came aboard the *Dolphin*: reclining on the gilded sofa, her slippered feet stretched out on the cushions. She was no longer looking in my direction; indeed, she appeared to be composing herself for sleep, seemingly uncaring of the black waters that were already lapping over the edge of the pretty pink upholstery.

Up on the boat deck, we met the awesome vision of great peaks jutting hundreds of feet into the night air. The doomed yacht was drifting close to a rocky headland. The roar of the waters shut out all else; when I had helped Dr Weems to lie down on the more sheltered side of the deck, I had to bend my head almost to his cheek to catch his words.

'Don't try to talk,' I cried. 'Rest yourself. They'll send life-boats after us, for sure, and we'll be picked up by daylight.'

'I'll never see another dawn,' he said.

'You will – you must!' I told him.

Presently he said: 'I loved her once, you know. Her beauty drove me mad. I wrote letters to her. Innocent letters – but capable of being twisted into something evil in the mouths of clever lawyers. "Unprofessional conduct" – and Melloney little more than a child, though already far gone in vileness. She was quick to see her advantage and make use of it: tormented me with the threat of disgrace and ruin. With imprisonment. In the end, I became her ... creature.'

'You've no need to tell me this,' I said. 'I'm not your judge, Dr Weems.'

He appeared not to hear me. 'I connived in all the lies,' he said. 'About her condition, about Harriet Cadge – everything. Only in one thing I defied her. I defied her about you. And even in that, I showed no constancy.' The thin moonlight momentarily brightened a tear as it coursed down his cheek. 'Forgive me, for I found her the Arab assassin, gave him her order to kill you.'

I pressed his hand: it had grown cold. 'You repaid the debt,' I whispered in his ear above the crash of the breakers. 'You saved my life just now.'

'When she heard that the attempt had failed,' he said. 'When she knew that you were alive and in Sidi-bel-Abbès – with Saltram – I think she went insane. You were to be brought back immediately, and you were to die. I lost my nerve then; gave her a powerful soporific to prevent her from doing any harm, to give me time to think. I fled ashore – away from it all, where I could decide what to do.' A weak smile touched a corner of his lips, from which issued a thin trickle of blood. 'I decided for you, Annabel. I came back, to try to save you from her.'

'And you did save me,' I reminded him.

His hand clutched mine. There was no strength in the grip; the life was fading out of him. A choking cough racked his body, preventing him from replying. When it was over, he whispered, so faintly that I had to lay my cheek against his cold one.

'Sometimes,' he said. 'Sometimes, when I looked at you, I had a vision of what might have been. The love that I might . . . might have . . .'

His voice trailed away into silence. He was gone.

The *Dolphin* was dying.

I sensed it. Barefoot now, I felt it by very contact with the woodwork of her deck. Her movements were sluggish and sick, like those of an animal in mortal agony as it crawls away to die in a dark corner. The sirocco continued to drive her on, wallowing under the burden of the water within her, her foredeck awash and the gilded figurehead out of sight.

Under the long rock wall of the headland, before she had time to sink, she struck again. Again, the terrible grating of tortured metal on splintering rock; followed by the un-forgettable sound of her back breaking.

The *Dolphin* split in two parts at the rear end of the boat deck, close by the companionway leading down to the saloon. The rear portion immediately slid off the rocky shelf and plunged out of my sight into the roaring waste of water.

With it went the saloon.

The remainder – bearing me – stayed in the grip of the rocks; no longer a proud yacht with a soul of her own, but a corpse – the wreck of the *Dolphin*. And even in death there was no peace: the wolfish seas fought over the remains; pounding down upon the wreck in order to tear it from its uneasy perch.

Crouched on what was left of the boat deck, clinging for my life to a metal upright, I waited for the end. With every onslaught of white water that came crashing along the heeling deck, my grip grew weaker. Dr Weems's body had been carried over the side, together with the remainder of the boats and everything movable. Everything but me.

I stared up at the cliff walls, and then at the spent breakers that clawed with long white fingertips up its rocky face. When I lost my grip, as lose it I soon must, my end would come in that maelstrom beneath the cliff.

Images came and went in my mind: the recollections of times past that are traditionally granted to the dying. I saw my half-sister Harriet as she said goodbye to me for the last time, before returning to her willing martyrdom; and I wept for her. Then I was back in St Finn, where Lumley charity had established me, and where, but for Sir David Lumley's whim, I might have stayed, eking out my grey days as a spinster teacher.

Do something for that poor child Annabel Trewella when she comes of age.

Those words, addressed to Jason Saltram, had been enough to deliver me out of obscurity to – what?

To a nightmare death on a desolate scrap of coast in a part of the world that, but for chance, might have remained a place in a school atlas. To the agony of a seemingly hopeless love that would now never be requited. To oblivion.

Why, then, did my heart sing?

Why, when my hands were only holding on to life by the slenderest thread of energy, was my whole being coloured with a glorious radiance?

Because I loved, and was loved.

The tears and misunderstandings were behind, the doubts

and sad hopes forgotten. I had triumphed over my fears and frailties. For this was the truth of it: I would not have retraced my journey by one single step. Given the opportunity of a second chance of life, I would have chosen to make the same journey all over again.

Suddenly, I was very tired, and a great roaring filled my whole world. Everything was drifting away from me, all feeling turning to numbness. I was beyond hurt, beyond pain. My journey was all but finished: all that was asked of me now was to make one small step across the gulf that seperated life from death. To let go with both hands.

I breathed his name – Jason – savouring it. And I spoke it again when all the waters of the world rushed in and bore me off, through days and nights that were filled with the sound of many voices – all calling to me.

The voices grew louder. One of them was strangely familiar. John Bennett's voice!

'She's alive! I've got her breathing again!'

I opened my eyes to darkness. My cheek was pressed against wet woodwork that smelt of rotting shellfish, and someone was pressing hard against my back and shoulders, forcing water out of my lungs. I choked, and drew in a sobbing breath of air that tasted like the rarest nectar.

I was saved. I was alive.

We were in a large boat, a sort of lifeboat, pulled by five oarsmen. At the tiller crouched the small, stout figure of M. Cambronne, the harbourmaster of Oran. As the craft was lifted high on a passing comber, he pointed back the way we had come and shouted something to me in excited French that was immediately snatched from his lips by the tearing wind.

I was huddled in the stern, wrapped in a thick blanket, with John Bennett's arm round my shoulders.

'He's pointing to what's left of the *Dolphin*,' said John. 'Take a look, Annabel.'

On the next rising wave, the dark cliff wall came in view behind us, with white water lashing at its foot and among the tangled rocks. Half of the poor *Dolphin* – less than half – see-sawed perilously upon the rocks with water breaking right over her. How I could have survived there for so long, how they could have got close enough to rescue me, was beyond all belief.

'The sirocco was blowing from the south-west,' explained John. 'And it carried her right out of the harbour and across the mouths of two shallow bays, towards that headland – the Cap de l'Aiguille. A few feet to the left and she might have cleared the headland and continued on her way into the relative safety of the open sea – which was what Jason was hoping would happen. But I guess the *Dolphin* was right out of luck.'

I shuddered. There was something I needed to know.

'John . . .' I began.

'No need for you to say a thing,' John said, hugging my shoulders fondly. 'That can all wait. One thing I'm going to tell *you*, though: Jason Saltram and I had plenty of opportunity to talk while we were waiting for news in the Villa La Blanca. And before you start accusing me, I'm going to tell you that red-hot pincers wouldn't have dragged your secret from my lips. I never gave Jason a hint of your feelings for him – neither before nor after he confided in me. Now – can you guess what he confided in me, huh?' The first light of dawn was lightening the tumbled sky above his head, and showed that he was grinning down at me.

'Yes,' I replied.

His face fell. 'Oh, you can?'

I nodded. 'I found out tonight. Where is he, John? Where is Jason?'

'Well, I'll be –' cried John.

M. Cambronne was shouting and pointing to somewhere away on our right. When we rose on the next wave, another and similar boat could be seen coming obliquely towards us. The morning light touched the men's oars as they rose and fell in unison.

'Monsieur le Commandaire!' cried Cambronne.

The lean tallness of Jason Saltram marked him out from the others. He stood by the helmsman, dark-cloaked and sombre like a bird of prey, with a great weight of despair hunching his broad shoulders.

'Jason insisted on taking the seaward search,' said John. 'He believed that the *Dolphin* would weather the Cape, but he was wrong for once.' He stood up in the boat and, waving his arms wildly, he shouted across the foam-clad wavetops that separated us. 'Do you hear me, Saltram? – it's all right! We've found her, do you hear? She's safe! Annabel's safe!'

'*Annabel's safe . . .*'

I shall be grateful to the end of my life that I was close enough to see the effect of those shouted words upon the dark figure in the stern of the other boat: to see the heavy burden sloughed from those bowed shoulders; to see him raise his head; to know, from the way he spread out his arms, that he was shouting his thanks to the heavens for my deliverance.

M. Cambronne put over his helm, and the man steering the other boat did likewise. The two craft slanted towards each other. And with every foot that we drew nearer to each other, I strained my eyes for my first sight of his face.

epilogue

The wreck of the *Dolphin* remained for many months on the rocks beneath the towering walls of Cap de l'Aiguille. On the calm days that followed the terrible sirocco they went out and salvaged all that remained – including my personal belongings from my cabin. Shortly after, another freak storm finished the sea's work and drove the half-hull off the rocky ledge and into deep water.

The after-end – the part containing the saloon – was never found and likely never will be; though divers sought, they sought in vain. The sea bed shelves sharply just off the Cape; somewhere, five hundred fathoms or more beneath the Mediterranean, lies the tomb of Melloney Lumley and her faithful nurse.

The day following the final disappearance of the wreck, Jason Saltram and I were married by the British consul in Oran – with John Bennett acting as best man by Jason's request, thereby indicating that all ill-feeling was at an end. For the man I loved possessed his full share of human imperfections, and a tendency to jealousy was prominent among them. I well remembered his fury after John had escorted me to see the police inspector in Gibraltar and taken me to tea; not to mention our conversation on the way to Sidi-bel-Abbès, when, the flames of his jealousy having been fanned by Melloney telling him that I was scheming to marry John for his money, he as good as sent me packing!

Melloney – the name keeps coming back. I suppose we shall never entirely be rid of her memory. Sometimes I seem to heard the sound of her laughter and sense the curious magic of her presence. With benefit of hindsight, we all now know that her attraction had been like that of an exotic and poisonous flower: it spelt death to touch her. We shall never know how many suffered from that fatal touch.

My talisman against her memory became, and will remain, the memory of my half-sister.

Poor, ordinary Harriet whom I never really knew, or even liked very much. Her actions shine out like a beacon in the darkness of evil that surrounds her end. The thought must have preyed on Melloney's and Nurse Bagley's minds that Harriet had written a true confession – handed it, sealed, to her lawyer, perhaps, to give to me after Melloney's expected death. But Harriet had done no such thing; her sacrifice had been total, complete, unsullied by second thoughts, recriminations, regrets. An act of love.

Immediately after the wedding, we all went our separate ways: John Bennett boarded a westbound P & O liner for the first stage of his journey home to Boston – his mission a failure; for though, as it transpired, the directors of Lumley's had voted unanimously to accept the American offer, Jason went against their advice. As he put it, it behoved him to look to the future and provide his heirs with a business; and unless the approaching twentieth century was to be heralded by the promised war with Germany, the Royal Navy would see him no more.

One day we shall return; retrace the footsteps of the *Dolphin* summer. Armand de Belleisle offers us the Villa La Blanca for as long as we please. One day we shall walk in its cool gardens, and the ghost of the old lady will smile upon us.

But not yet – not yet.

Carola Salisbury
Mallion's Pride 75p

Castle Mallion, the great house on the wild Cornish coast, held many
secrets for Joanna Goodacre, transported there from Jamaica by
Benedict Trevallion, Mallion's new master . . . Benedict makes
Joanna his bride – but a bride in name only. She is threatened by
Benedict's servants and tormented by Mayana, the half-caste who
visits her husband in the dead of night; and, against her will,
Joanna comes to suspect her husband of past murders . . .

Dark Inheritance 75p

The dying words of her father cast a shadow over the strange
destiny of Susannah, alone and friendless in a dangerous world . . .
As governess at Landeric, the Cornish home of the Dewaines,
Susannah becomes aware of dark secrets and hidden enemies — and
she meets Mark Dewaine, handsome young cavalryman. The tide of
fortune then sweeps her to Venice and more intrigue . . . then back
to England, and the London of Victoria's heyday.

Barbara Michaels
House of Many Shadows 70p

Meg's mind still played tricks on her after her head injuries from the
accident had healed. When she tried a change of scene by moving
to the old house cousin Sylvia had inherited, the hallucinations
would not go away. The shadows and presences of horror came
more often in the silent rooms . . .

'A heady blend of romance, murder and the supernatural'
OXFORD TIMES

Phyllis Whitney
Spindrift 70p

Christy Moreland returns to Spindrift, the great mansion on Rhode Island, determined to discover the reason why her father died. Was it suicide or murder? Why is Theodora, the mistress of Spindrift and Christy's mother-in-law, so insistent that it was suicide? And why is Christy warned not to investigate further — on pain of her life?
As she unravels the mystery that Spindrift holds, Christy exposes a tightly woven web of passion and deceit that only another murder can conceal...

The Golden Unicorn 70p

Courtney Marsh came to the great ancestral estate on Long Island in search of an answer to the question that haunted her life: who were her real mother and father? Round her neck hung a tiny golden unicorn and they say that when the shadow of the unicorn falls across the moon, someone in the house will die...

'A top class thriller in an eerie setting'
MANCHESTER EVENING NEWS

Juliette Benzoni
Marianne and the Lords of the East 80p

Beneath the red silk canopy of the royal barge, Marianne crosses the Bosphorus. In her womb she carries the child forced upon her by the sinister Matteo Damiani. In her trust is a vital mission for her Emperor, the conquering Napoleon... A mission that takes Marianne through palaces and prisons, from Constantinople to the shores of Russia itself.

Jessica Stirling
The Hiring Fair 80p

This magnificent sequel to *The Spoiled Earth* is set in the Scotland of
the bleak 1870s. With her father and two brothers dead in the
Blacklaw mine disaster, Mirrin Stalker, the restless firebrand of the
Stalker family, takes to the road. Through tinker camp and hiring fair
she finally emerges on the stage of the music-hall in its bright-lit
heyday.

The Spoiled Earth 95p

A powerful and exciting love story set against the loyalties and
oppressions, catastrophies and ambitions, of a nine teenth-century
Scottish mining community. This haunting saga traces the joys and
despairs of Mirrin Stalker, radical firebrand and tantalising beauty,
who is unprepared for the directions which her passions take . . .

Susan Howatch
The Rich are Different 75p

A great fortune and the struggle to control a worldwide business
empire ; an ambitious and beautiful woman who is one of the most
provocative heroines in fiction ; a love that spans ecstasy and
anguish and a story that reaches from the quiet Norfolk countryside
across the ocean to the New York of the Roaring Twenties.